£3.

MISS

Can you help?

Sipho Madini was last seen in November 1998, staying in
Braamfontein. If you have noticed him please call Homeless
Talk on 838 2143, or come and see us at 2nd floor, Longsbank
Building, 187 Bree Street (cnr Bree and Rissik)

Finding Mr Madini

Directed by
Jonathan Morgan
And other Great African Spider Writers
Virginia Maubane • Robert Buys
Valentine Cascarino • Sipho Madini
David Majoka • Steven Kannetjie
Gert • Patrick Nemahunguni
Pinky Siphamele • Fresew Feleke

ink  inc.

First Published in 1999 by Ink
an imprint of David Philip Publishers
208 Werdmuller Centre, Newry Street,
Claremont 7708, South Africa

Character portraits by Sanae Sawada
Photographs by Jonathan Morgan
Cover design by Fiona Royds
Printed by CTP Book Printers, Parow

PART I

I

Tips to Survive on the Streets

July Tip 1: You need a place to sleep, not just anywhere in Winter. You don't want to be like one of those glue-sniffing boys who live with their heads in their walking blankets. And you don't want to mess around with the security guys, they are an unreasonable lot. They cannot see the difference between a criminal and a cross-eyed baboon! We might as well also be careful of the cops. Some of them suffer from Rodney King Syndrome.

July Tip 2: Location is of utmost importance. City centre, or close to it, is most preferable. There garbage cans have got a variety to offer. Fruits and vegetables the vendors leave after a day's work. If you are afraid of becoming a vegetarian, there is a lot of meat. Pigeons. It's a pity most malundas are not into it.

(Sipho Madini, *Homeless Talk*, Johannesburg, July 1998)

My name is Jonathan Misha Morgan. The last time I stood with ten other people was in long socks. It was in the sixties when I played right wing and could curl the ball into the net from the corner spot. For hours I practised by myself, well into the dark. Sometimes the yellow ball, a Lion, hit the cross-bar. Six out of ten times, it swung in. Our swimming pool was at the bottom of the garden, which was eleven houses from the school, which was a block away from the Wanderers Cricket Stadium. The world then was holdable in my head.

No one's homelessness is quite like anybody else's. Eleven of us pulling down seven stories each. Tying knots in our tales, this one to that one, my one to your one. Sipho's first is about eating cat meat in a township outside Kimberley. He and the other boys spit and vomit, but it's too late. Tied to Valentine's mermaid in Cameroon. Tied to Virginia's immunisation scars

3

in Transkei. Tied to workshops and reef knots and what-what's and what-nots.

*   *   *

Cooking cocaine into crack is harder work than you think. You got to bend over the tiny pot on the portable primus. You got to mix and pour and stir it just right. You got to take care not to spoil expensive ingredients.

Ike gets up, stretches and looks down. He likes looking down. Most of his life he's been staring up, gaping, squeezing his eyelids shut, regretting, forgetting. This vantage feels new. Just above his head a giant red and white neon light flashes, 'Enjoy COKE'.

It's aimed at the Ellis Park rugby fans and the Africa Stadium soccer spectators. Down in Bezuidenhout Valley, they sit in the sun on most weekends, or under powerful spotlights at night. Ike can't see the words but he can see the light. It flows and pulses over him. It comes from his building, from above his roof, his head. In a way it comes from him, or at least from a part of him. He's worked hard to get here.

The apartment belongs to Wallet but Ike spends lots of time here. He looks after the place whenever Wallet is away on beezness, which is often. I'll move over here to Ponte soon, just watch me.

'Ponte. Ponte,' he now says aloud. The tallest residential building in Johannesburg, and on the top floor. To be here. This makes him proud. So far South Africa has been good to him.

Nearly every apartment in Ponte is inhabited by a makwerekwere. This is what the South African Africans call the immigrants from up north – Mozambicans, Zaïereans, Angolans, Kenyans, Ghanaians, Senagalese and us.

Standing on the carpeted floor of the lounge, at the window, looking northwards from a great height, with a long-tom Black Label beer in his hand, Ike feels as secure as any immigrant can expect to

4

feel. Once his South African passport is organised, which will be soon now, and once this flat is his, he'll feel even safer and prouder.

Squinting into the sun, looking southward, from the Imo state in Eastern Nigeria, is his mother. She sees her last born, Ike, her favourite, standing in his own apartment in a new land.

'Why not?' he asks himself, 'it's a big motherfucker, I mean mother of a sign, and anything's possible.'

* * *

Ice-cold drops from the brass tap are dripping down my neck. I'm wondering where the man walking down the freeway, carrying an avocado pear seed with matches stuck into its sides, can fit into my novel. The pink pip is suspended in water in a plastic 1,5 litre Fanta bottle whose top has been cut off. Walking very slowly, holding the container with both hands, so as not to spill any, he became smaller and smaller in my rearview mirror. I should have stopped to talk to him. I need a character like that. A good guy to stand against Ike and the sifrats.

'How's your book coming on?' asks Kyoko who is sitting opposite me in the bath with her knees up.

It's about a stash of drugs which go missing. The main characters are Ike, the Nigerian crack dealer, Kingsley, a Ghanaian street barber, Shadrack, a Venda gardener, and a Boksburg teenager called Kriek. Maybe I need a woman or two?

The Venda gardener's church, the Zionist Christians, dance and pray on a cement circle on the koppie near my house. The koppie is this raised spot where all these cultures collide. It's on a favourite nature trail, it has an Iron Age furnace, it borders on the cemetery where all four of my grandparents are buried, and it's a preferred after-midnight drugging posi. The missing drugs are buried there.

I take a deep breath, shoot my legs out and pinch my nose. For a full half minute, I stay under listening to the house through hot water. In Kyoko's tummy is someone who is four centimetres long and whose fingernail pads will be complete by tonight. Something pushes my legs apart, then I feel Kyoko sliding up my chest. The one lion claw of the bathtub is shorter than the others, or maybe it's the tiles which are uneven. When we move, the tub rocks.

'This novel doesn't know what it wants to be,' I tell her.

'You and it,' she says shampooing my bristles.

'More than anything else I want it to be a description of Jo'burg-Africa, from the margins, just before the end of the millennium.'

I dip under again.

'DubBiL, Jonji, DubBiL,' says Kyoko poking me.

'What?' I say struggling to surface, feeling the weight of her on my chest.

'There's someone at the doorbell,' she says.

I get out dripping, put on a towel and stop in front of the green door leading out to the street.

'Who's there?' I ask.

'Given, please help me.'

With all the rain, the door has swollen in its frame. I leave the chain on. Outside is a man holding his thigh in pain.

'Yes?' I say.

'Sir, I have been walking all day, asking for a job. I walked from Soweto and through Parkview, Greenside, Emmarentia, Parkhurst, Melville. That is why my leg is like this.'

'A old lady down the road, just there,' he says, 'she has promised me a painting job, but last week someone began that job and stole her stepladder and wheelbarrow. She wants my ID book before she gives me this job but I left it in Pietersburg. I need R45 for taxi to fetch it so I can begin tomorrow. I will pay you as soon as the job is finished on Friday. Here is my brother's number in Soweto. Please.'

I take a torn piece of brown paper through the crack, glance at it and hand it back.

'I'm sorry,' I say closing the door, taking care not to catch his fingers.

'PLEASE! BAAS! PLEASE!' he says getting down onto one knee. He clasps his hands as if praying at me, face all grimaced up, tears in the whites of his eyes.

'Who is it?' shouts Kyoko.

My wallet is next to the front door. I separate out and part with a red fifty rand note.

'I will give it back to you on Friday,' he says.

As I'm climbing back in the bath, that feeling when I know I've been lied to hits me where it always does, in my neck. My fists shoot up to tuck in and cover my Adam's apple.

'Who was it?' asks Kyoko.

'Even kak stories are powerful,' I tell her.

Maybe the guy who witnesses the drugs being buried on the koppie should be some poor homeless fucker …

I listen to the springs of my mattress zing as Kyoko and Masego breathe on their backs. Masego's foot flexes against my hip and her kinky fro rests in the space between our pillows. A West Indian Buddhist friend of Kyoko's from London, who also has very curly hair, taught us that word. Fro from Afro. I get up to check that I locked the door and the garage gate properly. When I switch on the florescent light, there is a long pause I can never get used to before the long tube goes *tink* and sparks for the first time. My eyes expect to see but don't. Then everything, including my sparkling blue automatic Mazda, is on my retina. I scroll up the door, the outside security light switches on automatically and I see loose soil on the driveway and in the street. Someone has stolen the two little trees with variegated leaves that I planted in February. I'm certain that they were there when I spoke to that Given.

Before it is light and before Masego wakes up, I sneak out with my Montana mountain bike. Masego loves standing shoulder-to-shoulder with the hissing geese, not giving them the bread we have brought for them. Without her I am able to get some real exercise. On a lamppost just outside my house is today's headline – 'STORM IN SPACE'. We are trying to have our dam declared a nature area but our councillor doesn't attend our meetings or return our phone-calls. The neighbourhood committee have threatened to declare him a missing person.

With one foot on the near bank of the dam, I stop for breath. Only last week, right here, I saw an Egyptian goose with a steel-tipped arrow through its webbed foot. Who would do that? Some kid or the guy who I often surprise while he is spraying the willow tree with potent smelling piss? The first time, as I lurched past the trunk, pedalling like mad and sucking air, I startled him. He put his penis back in his trousers, mid-stream. His left leg kept on quivering. Our conversations are getting longer.

'Do you know who lights these fires under these beautiful old trees?' I ask as the sun comes up behind the university.

'It's those other guys who care only about themselves,' he says.

Robert is his name and he comes from Upington.

'I'm a Coloured,' he continues, 'but there's no such thing. Firstly, properly translated from Afrikaans, it's Colour*ling*, and second, we are all human beings.'

Johannesburg has had him for only two weeks. I get to meet two of his friends. The one, whose name is Portuguese sounding, is from Angola. The other, Gert, was born near here in Mayfair before it was declared an Indian area. Gert knows

8

things about Westdene. His grandparents lived in my street. He told me that as a naughty white Afrikaans boy, he used to steal horses from the coloured township just over there and ride them till their tongues hung out.

*   *   *

'Come read this,' I say to Kyoko. 'It's the scene where Kriek, the in-patient in the rehab, jumps the wall and goes to Hillbrow where he finds the stash of drugs hidden behind a fire hydrant.'

She sits on my lap and begins reading off the monitor, scrolling down ever-so-slowly.

I always dress like this. Black. Looks evil against my pale-pink-pigskin as Bongani, that daggarooker, calls it. You can't insult a punk. Never take my knee-high Docs off. Fully ripped jeans full of safety pins and key-rings. And this favourite Mega Ded T-shirt I lifted from Moola's at the Carlton Centre. The bubbly, plastic silk screen stuff, scratches my pierced studded nipple lekker sore.

The video machine, wrapped in my leather jacket, is in the bushes on the other side of the wall. Sister Stella schemes I'm picking up cigarette stompies. She's so fokken surprised she hasn't told me to get away from here. An ex-junkie called Steven is coming to tell us how he managed to come right, and how the only way – it's been proven time and time again – is to go to NA meetings. Boooring. Sorry can't make it.

The Hillbrow tower is where I've been for close to an hour. The sun disappeared right behind it. In ten minutes the whole place is going to be shadowless. I'll jump, meet Ike, and trade the video for five fat rocks, minimum. Wanna deal with me, deal with my disease.

'I like it,' Kyoko says getting off my lap, 'but the character sounds too much like that boy Nick in the rehab.'

'I'll disguise him later,' I tell her.

* * *

The MTN shop with the tightrope stretched across the totem poles used to be an art gallery. The phone will help me keep in touch with Kyoko when I'm out hunting and gathering stuff for the novel. It's a Nokia 5110. Outside the shop I punch in our land-line number.

'Howzit, Kyoks, I bought one. A cell phone. Six-ninety-nine on a special. Free voice mail retrieval and a free charger.'

'You're a fish called cell,' she says.

Maybe I am selfish.

'I'm at home looking after Masego,' she goes on, 'I need to prepare for my next lesson, and you're out doing what?'

'I thought you supported me being a writer,'

Click.

In seven months there will be another mouth to feed.

I look up at eight pigeons on the tightrope between the totems, past obscenely white banks of clouds, into the sun itself. I know there's a satellite up there that connected us and then disconnected us. I think they work off satellites and those fake trees that you see around are the aerials that beam up the messages. We've only been married one year now.

* * *

Kyoko's gone to a squatter camp in a place called Stilfontein. To donate chalk boards and world maps to a primary school. The school operates from a bus without wheels. The other classrooms move with the shade around some thorn trees. The yen that bought the board and maps was raised by Japanese post office savings account holders. They donate one per cent of their savings to the Third World.

I take the gap and decide to visit the Mimosa International. It's a hotel in Hillbrow inhabited only by Nigerian crack dealers. I met Lea when I worked in the rehab. Yesterday I got a phone call from the person I'm basing the wall jumper on. He keeps in touch.

'Lea's working as a prostitute in the Mimosa,' he says, 'the Nigerian who owns her supplies her with cocaine to freebase, and a loaf of bread every day. The cunt keeps the key to her room.'

'I'll try get out there,' I tell him thinking about the novel.

Just before Kyoko's lift comes I decide to tell her where I'm going. Just in case something happens.

'Are you going to smoke crack?' she asks.

'No. I'm going for research.'

'Remember when you took ecstasy at that rave,' she reminds me, 'also for research, you were depressed for a month afterwards.'

I find the place but I can't find Lea. That night I dream about the peeling wallpaper, the tilting, waiting to crash chandeliers and the expensively printed obituary on the glass door of the hotel's entrance. On it there is a colour photo of the now dead man leaning against a recent BMW. He came from the Kanu State in northern Nigeria and he was a Christian.

*   *   *

'*The important thing when building a house is to run bundles of conductors of fibre optic cable to every room while the walls are still open*' says Bill Gates in his syndicated column. I'm in the Mazda, reading *The Star*, waiting for Kyoko to finish teaching Japanese to the Taiwanese boys. On another page I read that if the same Bill wasn't so busy buying out and closing down his competition, my computer would work better.

I finish the main section, 'Trends', the 'Financials' and the 'Motorist'. It's a toss-up between the 'Classifieds' and *Homeless Talk*. I still buy it but no longer read it. I used to but then it began interfering with my anti-depressants. Got tired of the whinging as well. Now I fix it to my dashboard as a homeless person repellent. On the top of the second page it says, *'Ads and Appeals'*, even though there aren't any ads.

'Due to financial difficulties, *Homeless Talk* is in danger of closing down. If you can help please phone Pinkie on 838 2143.'

And below some photos, 'Some of Our Writers'.

'Every Monday between 5p.m. and 7p.m., *Homeless Talk* writers meet at the Writer's Workshop to discuss topical issues and receive training. If any of our readers would like to hear more about specific street/homelessness/other issues, please drop us a line.'

I turn the page and find out why homeless people sleep in parks on their stomachs. It's obvious – it makes hunger go away. Another guy, drunk outside a shebeen wearing a stolen bullet-proof vest, dared this other guy to shoot him. *Bang* and he was dead. By Sipho Madini. Not a bad writer.

Maybe I really should make one of my characters a homeless dude? His point of view is the angle from which this shit-hole looks most potent. These okes can serve me for once. Fuck knows I've handed out enough one and two rand coins.

* * *

Kyoko and Masego are doing the deep breathing mattress spring zing sing thing again. When Kyoko exhales, Masego inhales. Under the duvet, I stroke our striped cat Sushi vigorously and watch sparks fly from her fur. I think about getting up to make a sandwich. Instead I try lying on my stomach and within minutes I fall asleep.

At 7, I wake up and I go get the *Homeless Talk* from the car. It is too early to phone so I slash at the lawn with an angled panga thing. At 9, I pick up and dial. The number just rings and rings. Maybe the place has closed down?

At 9.30, an English voice answers. 'You can try come on Monday but we may be closing down, things are in the balance.'

It's been around for about five years now. My fucking luck.

*   *   *

My last patient won't leave. She leaves the bombshell for the last minute like they always do.

'We'd better talk about that next week,' I say herding her out the door.

Town is almost empty, but still I drive too fast. The July edition sits on my dashboard. I wonder what they will be like.

In the lift I squint at my diary:

'5.30. *Homeless Talk* writer's workshop, Bree and Rissik, Longsbank Bld, 2nd floor.'

I burst into a big room, half full of seated people, crowded around a table. Everyone is black except for me, a guy in the corner and a woman with blue and green flashcards who stands in front of the writers.

'Trash to treasure can work. I'm convinced of this,' she says, 'three separate bins and mind over matter is all it takes. And people do care. Recycling is big in Europe and the States. It'll catch on here, you'll see and Madiba didn't get to be president by sitting on his bee-hind.'

'Did,' says a young man into his hand. He is sitting two away from me and he's wearing a leather jacket and a balaclava.

'We all gotta lose the victim mentality,' the woman continues.

'Hi,' whispers a woman sitting on the other side, 'I'm Helen, we spoke on the phone.'

I recognise her English accent. She tears off the bottom of a page with a ruler, writes me a note and passes it over.

'That guy in the corner is Clive, it's his writing workshop, he's been running it for years. I'll introduce you later.'

I look over at Clive. A very fit fifty-five. White hair and a barrel chest. His legs are crossed. He's biting his nails and creasing his face. Then I feel my chair on coasters sinking and sliding away from the table. Looking down, I notice a child fiddling with the lever.

'Hey, stop that,' I whisper separating his hand from the lever.

The boy goes back to his drawings. I have an aerial view. A sequence of running gun battles on A4s, executed with a short black crayon.

I've lost what the recycling woman was saying and try tune in again. Opposite me, a well dressed guy in a mauve zip-up shirt with leather padding rolls his eyes at her.

'People get really clumsy over this homeless issue,' he says just loud enough for some of us to hear. I notice that his skin is very very dark and that he's got a heavy gold ear-ring in his left lobe.

'Well, who's coming with me to present this thing?' asks the woman, 'I know it can work. We'll stand outside Madiba's office, knock-knock-knocking on his door, until he answers.'

Clive jerks himself off his chair. He slams his palm down on the table. 'These people are writers and this is a writing workshop. You're patronising them,' he shouts jutting his chin at the woman.

She recoils as if shot in the belly.

Someone sniggers. In front of the desk, lampooned, she rotates her neck to take in the consensus. No heads are up and there are no eyes to be met. Red blotches develop on her neck in dark-room time. Her flashcards and her files are gathered up, she apologises, and she runs out. I quite liked her voice and her face. This guy is a bit heavy. Like her, I can't read what the others are feeling.

Clive's hands go to his throat to adjust the tie he isn't wearing. He is in front of the huge newsprint flipchart on the tripod. He slashes the page with a dry, black marker pen. Then he turns to me, leaning forward onto the table on his big hands, 'Do you want to introduce yourself? I'm Clive.'

I think, 'Fuck', but stand up, and swallow, 'I'm Jonathan and I used to enjoy reading *Homeless Talk*. Some of the writing is great. I'm not a full-time writer but I write and I've been published. I sometimes attend another writing workshop and I'm interested in coming to this one or starting another one with you on another day. I'm also prepared to act as a contact person and submit your pieces to magazines I have relationships with.'

I stop there, deciding to say nothing about my novel or using them for research. Clive smiles at me, and so do a few others, which makes me sit down and begin breathing again.

'This is the outline for the courses we discussed last week,' he says to the group.

On the flipchart he writes.

Mondays: 5–7: Feature Writing

Tuesdays: 5–7: Investigative Journalism

Wednesdays: 5–7: Fundraising

Thursdays: 5–7: Photojournalism

Fridays: 5–7: Free Writing

'Would you like to run the Free Writing one?' he asks me.

'Ummm, can I get back to you? I need to ask my wife,' I say instantly feeling stupid.

The rest of the workshop is spent discussing *Homeless Talk* organisational difficulties. Only at the end is writing mentioned.

'Quickly tell us,' Clive asks the group 'what the piece you're presently working on is about. Remember Thursday 1 p.m. is deadline.'

Pieces of paper shuffle. Cassius, wearing a school blazer, says, 'Burning love'.

Temba, in the corduroy jacket, mumbles 'How to catch AIDS through the top of your head. It's about street barbers.'

Laughter.

Steven, the older guy in the grey jersey, grinning, announces, 'Malunda teaching street kids boxing in Commissioner Street.'

'What is a "malunda"?' I ask the man sitting next to me.

'A homeless person,' he whispers waving his finger around.

Elizabeth, one of the few women present says, 'Final eviction notices, Doringkop squatter camp'.

'I'll do the free writing course but I can only do it on Saturdays,' I say just before we break up.

'Can we start this week?' asks the guy in the balaclava and the leather jacket.

II

Tips to Survive on the Streets
August Tip 1: Speaking about a place to stay in winter months. There are
some churches and soup kitchens around. If you don't have ambition,
just sit back and relax.
August Tip 2: Now my friend, we cannot live on bread alone. Tito
Mboweni, a brother, is now in charge of the Reserve Bank, but so what?
Parking cars is one of our only options. If you can find a spot.
(Sipho Madini, *Homeless Talk*, Johannesburg, August 1998)

Saturday morning is month-end and everyone is shopping. The building looks very different in the day. I park outside near the licensing department. When I step out I get mobbed. By parkers, by men wanting to take my photo and by men selling number plates. The women just sit with their backs to the wall and their legs out straight. They hang back. Behind their single chocolate éclairs and cigarettes. Roasting mielies. Tomatoes displayed like molecules on coloured plates. Butternuts and cabbages with prices in rands, written with marker pens onto the skins and outer leaves.

The entrance on Bree Street is between a shop that sells discounted child tombstones and Mama Temba's Café. The pavement outside the café is full of very reasonably priced hoe heads, hammers and pliers. It is an extension of the hardware store around the corner.

A Shangaan woman with unshaved armpits and a barrel full of holes and red coals on her head, forces me off the pavement. Black smoke clouds her head, but it is me who coughs and can't stop – even in the lift where I join a young guy in a leather jacket. He presses the button, the doors begin to close, but they fail

17

and he presses again. This time they shut. We are jolted as the lift lurches upwards. The young man looks at his feet and my gaze is jerked from the floor to the numbers above the doors. I'm not sure but I think he is the person who blasphemed Madiba and who asked me to begin as soon as possible.

'I'm Jonathan,' I eventually say.

He looks up and smiles, 'Sipho.'

'Where are you from?' I ask him.

'Kimberley.'

'Are you Sipho Madini?' I ask really looking at him for the first time.

'Yes,' he answers as we step out.

He is younger than I expected. Could be eighteen but there's something much older about him too. We walk down the passage and I try and open the heavy glass door to get into the *Homeless Talk* offices. It doesn't budge.

'Is *Homeless Talk* closing down?' I ask Sipho.

He shrugs.

'Did you know the guy who ripped the paper off and defrauded the trust fund?' I ask.

'Ja, he was like smooth, he took us all in.'

A few minutes later an older man gets out the lift. His shoes are heavily polished but have no tongues. I notice his laces, which are pulled tight across his bare skin.

'Hi, I'm Jonathan.'

'Eddie.' We shake hands.

'I once produced "Waiting for Godot" at the Market Theatre,' he immediately tells me. 'I'm tired of begging for work. Next week I'm auditioning for a minor part in "Long Walk to Freedom", the movie, but all I expect is more empty promises. They can't decide between Denzel Washington and Morgan Freeman to play Mandela. I think I look a lot like Mr Mandela, don't you?'

18

I smile. 'And you Sipho?' I ask, 'why did you come to Jo'burg?'

'I've got a matric but there are no jobs,' he says.

'Have you always liked writing?'

'I used to come number one in class, especially English.'

'And how do you survive here. Do you park cars?'

'No, I'm a writer.'

I remember Helen telling me that for three poems in *Homeless Talk* they get sixty bucks, and for one story, eighty. The paper only comes out once a month.

'You write that column about survival on the street, don't you?'

He smiles and nods.

'I've also seen some of your poems,' I say, 'even though poetry is not really my thing.'

For ten minutes we sit on the floor not saying much. Three is almost a group but not quite, and it feels like my blood sugar is down.

'Let's see how many come next week, and bring some writing with you – anything,' I say to Eddie and Sipho whilst getting up.

As I pass bunches of bananas on the pavement, I think maybe I should buy a whole lot of them before the workshop next week. Or even a few loaves of bread and some peanut butter. Naaa, they'll think I'm getting all soup kitcheny.

I'm relieved my car is where I parked it. And that the baby seat is still there. As I dig into my pockets to get my keys I notice Sipho standing behind me. I smile at him and open the front door, which prompts the leopard at the back to bob its neck. I bought the carving from a Zimbabwean where the freeway ends. The leopard is wood and the detachable head is weighted with a piece of steel.

'This is my chorrie,' I say.

19

'She's a beauty,' says Sipho, walking away backwards, his hands shoved deep into the pockets of his black leather jacket.

*   *   *

Traffic lights only change in good time if you breathe deeply. I'm tuned to Classic FM. If no one comes today, that's OK. My head's taken enough photos to paint a good homeless character. Will base him on Sipho.

'Strongarm Security – Hang em High' says a sign on the bakkie in front of me. I can see the driver, in his driveway on a Sunday afternoon, fashioning the advert with red insulation tape. The company emblem is a hangman's noose which is dangling from a vertical stick gallows.

'BOOM BOOM BOOM.'

I take my hands off the steering wheel, jerk my head to the left and put a finger from each hand into my ears. From behind the dark windows of a navy BMW, blasts this incredibly loud music. The extra heavy tints, the kind you can only see out of, were popular amongst taxis just before the election. Then they were banned. Too many white traffic cops, trying to issue fines, were shot dead by unseen assailants. The music, which I think is called Kwaito, is truly shuddering. I close my window and turn off my radio. In the BM two feet away from me, I can sense the passengers. A feeling of not belonging in Africa wells up. As my window closes, one of theirs rolls down. A guy holding a Castle long tom, flashes gold teeth at me.

'Hola,' he says toasting me.

❞

When I get there, the room has, one-two-three-four-five-six-seven people in it. The boardroom is a huge space, divided into

20

two by a dirty seventies style screen that concertinas open. Both sections are bare, save for piled rolls of industrial carpet in one corner and some donated seating arrangements. Large windows look down onto a roof which is covered in silver insulation material. Five noisy industrial air-conditioners stand there humming. The space has a not-much-happens-in-here feel to it. If this is the boardroom, what does the board look like?

I take a seat around the four, shaky tables. They are arranged to form a space in the centre. Some of the chairs are bar stools, and some are low-slung, shredded foam and vinyl. A regular plastic veranda chair has been left for me.

'I'm Virginia,' says the woman with a young boy, the one who lowered me, 'and this is Prince.'

'I'm Fresew from Ethiopia,' says the tall man with the Semitic face.

Teketay, Messai and Sampson, the three men sitting next to Fresew, are also from Ethiopia. In broken English they are able to communicate little more than their names.

'They publish a monthly newspaper in Ethiopian,' says Sipho.

'We used to sell cassettes and shoes from stall on Bree Street, but we are, umm, how you say it, robbed many times,' says the one called Sampson.

'I'm Valentine from Cameroon,' says the young man with the gold ear-ring.

I admire his mauve and blue zip-up shirt jacket, which I noticed before at the Monday evening workshop.

'Steven from Ciskei,' says the older guy with the Kaizer Chiefs T-shirt.

'Eddie from Soweto,' says the Mandela wannabe.

It's been a bit of a sweat but this is going to pay off. Through these okes I've got access to stuff most South African writers can only dream of.

I lean forward.

'Thanks for coming. I'm Jonathan. I'm happy you came. I don't believe writing can be taught but it can be learned. The most powerful writing stuff I've ever learned was around a ping-pong table in a room like this. Around the table were grannies and schoolgirls and poets and novelists and good writers and bad writers and cool people and uncool people. Everybody reads something they've written and then they get feedback from all the others. This way, in one shot, you get to know how your stuff goes down to a broad sample of readers. Has anyone brought anything to read?'

Messai, the Ethiopian man with a bokkie and a desert complexion, holds up a tattered sheaf of photocopies.

'I'm a chemist. This scientific. About the cloning sheep.'

'Did you write it?' I inquire.

'No.'

Valentine saves me, 'I wrote something.'

From some hand-written notes he begins to read. All I can hear is accent. No words at all.

To me there are traces of pidgin English, American and West African, but also some Latin.

'Sorry, Valentine. Can you please slow down and read as clearly as you possibly can.'

He begins again.

 THINGS FALL APART
by Valentine

Who did not envy sumptuousa Albert Cascarino? At 45 he was a multi-millionaire. He owned fifteen bedroom Italian villa in Victoria called 'Golden Grape'. He owned a Mercedes 500, a Renault Safrane and a stationwagon. He was also the proprietor of the town's most impressive supermarket. Women flocked behind him the way the Israelites flocked behind Moses. Apart from his numerous relationships, he had married six times, and came out with three children, each from a separate mother. Me (Valentine), 23; Susie, 20; and Harry, 18. He was popularly known as Lord Albert and loved to be called that way.

But the source of his wealth was a shocking tale of combined treachery and roguery. He had been a brigand from his early youth. He had taken part in many interceptions on the Johannesburg–Durban highway. He used to forge letters and blackmail women of high standing. Personally, he led the gang which ripped the Johannesburg branch of Barclays Bank of two million rands in one of his bloody hold-ups. It was him (then working under false identity) who had duped four French tycoons coming to invest in South Africa and it was him who enjoyed their money. Lord Albert took cover then in Bulawayo for police investigation to follow before returning to settle in Victoria, Cameroon.

There was no time for his family and so he never knew what characters his family children were developing. He never knew, for example, that I loved gambling and wine in smoked-filled games departments and in expensive hotels. That Susie (his sweetheart amongst his children) was in love with cocaine. And that Harry was becoming the most expensively dressed person in the world. We crumbled the supermarket that was under our care to satisfy our obsessions.

When Lord Albert realised he had reared an army of noughts, he closed down the supermarket and stopped giving us allowances. The three of us had already developed our geniuses for top class trickery, decision and courage. We immediately retaliated. She stole our dad's business documents, made statements about projects, forged his signature and transferred two thirds of his millions into her personal account. She also got involved with a Nigerian drug cartel and pushed her money into that business in the hope of becoming super-rich.

Harry, who had finished his millions in Europe's fashion houses, burst into our father's hotel room with a pistol. With the gun, he threatened to shoot his dad down, and collected a suitcase full of money. He also took Lord Albert's sixth wife, who was just his age, and with whom he had fallen in love. They went to Milan for a peaceful flirt.

I, who was stranded in Abidjan, arranged a gang, and before Harry burned down the 'Golden Grape', I stole all the saleables. The marble statuettes, the gold-plated kitchenware, electronic gadgets and his luxury car.

Lord Albert returned from his sunny sand splash. He used his remaining money to restore the house, then went bankrupt. He began living on borrowed money. The hotel was seized and sold to pay back his debt. Patching up life in a one room apartment was begun. His girlfriends fled, and our relatives ignored him saying that when he had money he did not think of them. Life suddenly felt bitter, then he fell sick. He had contracted the deadly killer disease Aids and had a heart attack. He lay on his bed feebly doomed to die.

How do I feel about him?

He should have the courage to look himself in the mirror and say, 'I deserve everything I have got, and I am responsible for the plague that hit us all.' After all, he was once a thief, the world merely returned him the very coins he'd introduced to the world.

Valentine stops reading and looks up.

I begin the clapping and the others follow.

'Is it true?' I ask.

'Every word,' says Sipho.

These two seem close.

'It's brilliant,' I say, 'did your father, Lord Albert, really intercept money vans on the highway between Jo'burg and Durban?'

'My mother told me that in Cameroon,' says Valentine, 'before I even knew what and where Johannesburg was.'

'It's an attractive history,' says Fresew.

'Maybe you still have some of that money,' says Steven.

Eddy's head has dropped and he's snoring. I reach over to wake him up but Sipho stops me saying, 'let him sleep, most homeless guys talk at night and sleep at this time.'

'Why's that?' I ask

'Because we sit around the fire in the cold months, and we go to sleep when it gets warm enough to lie down without freezing,' he answers.

I want to ask where they all sleep. Sipho and Eddie look like they live rough, but none of the others look too bad. Valentine's outfit is on a par with mine.

* * *

The next week, Fresew is the only one who has brought anything to read.

 JACQUI
by Fresew

When I left, I said goodbye to everyone – my mother, my father, everyone, but not my dog. This dog, his name is Jacqui, he begins to misbehave. I get him from the rural area. Sometimes I wrestle with him for one hour when he misbehave. One time he bites me and I decide to kill him but stop

25

because I tell myself he is an animal. When I leave he cries and cries so I have to tie him to the bed with a rope before I fly away from my compound in the aeroplane to South Africa.

I can see the page he's reading from and it's not written in English. I point at the squiggles on the paper and ask, 'what is that kind of writing?'

'Amharic, the Ethiopian alphabet,' he answers.

Sampson shoots Fresew's story down in a blaze. 'No story, no development. No climax. No scoop.'

Sampson was a journalist in Addis Ababa.

'I think it's a powerful story,' I tell him, 'about a man with unfinished business. But I agree with some of what the others have said. There's so much undescribed I want to know. What the compound looks like?'

'And the dog, is it big or small? And when was it set? Which year? And more physical description,' says Sampson.

'I've been thinking,' I say, 'how about we try give this group and this project some structure and purpose, and we aim for a book. A bloody bestseller.'

I seem to have their attention.

'Right here in this room we've got more raw African writing talent than perhaps anywhere in the continent. Let's begin documenting all of your life stories, beginning with say your ancestor-history-kind-of-story, going on to an early childhood story, then a teenage one, etc., etc., till the here and now?'

Fresew's smiling broadly. Valentine's eyes are shining. Sipho is scratching his head, the corners of his mouth sending outwards ever so slightly.

'Well?' I ask.

'It's feasible,' says Sipho.

'I like it a lot, a lot-lot,' says Valentine.

'It can be most attractive and interesting,' says Fresew.

On the flipchart, with the almost dry red marker, I scratch:

WINDOW 1 – where and when in Africa did your story
            begin, a family history story
WINDOW 2- an early childhood story
WINDOW 3 – a teenage/rite of passage/definitive movement
            story
WINDOW 4 – some of your life before hitting the road and
            becoming homeless
WINDOW 5 – hitting the road
WINDOW 6 – homeless living
WINDOW 7 – signing off

Windows are good, I think, it is a license to just glimpse and to
be incoherent.

'Perhaps we should work it the other way round,' I think out
loud. 'How about we start with a physical description of each
one of your sleeping places, then as a kind of voice over, we
begin with window 1 and move forward to how you got here?'

'That is better,' says Valentine.

'I believe the fact that you are all homeless and that you are
all writers is going to be a big selling point for the book,' I say,
'and I don't think we should pussyfoot around this. Let's jump
right in and show the readers from the start where it is you are
sleeping. You were not always homeless. These stories can be
partly about how this happened.'

It feels like the book already exists. It hangs in the space
above our heads. A big fat hard cover:

OVER 1,000,000 COPIES SOLD,
TRANSLATED INTO 11 LANGUAGES …

With a whole gang of us writing together, who says we can't
write a duk blockbuster in one tenth of the time it would take

27

one of us to write?

'Ok, I'll drop off some clearer guidelines for your writing. You can pick them up on Monday before your 5 o'clock *Homeless Talk* workshop. Try write the first two windows and please try visit someone else's home and describe it.

Didn't even need to bring food to draw the crowds, I muse, as I demobilise, unlatch my gorilla lock from the steering wheel, and then my VISA approved gear clamp from the gear lever.

III
Sipho & Valentine

THIS PACT OF OURS
It's so hard to be good
It nearly hurts my Lord

Had I not promised thee
Never to commit crime no more?
But it's hard
In such a poverty

My soul is clouded, dreams are murk
People having a blissful life
No worry, no pangs,
No cure my Lord

I want too, to live like them
The easy way, no concern
For crime at least I do understand
And what I don't, I just might learn
(Sipho Madini, *Homeless Talk*, Johannesburg, August 1998)

It is 10.30 Saturday morning and Kyoko is making *norimaki* from last night's rice. The workshop begins at 11. Her hands pat and rotate the sticky rice into flat triangles into which a pickled plum is stuffed. The rice is then wrapped in a sheet of *nori* seaweed. This is lunchbox and padkos.

I stuff it into my mouth and push the tupperware beneath the seat. I'm waiting at a red robot opposite the graffiti wall honouring dead hijack victims. You can fax a photo plus an obituary to *The Star*. They will pay for a Fine Art student to paint your dead relative up on this wall.

My best parking yet. Right outside Longsbank. The pavement hardware store is open. A woman in a blanket holds a carbonated invoice book. Creative Marble and Granite Solutions are still running the special on child graves. I stop and look in the shop. Through my own reflection, I see short rows of polished granite, an aisle, plastic flowers and a cash register. On the pavement beside me, an Indian vendor with patches of albino, loudspeaks fabric bargains to be had in the next-door basement. In Longsbank, the huge security guard in his very smart uniform, signals to me that I have to sign in. I shift from foot to foot and breathe as each of the five people in front of me painstakingly negotiates the ledger's columns.

On the second floor the door is closed and on it the paper 'BOARDROOM' sign, has come unstuck. I borrow some presstik from the bottom corner and stick the page back. There is no one inside.

Outside I can hear a choir practising. For fifteen minutes, I arrange the tables, and open and close windows. When Sipho and Valentine come in, I'm sitting down with pen and paper. Sipho just smiles.

"

'Hi, Jonathan,' says Valentine.

He is wearing his mauve and blue shirt jacket, and his sunglasses have dollar signs sandblasted into the lenses.

'When you look through those things do you see dollars?' I ask him.

'No, I cannot,' he says.

'Can I try them?'

He takes them off. He's right. When I look at Sipho I see

only this guy in his leather jacket and unwashed jeans.

Virginia arrives and then some new ones. Steven and David and Patrick. This is not bad.

'Are you Steven Kannetjie?' I ask, noticing he walks with a limp, 'I've seen your articles and your poems.'

Patrick draws the cartoons and David is in charge of advertising. I remind them, and myself, that the brief was to visit someone else, to write about it and to have a shot at Windows One and Two.

'I went to visit Sipho. I walked there from Yeoville,' says Valentine.

Sipho is smiling at me as Valentine begins reading.

 ## VALENTINE VISITS SIPHO
by Valentine

I, Valentine Eboh Cascarino, leave home at 9 o'clock. Some guys are playing soccer in the park under the Ponte building. They're passing a joint around as they play. When I walk through them, they surround me. I ask for a puff and blow the smoke up at the Coke sign on top of the towering round building.

'Thanks gents,' I say and walk on.

The hit makes me dizzy. Down Abel Road I feel safe because I live with Nigerians and many of them know me. Already at 9.30 in the morning, addicts are coming for their zooms, moving in to buy crack. They look thin and dress poorly while the Nigerians all look very healthy and wear tweed pants and latest dressings.

Past the old Fort Prison, I walk down the hill toward Wits University. One street behind the university, in a drain ditch covered with a steel grid, and covered again with big sheets of plastic, I get on my knees. Into the drain, I push my head.

31

Inside the ditch is a pipe which runs like a shelf down the length of the place. Some clothes and magazines are balancing on the shelf. Five bodies in a line lie under blankets. Which one is Sipho I ask myself.

'Mfowethu, it's me Valentine,' I whisper very loudly.

The others don't even move but the one nearest me stirs and I see it is my man.

Valentine stops there. I have been watching Sipho as Valentine reads. His lip curls and his feet dance on the balls of his worn Doc Martens.

Everyone claps loudly.

'That's great, let's save feedback till after the stories themselves,' I say. 'Now can we go straight into a kind of movie camera portrait, and then into a voice over. I'd like you to choose a partner, pull your chairs out so they face each other, and spend five minutes each getting down a physical description of your partner.'

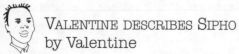

VALENTINE DESCRIBES SIPHO
by Valentine

Sipho is wearing a thick-weight black leather jacket and a loose paper-thin T-shirt under. His jeans are baggy and held up by a brown belt which is very long for him. He has high cheeks, and a yellow and green balaclava, which is his registered trademark for some time since we met. It makes his stature higher. His face looks twisted and full of sleep.

Go for it Sipho, read your first and second window,' I say once Valentine has finished.

Sipho takes a sheaf of dirty folded papers out his jacket and reads from the sheaf of disorganised papers. They slide off his lap and he is so doubled over, that I struggle to hear him.

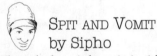

SPIT AND VOMIT
by Sipho

The whole rainbow is inside me. I'm sitting on the step of my grandmother's house in Mankunwane township just outside Kimberley. Beside me is her Bible and her religious booklets. Yesterday was her funeral full of relatives. Blue eyes and brown eyes and transparent eyes. Crinkly hair and blonde tints and nearly all eleven official languages.

'Sorry to hear about Gogo,' Mbuthana says to me.

Mbuthana is a local gangster. His black and white mafia shoes stop in front of me. I blink. The sides of his trousers are ironed into a razor sharp crease and his shirt is tucked into a crocodile skin belt. On his face are many scars.

I shrug, mumble, but I don't get up. We fall into remembering the day three gangs with every kind of conceivable weapon stood poised to attack each other right here outside Gogo's kitchen.

'Hey what are you about to do? Go home! Hamba! Voetsek!' my grandmother screamed at them.

There was not a hair of fear in her head and she had the conviction of right. Even Mabuthana, who had felled four with a knife, bumbled like a boy.

Sitting around the mbowula, a tin drum punched full of holes and filled with burning coal, Gogo used to tell us stories without the need to convince. She was born somewhere in the Free State in 1919. We used to call my grandmother Gogo. When she came to Kimberley, she married a Zulu who was working on the diamond mines.

Gogo opened a shebeen selling traditional beer. She would never put acid or other undigestibles into the brew to give it extra kick. She would never follow her bad debtors with sjamboks and threats. Eventually they always paid. At her funeral the whole street outside her house was full of people, some even from Namibia. Now it is me who must remember.

There is one is about my uncle Thabang. He had a lot to do with meat. Not only the cooking but the catching too. In Kimberley, most people believe Xhosas are thieves, most especially sheep thieves. In this respect Thabang did not disappoint them.

'I want the head and the hooves.'

'I want the rib cage.'

'Me the rump.'

Every day people would place their orders to be collected the next day. In this butchery business, Thabang's little brother, Tsepo, united with him. Both of them had independent professions. When we saw the two of them wheel out their bikes with front carriages, like those used for deliveries, we knew a sheep was coming. They delivered other people's sheep to their own house. Sometimes they would slaughter the beast in the field of the white boer's farm. To make it less heavy to deliver, the intestine would be left behind or scattered to confuse the dogs. The two of them would even sometimes don the sheep in coat and cap and sit it up on the seat of a bike tied with rope.

One evening in 1989 they got caught. I was standing in the street and I saw a white man in a bakkie stop them. The two brothers left their bicycles in the gravel road and ran like crazy. Tsepo managed to get away. With blood dripping from his eye and his nose, Thabang came crawling into the yard. The boers gave him a grey lump of meat where his eye was, but he wouldn't squeal on his brother.

Sipho pauses and looks up. Valentine begins the clapping.

'I'm not finished yet,' Sipho says skeefing us.

Sorry, it did seem like the end of one story,' I say.

Only when there is complete silence, does he resume. The words fall out his mouth like a slowly dripping tap.

As hungry young boys, we were often tempted to accept dishes from Thabang. Even with one eye, he didn't stop this meat business. I must have been 8 or 9. The sun is down and we decide to finish the game of street soccer in the faint light.

Only when we are kicking at nothing do we give up and get to my yard. Over an open fire stands a heavy steel pot. The smoke coming out from under the black lid smells of onions and tomatoes and meat. It plays havoc on our empty stomachs. We kids crowd around. The cook is Thabang himself.

He motions for us to get plates from inside. The cracked enamel ones we come out with, are held like shields and steering wheels. When the food is well, he lifts the heavy lid and scoops for us. Thick red gravy over big lumps of meat. We eat fast and when the last one of us is about to finish, Thabang asks, 'Do you know what this is?' stabbing the meat with a long wooden spoon.

'Of course, it is meat,' answers Tsepo, whose bellybutton sticks out like a branch.

'Yes but what kind mfowethu?' asks Thabang grinning.

We all stopped chewing, and our heart-beats were the only sounds our ears could know.

'Cat meat,' Thabang said spluttering gravy.

We tried to spit, to gurgle, to vomit. We ran to our mothers crying.

Amidst the clapping, Virginia and Pinky ululate.

'So you have Basotho in you. Eaters of cats,' says Virginia.

'I really loved the gentle flow of ideas and incidents,' says Valentine.

'Me, I liked the part about the meat,' says Steven. 'Do you know what we call the goat of the mountain?'

Nobody answers.

'Baboon,' he shouts out, patting his thigh.

We take a break and go downstairs to buy vetkoek from a vendor at the corner. Twenty minutes later we are sitting around the table again.

Sipho is now sitting right next to me. He begins reading his second window.

 CAMOUFLAGE
by Sipho

Growing up we would always go to the dumpsite, but not out of necessity like the female vultures who were always there in old dresses. Most of us came out of well-off families, in the location-sense of more than one breadwinner and all the conveniences. We, the youngsters, were looking for thrown-away toys, rubber tubes to make slingshots and any kind of thing. Sometimes we'd find reject dough from the big bakery in Kimberley, or reject meat, and we'd take it to our camp. I would always be the one reluctant to relish on it, expecting it to be poisoned. Who would throw away good things? I told myself. Every couple of days later I'd regret it, for nothing wrong ever happened to them.

As my friends scavenged around for whatever, I'd be looking for magazines and books. Once found, I'd squat oblivious to the burning trash and my friends sliding somewhere down a slope. Nothing made me more content than to find a loadfull of books.

Our treasure was dragged to our camp which was an old car. A place where stories and dreams were crafted, mockeries dispensed, adventures planned, fights instigated and smoking tried out. But I'd only be of their world when I had nothing to read.

'Hey, you are a bookworm,' they'd say or they'd call me 'Prof'.

Not far from there, across the tar road, was the coloured area. Before you reach this, there is a hole in the ground. Every time in the rainy season it would fill up with water and also with kids from all over, including ourselves. More than likely, one of us would be chased by the coloured kids with stones or dogs. Once we passed the tar road, we'd make a stand and hurl back both stones and insults. Neither side was keen to cross the road which formed an unnatural boundary.

Parents were lenient about the dumpsite but about the dam they didn't want to hear anything. In a way this spurned us on to go there. On a hot burning day, we slipped away to indulge in the coolness of the brown water which left you grey if you had not the foresight to bring some Vaseline to smear over your body. Most of us could not swim, but we pretended to by walking in the water, thrashing our arms about, or just submerging for short periods.

One time I was doing this and the laughter and joyous noise ended abruptly. I looked back at them through muddy eyes thinking, 'What is wrong. Oh, I'm the centre of attention so I'd better take another dive.'

When I emerged, I knew I'd been right the first time. There, on top of the hill stood my aunt, like a monstrosity, with my clothes held up high. Meekly I climbed the bank and held out my hands.

'Go!' is all she would say as she prodded me with stick, keeping my coverings at more than arms length.

Naked, pushed by her, I led the entourage down the street. My friends soon forgot the plight and reckoning that awaited them at their homes, and started laughing at me. My humiliation swallowed me as I limped on. Then I told myself, 'This is shit. Imagine you are a soldier. They wear brown like your colour.'

My head shot up and my posture changed like a soldier on parade. I marched on with a smile on my face. The kids stopped laughing at me, and rather at what I was doing. The sadistic enjoyment wiped off my aunt's face. She never knew what hit her and how I subtly changed the board.

This is better than I expected, I think feeling very excited. This boy can write.

'I've got a friend Roy who is writing a novel much of which is set at a dumpsite in Johannesburg, which is exactly where he spent much of his youth,' I say. 'I bet you and him could have some good conversations.'

'I loved the part about the bread dough and the bit when you used mind over matter to fox your vicious aunt,' says Steven.

'You write beautifully,' says Virginia, really looking at Sipho.

'I love it, Sipho is a pathetic writer,' says Valentine.

The room goes quiet.

'Pathetic?' says Virginia aggressively, 'I think he's brilliant.'

'Do you mean sympathetic, sort of like sensitive?' I ask Valentine.

'Yes of course,' Valentine replies, 'his writing is full of pathos.'

It is 12.30.

'Virginia, will you read us your physical description of Valentine?' I say.

We take a moment to shift gears, then she begins.

VIRGINIA DESCRIBES VALENTINE

Valentine sits with his feet almost one metre apart. His navy corduroy trousers cascade onto white takkies. They are so clean they could be foam at the bottom of a waterfall. I am stealing this image from his story he has shown me already. His white shirt has pleats around the cuffs, and one of his hands is tucked into his neck to rest on his collar-bone. The gold earring gives the impression of influence, even though he looks like a boy. When he talks, his dreadlocks follow his head as if to confirm his statements. When he smiles weakly at me, I want to return it with thrice as much volume.

'Ok, Sipho, the floor is still yours,' I tell him when Virginia finishes, 'can you go straight into your description of Valentine's home now?'

SIPHO VISITS VALENTINE

After Valentine visited me, we walked back to Yeoville together. His place is lekker. He shares a place with two Nigerians who were there listening to music. They sell cell phones and there were some lying around on the low table. Except for this table, the TV, video, CD player, and a pillow-like soft couch, the living room is very cavernous. He lives near an old steel water tower that looks Russian or something. Like a Sputnik I saw in a second-hand book. He has got a double bed with a duvet full of slices of watermelons. Below a picture of a shrine, are his Bible, a book of Saints (Catholic) of Italy and some magazines. This is where Valentine meditates before going to bed and in the morning. On the floor next to his bed are two fax machines, but they are not plugged in. His trousers hang out the window. I go without saying goodbye to his mates. Ja, his place is OK.

Sipho looks at me and indicates that he is finished. I nod at Valentine.

Beside him on the floor is a newish-looking black leather shoulder bag. He leans over and hands me a copy of his writing which he has printed out on a computer.

In his thick accent, which I am beginning to get a handle on, he begins.

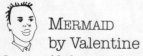

Mermaid
by Valentine

My grandfather taught me how to catch a mermaid with certain herbs. He was an overseer at a British rubber camp called Mbimbia on the south-west coast of Cameroon. In 1950 he was one of only three high-ranking blacks in the country, and was invited to month-end feasts in the homes of the British officials. He would keep the beer bottle tops for the others to smell what the British drank.

As a boy, Grandfather was drilled in superstitious schools of thought. He scared me by speaking about a half-human, half-animal with a very long tail. This creature threw sand on roofs and lured young people to become fighters against evil spirits or traditional healers. Grandfather would eat gorillas but not sheep. Killing gorillas was very heroic then.

On this journey through the forest, Grandfather was carrying wooden luggage which was considered first class. Mine was a small bag made up of a few of our dresses. He also had a rifle and a few cups of gunpowder. Gunpowder, he told me, was supplied by a French cloth-seller called Jacques Straw, who also bought dried skins from the villagers.

'To catch a mermaid it must be between 12 and 1 in the afternoon and there must be a waterfall around,' Grandfather told me. He kept on reminding me that seductive as they appear, these creatures are workers of iniquity.

'We will never drink cold water again Amajoh, since the British took over from the Germans,' I remember him saying, sitting over me beside a stream near the village of Tonkilo. He liked to call me by my middle name which means hard boiled.

We picked up our luggage and further on, near a collapsed bridge, Grandfather took my palm again and laughed aloud, 'No creature on earth is having half the luck you are having.'

It was 1979. I was four years old. My mother was in Nsanke, the village we were travelling towards. Grandfather had insisted she wait there whilst he fetch me. I was born in Cameroon, but had gone to France with my father when I was a few months old, as a pawn in my parent's many separations. This was my first time back. When my mother heard I was in the country, she sent my grandfather to fetch me, and bring me deep into her village. She was afraid my father would take me away to France again, never to be returned. She also knew his other wives in France would not take care of me like her. Father had taken me when the country was divided between the French and the British. He wanted me to be one hundred per cent French.

Most of the journey was on a wagon, but at some point the road became inaccessible. We were dropped off to walk some ninety kilometres through wild forests and having to cross many rivers.

'Taste this water. Taste it,' said Grandfather.

He carried it to my mouth in his palms, letting it into my

mouth through his fingers. It was warm, almost hot.

'This water used to very cool,' he said, 'most travellers would rest over there in the shade and quench their throats.'

I looked over and saw a waterfall but no shade.

'The British who claimed to be constructing roads, destroyed forests as well as perfectly sturdy bridges,' he said in French.

I only wanted to know about the mermaids but I had to wait. He had no love for the British. The North-West belonged to the British, while the coast had gone to France when the country was first partitioned in 1919. Some minutes later he came back to my interest.

'In our village, Eboh, mermaids usually catch little children who come to fish. You can marry one if you like, but there are certain conditions,' he said.

I had no interest in marriage. My mother and father had tried it, and already lived separately most of the time. As I said, this was much better. Grandfather pointed to the bubbles where they spin around and make a hole under the waterfall. Then out of a pouch, which he carried on his belt, he sprinkled charms and herbs into the sucking water. A black mermaid jumped out and she lay on the surface facing the sun. We just looked at her and she at us. My eyes did not know whether to stay on her wet breasts, or her fish parts, or to meet her turquoise eyes.

'Mermaids always have long hairs and can be black or white,' he told me, holding my hand.

He seemed quite stuck to the idea of having one in the family because he said, 'If you marry one, you will have to take them out every night to the river when others are asleep, and return early before the cock crows. This bores many people. Once you are married, you will find it hard to drive her away.'

The mermaid said nothing and eventually rolled over and swam down another bubble.

The clapping is especially loud this time. Oh, to be in the right space at the right time.

Almost forgot him. Halfway through the reading, a man with a shaven head and a striking face, burst through the door. Valentine had reacted with an intense look of irritation on his face, but he didn't lose his stride.

'I'm Jonathan, welcome,' I say to the newcomer, now that the reading is over.

'I'm Victor,' he says, reaching over to African triple hand-shake me.

The others appear to know him from the newspaper.

'Great story,' says Sipho to Valentine.

Patrick laughs, and sprays the table with spit, 'so you have these superstitions all over Africa.'

'This thing is very much interesting,' says Victor, the newcomer, jumping right in, 'these man-mades are fucking people around.'

'What do you mean by man-mades?' I ask.

'He means mermaids,' says Virginia grinning generously.

Victor nods. 'One time I was selling ice-creams and guava juice on New Year's Day. The sky became black. Then out of my corner eye I saw a man-made fell out of the dark cloud with hail, BOOM, into the Marula Sun dam. Shacks were thrown up off the ground and landed far away. I'm telling you these man-mades fuck people up.'

'In Cameroon,' says Valentine, 'usually there is rainbow in the sky.'

'There was one,' says Victor pointing out the window, wide-eyed.

The only reason I can make sense of this conversation, is that last week, while Hurricane Mitch was wreaking havoc in Mexico and Guatemala, a spiralling tornado hit Harrismith in KwaZulu-Natal. Local people blamed white-owned aircraft which, they said, had disturbed a giant snake in a dam.

'Before I forget,' I say, 'someone must visit Victor for next week.'

He seems like a real character.

'Where are you sleeping?' I ask him.

'I was kicked out of the unused servant's rooms in the Rosebank old-age home, and now I'm staying in the Wits Library.'

From his back pocket, he pulls out a current student card.

'It's open twenty-four hours and they let you doze a bit,' he says, 'I just put my bag under the table and sleep. I've been there two weeks now.'

'How did you get that student card?' I ask.

'I'm a student teacher at JCE in my second year. I had to cut my dreads. They told me I cannot teach the youth if I am a Rasta and smoke dagga. I have lost my strength and I am failing my tests. Before I was passing very well.'

The rest of the group have become very curious but I can see Valentine is impatient. The focus has been shifted away from him.

'OK, hit us with Window 2, Mr Valentine.'

 ## Haunted by Old Decadence
by Valentine

The last ashes from the burned fence were still falling early the next morning, even though the smoke was weak and scattered. Near where the fence had been, stood my headmaster, in mute amazement. This fence, which was seven years old, was made from thick brush sticks. Even the wildest sets of students, long before I started school, had been afraid to touch it.

'Get me Cascarino,' he ordered. I was to the side behind a mud classroom. He was right in his judgement. The morning before he had flogged me for wooing his daughter.

Corporal punishment was at its peak in Cameroon. A teacher was regarded by the natives as a demi-god just because he could speak the white man's languages. With this status, a teacher could hit any child for whatever he wished. The principal was God himself, and I had angered him. When I burned that fence, I became a wanted boy by the whole village. Some older boys fetched me and made to bend over a low stool. I was publicly flogged to a standstill.

'Go and collect even stronger bush sticks to reconstruct the fence,' the principal bellowed.

Sweat was dripping into his collar. Every day he wore a different tie but he wore the same shirt for a week.

Gabriel had encouraged me to commit the act. I was therefore not surprised to see him come to join me in the mosquito forest where I was chopping. But he came crying.

'Why are you wailing?' I asked him.

He took out his penis and showed me where the principal had rubbed pepper into the tip marked with a razor blade. Gabriel too had been accused of making love to a girl and had been punished for his sexual immorality. I don't know how I escaped this but questioning luck is bafoonish and the gambit of beggars.

Rebuilding the fence, Gabriel and I named ourselves 'Tom and Huck'. Thick in the forest at that time, we fed on their adventures from memory. When we ran out of bush sticks we intruded into even deeper foliage, finding and concentrating more on wild mangoes and plums. Cutlasses were our only weapon. After some weeks we satisfied the wrath of the headmaster with bush sticks. But through our excursions, Gabriel and my friendship was cemented and we had gained the reputation of Romeos.

In the evening we would be double exhausted but sometimes,

if our mothers were short of food, we would be sent through the wild rain to harvest extra maize. These would be roasted as the rain thrashed the thatch. Through this sound, my grandmother would talk above the cracking fire. No one would dare interrupt her and no modern man has the faintest idea of what she said.

Clapping, I motion for the others to give feedback, 'Just say what caught your attention.'

'The way teachers could do anything reminds me of the way men teachers think they can sleep with girl scholars here in South Africa,' says Virginia.

'You turned your punishment into an adventure just like I did,' says Sipho.

'Gabriel's punishment reminded me of circumcision practices,' says Patrick.

Time is up. We disband.

"

My car is still there thanks to Khadim, a man from Sudan who is selling fake designer caps and hats on the pavement. For a few rand, he keeps an eye on my wheels for me. If I didn't need him so much, I'd ask him to join the group.

IV
Virginia & Pinky

TIPS TO SURVIVE ON THE STREET
September Tip 1: If you do not succeed in finding a parking spot, try
recycling although it may not pay as well. Next time you pass through
trash, look at it positively.
September Tip 2: If you fail at parking and recycling, I guess you have to
get down with it and beg. It helps if you are visibly crippled
or have a spare baby.
(Sipho Madini, *Homeless Talk*, Johannesburg, September 1998)

On Sunday morning at 5.45 Masego opens my eyes from the
outside. Her little thumbs are inside my eyelids, 'Duddy,
Duddy.'

'Let's go to the zoo today,' says Kyoko, stretching both her
arms up towards the pressed steel ceiling.

'No, I want to go to the koppie and dance with the ZCC. For
my novel. Wanna come?'

Right outside our house, in the middle of suburbia, in a
nature reserve, there are plus minus one hundred cement circles. Every Sunday and sometimes through the night, people
wearing khaki overalls, or blue and white embroidered robes,
dance in a way that is hard to associate with Christianity.
Kyoko, Masego and I have become semi-regular members.
Without Masego, who is half-Tswana, I would never have had
the courage to apply for temporary membership. I haven't told
the Zionists I am a Jew and that Kyoko is a Buddhist. So far we
have been invited into five different circles. The one with the
huge rocks around it. The one with the tin cans. The one in

47

the thicket. And the one, on the top, overlooking the cemetery.

We climb up the slope. I recognise the priest from last week. A woman sits in the shade of an aloe, beating a cowhide drum. Wearing a blue robe, and wearing white shoes with car tyre soles, another man stamps his feet and leads the singing. A cross and a dove have been embroidered onto the back of his garment. I carry a hand-held tape recorder to capture some of the singing but I never get a chance to get their permission.

*   *   *

Kingsley is Kyoko's Buddhist friend. He is the Ghanaian street barber, my book's main character.

I park my car on the corner of Bree and Quartz, across the road from an escort agency, not far from the *Homeless Talk* offices. On the pavement is a hand-painted sign, on which a Kenyan trained doctor alphabetically advertises all the diseases he can cure. Aids, Impotence and Heart Attack are underlined in red. Kingsley, whose muscles are bulging out a sleeveless shirt, is standing on the corner, talking to a man who is sitting behind a sewing machine. Kingsley leads the way up some stairs. Across from the doctor's rooms, in a dark passage, he fishes a chrome plated door handle out the back pocket of his very baggy denim jeans. The handle is held against the store-room door and a key is inserted into the lock.

From the unlit space, he unloads some stuff. Downstairs, outside the Apangani Restaurant – *Where the smart people meet* – he sets up his barber stall. I sit on one of the small plastic stools. Shears are plugged into an electric chord hanging out the window of the bar. Both his mirrors are fragments and triangular in shape. A ghetto blaster is also hooked up.

'*Woke up this mornin', smile with the rising sun,*' wails Bob Marley.

From the front horizontal pole of his canopy, using orange synthetic twine, Kingsley hangs a pale blue, wooden barber sign. This one he brought with him from Ghana. It's also hand-painted and shows five heads in profile and five hairstyles: Ponk, One-Step, Gentle cut and Ford.

Between five rand cuts, Kingsley tells me how he taught himself to be an illegal immigrant. About the time he was in Lindela, the jail for illegals and aliens. All I know about it was that it was started by the wives of high-ranking ANC officials. Soon after the ANC came into power, it was awarded a contract for the processing and repatriation of illegal immigrants. The owners like to keep it full. Even very dark-skinned South Africans find themselves there and have to bribe their way out.

'Why don't you come tell and write your own story in my group?' I ask Kingsley.

'Ok,' he says rubbing his chin.

We agree I'll pick him up at 10.30 on Saturday.

* * *

The same week, Dioup, the Senegalese man selling leather stuff in Melville, tells me his story. And Paulo, from Angola, who paces up and down at the dam, tries to tell me his. The man I buy the mask from at Bruma flea market is from Zaire. And Ted, the editor of *Homeless Talk*, from Zimbabwe.

'Maybe I should capture the stories of how they all got here, one from every country on the continent. Wouldn't that be something?' I say to Kyoko.

'You're good at ideas,' she says folding Masego's Japanese-style-joined-at-both-sides cloth nappies.

'I'm serious,' I say, 'I think I'm going to give up my novel.'

'But you've put in hundreds of hours,' she says.

'This project has more value and the book will be better literature,' I say, 'I know what, I'll call it, *The Great African Spider Project*. GASP. All the story lines from all the different places in Africa can be the legs of the spider.'

"

Who visited who, and whose got what to read?' I ask.

Pinky puts up her hand, smiles at me, and points at Virginia. She takes out some notes, a back issue of *Homeless Talk*, and begins.

'Virginia lives in a converted warehouse. This is a story about the warehouse that appeared in the September 1998 edition. I want to read some points made in the article first, OK?'

No one objects, so she carries on. 'Cornelius House, a derelict warehouse in Albert Street, with the generous assistance of the Johannesburg Trust for the Homeless, and the Greater Johannesburg Metropolitan Council, has been converted into a living space for two hundred people. The project targets those who we think will improve their earning potential within six months. Residents must have a minimum income of R250 per month and a maximum of R1250. Rentals range from R60 per month to R180. There are communal cooking facilities and ablutions which are always locked.'

Virginia, David and Steven laugh the loudest. Pinky puts the article to one side and goes back to her own handwritten notes.

 PINKY VISITS VIRGINIA

Virginia and I talk about lots of things. At times, I hope no one is listening or recording. This time we were talking about our sons, Prince and Moosa. And men, of course! It makes me laugh how much we talk about men but are unable to strike a steady relationship nowadays. Is it age?

I decided to take Virginia to an Ethiopian restaurant. At least I had some rands that day. I ordered this flat puffy sour bread called *njira*, which reminds me of Venda food but Virginia doesn't like it. What kind of Venda is she? Afterwards she invited me to go to her place. I have been there before but that time I did not get inside because it was too late at night. It feels like the place is a mental institution. I did not want to go and wanted to make an excuse, an honest one if possible.

My armpits started sweating as we approached the place – as they do at my boyfriend's parents. The feeling of not knowing what to expect kills me. I started talking. Talking about nothing, my brain going empty. The security guard asks me to write my name in a book. He gives Virginia a card with number '5' on it.

The walls are neatly painted with a green stripe up the step. This is the kind of thing that makes it a mental institution. There is no noise as we walk up the steps. No one moving

51

around. An old guy passes me, and turns to look at my backside. Men! Now I am a piece of meat. Virginia talks to three people before we get to her room. She is popular!

I'm anxious to see the rooms. Lights are on inside behind closed doors. When she opens hers, I brace myself, and then in just four seconds, scan the whole room. There is a bed, the duvet cover is so beautiful and bright, a wardrobe on my right, on my left a mini hi-fi, and a vegetable rack and some containers. The floor is clean.

Virginia looks at me, 'What do you think?'

'It is not as bad as you said,' I say.

She points at the wall. 'But look there is no window.'

I feel bad. Maybe she thinks I do not understand how it feels. You feel trapped and angry. You want to get out and find a place you can raise your child. A window for a view of life. A window is all you want to give you hope. To make you smile. That is all.

I keep quiet for a few seconds. 'Put up a curtain and pretend,' I say.

She smiles. I still don't know what that smile meant.

She shows me the spaces where the walls do not reach the ceiling. When a neighbour turns on the light it affects you but they are needed for fresh air she tells me.

We go to buy a cooldrink in the Spaza shop owned by Steven. Some guys are playing pool outside the shop. Steven greets me but not like Rodwell, who notices women a lot. After two hours I consider myself a non-visitor. I stand up to prepare food for myself.

'Sit down and behave like a visitor,' says Virginia, as she slices a polony thicker than a normal slice of bread.

'The idea is to enjoy the polony and not the bread,' she says laughing.

I remember that it is my cousin's wedding. I totally forgot.

Rodwell and Virginia walk me to the taxi rank. Hey, who needs to be at a wedding with so many relatives when I can spend a day with friends?

At the main door the guard asks me for my number 5 card. I have forgotten it in Virginia's room.

'Go back and get it,' he says.

'When I come back,' says Virginia with a smile and we walk away with our bums facing him.

Cornelius House is not a good place for Virginia. It makes her sad. She just has to be patient. Things will be sorted out. A window will be there for you to open. You know it.

After she has finished reading, Pinky looks up grinning. The two women sit touching shoulders. Virginia wipes her eyes. Her hair is tied up today. Plaited dreadlocks sprout upwards like small bunches of daffodils. The braids are held together by a red and blue scarf. Prince comes over and whispers something in her ear.

'Sorry, he wants to go the toilet,' Virginia says getting up.

'Don't worry, I'll take him, you read your window,' says Sipho, 'I also need to go.'

'Yes, stay to hear my description of you,' says Valentine to Virginia as she watches her son walk out the door with Sipho.

 Valentine describes Virginia

Virginia's body looks well taken care of. Her plans to reduce more kilos are working. She is wearing a sky-blue, small-legged jeans for the first time. The hairdresser who had suggested her hair to be dreaded, added more edge to her beauty, which is matched with an Italian black shirt. Her actress voice has improved sharply as she reads from the A4 sheet. Virginia's smile is not fully expressed as she reads, even though it hangs on the left corner of her lip.

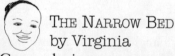 THE NARROW BED
by Virginia

'Gogo, why is everyone surprised at the size and shape of my immunisation scars?' I twist my neck and squint at my upper arm. The scars are long and white.

'Girl, yours are different because of your crazy mother.'

I am 4 and Gogo is 51 years old. We are sitting on her narrow bed. It is slightly narrower than an ordinary single bed. There is no space for any visiting boys. Even Boetie calls my grandmother his girl. Being black means you never age.

Evenings are when I can snuggle close to Gogo, looking towards the little one-plate iron stove in the corner. A ramrod metal chair, near the plug, does its job doubling as a lamp-post. On the chair is a chipped saucer on which a long white candle balances. My eyes follow the shadows on the wall and ceiling. Gogo's hand rests on my lap. Even though Gogo is scolding her daughter, my mother, I am glad to be talking about her because talking about her is usually taboo. I am always reminded that she is away drinking with men.

'She left you with strangers in Herschel. I came looking for you, just to visit, and had a hard time finding you. I ended up having to bring you here, thanks to the kindness of Miesies,' says Gogo.

It is 8 o'clock and Gogo has just finished serving Miesies and Baas supper.

'When I found you, you were as thin as a Lion matchstick, except for this arm which was double its size,' she pats the scars below my shoulder.

54

Later when I began reading comics and I saw Popeye's bulging forearms, I wondered if my arm had looked like his.

'Not only that,' Gogo continues, 'your one eye was sealed shut.'

'The arm, Gogo, what was wrong with my arm?'

'Those stupid farm people washed your inoculation with urine and it became infected. They believed the umlungu white doctors were trying to kill African children by inoculating them, and they believed urine could stop the poison. The fact that you fell ill but didn't die, they took as proof that you had been poisoned, and that the urine cure had saved your life.'

'And my eye, Gogo, what about my eye?'

'That's another story my child,' says Gogo cupping some snuff in her old hand. 'Herschel is a land of prickly pears. They grow wild all over the place. Since you had seen people picking them, your 3-year-old mind told you do likewise when the hunger pangs became too strong. You got a prick in your eye. As I said, I had no choice but to take you. Your guardians had made a mess of bringing you up, but I thanked them anyway and brought you here to Kensington. Miesies insisted that I keep you till you get well. Baas, God bless his soul, also saw no problem, even though this is against the law. Maids are not allowed to keep their children in the suburbs. You know he is a police sergeant, don't you?'

'Yes, Gogo.'

I had peeped in his wardrobe with Boetie to admire his uniforms.

Virginia finishes reading and rips her cardigan down over her left shoulder. She displays a rash of prominent pigment, which sits like a tattoo on her upper arm. We all take a look. David, who is also sitting next to her, rolls up his sleeve. He pushes his shoulder into hers saying, 'look at mine, look at mine!'

His scars, three rosettes, are also striking. Others begin straining their necks to look at their own marks.

'The narrow bed reminds me of a life full of disappointment,' says Valentine, 'it's like a symbol of deep alone-ness.'

He continues making analytic interpretations. To my surprise, Virginia's eyes sparkle then moisten.

'I never had a real home where I felt I belonged,' she says. 'I've tried many times and the first thing I always buy is a bed. Even now I sleep in a single bed, like Pinky said.'

Whilst everyone was bearing and examining their skin, I noticed how black all of it is.

'Do you know any white homeless people interested in writing?' I ask.

Heads shake.

'I once met a guy at Westdene Dam who had interesting stories to tell,' I say, 'there was one he told me about stealing horses from coloureds, and how he rode them round and into the dam. It might add some interesting colour and variety to have one more whitey in here.'

'I like the sound of this person, we should go find him,' says Virginia.

I don't tell them he also told me he was charged for murder at age 9. Something about koolies or kaffirs.

'OK, Virginia, hit us with your next story,' I say cocking my watch at my head.

Readjusting her dress, she starts reading.

 BOETIE
by Virginia

It's true I should be grateful to the Steyn family. They gave Gogo money to take me to Dr Shapiro near George Goch

Hostel. They took me in almost as though I was their own child. I try to feel grateful but I can't.

I should be allowed to eat at the table with them, on breakable plates if I'm almost their child. Don't get me wrong, I love this family. Most of the time, I just enjoy being a child. An Afrikaans-speaking child. I have all the toys and clothes I want. I eat everything I want, except I can't just go to the fridge the way Boetie does. I have learned to trick him into bringing me what I feel like eating, by making him think he's the one wanting it.

'Wouldn't you like it if a cup full of chocolate ice-cream fell onto your lap?' I'd say on the swing with my eyes shut.

'Girls are such dreamers. I'd rather fetch some real ice-cream,' he'd say, going to fetch my tin cup from the servant's quarters, and his real porcelain cup from the kitchen. They'd both come back full to the top.

What annoyed me the most was how my Gogo used to carry Boetie on her back every time we went shopping. That was supposed to be my place. People stopped in the street to admire him. To me he looked like an ordinary white child – red lips and a bit too fat. I always had to compromise for him. One day we bought multi-coloured chewing gum. I saw a black one which I quickly put in my mouth because I knew I wasn't allowed by Gogo to give things with my saliva to mlungu's child.

'I want it, I want it,' he cried and I was scolded and ordered to give it to him.

Boetie and I played the whole day together. We invented a lot of games, and in most of them I'd be the servant and he the master. He was colour conscious from a very early age. There was a gardener, called Simon, who was Xhosa and very fair in colour. There was another gardener, called John, who was just ordinary black.

Why did the Steyn's have two gardeners? Because these two were always in and out of prison for pass reasons. Whichever one of them was free, would come and do gardening and stay in the room next to Gogo's. Boetie insisted we call it Simon's room. Remember, Simon was the 'light' one and they both seemed old and a bit smelly. They wore lots of clothes all at once, clothes that included big heavy overcoats and big boots.

'Why is it Simon's room and not John's room?' I asked Boetie.

'Virginia, jy is dom,' explained Boetie. 'How can you not see that Simon is better and that he was once white.'

I tried staring at them to see them according to Boetie but I never could tell the difference.

Miesies was to me the most beautiful person on earth. She had a hive of purple hair and a skin so white it almost looked transparent. All her clothes were similar to her hair in colour. I never noticed the colour or her eyes. Her legs were always in high heel shoes.

To give them a taste of a better life, Mrs Steyn would sometimes bring a group of poor children home from the elementary school where she taught. The words they used would make the devil himself blush, and they climbed on every tree, window, pipe or wall they could. These rough children would tease me for being a black kaffir. Boetie would scream and punch them and tell them that I was a brown-kaffir, not a black one. Those were dreadful days for me.

So, when the shoeless ruffians visited, I stayed in Gogo's room.

Baas, Mrs Steyn's husband, never talked much except to tell visitors how I learned Afrikaans in three days. He'd sit on the stoep with a pipe in the corner of his mouth, surrounded by unopened packets of cigarettes on every available surface. For him pipes were the thing and he had quite a few. He died from lung cancer in the seventies when I was a teenager.

As I grew older the house no longer looked big and beautiful to me. It began to seem small and over-furnished, and the garden was overgrown with plants.

'You write simple but powerful,' says Sipho, 'straight to the thing, and the gardeners with all their clothes remind me of me.'

'The brown kaffir and the black kaffir got my attention,' says Valentine, pronouncing 'kaffir' in a unique way.

'The woman Nondomisa who helps us at home, carries my daughter Masego on her back, and her own daughter has to walk,' I say. 'Kyoko and I have tried to get her to stop it, but she won't, it's really embarrassing. In fact, it reminds me a lot about my own childhood and the women who brought me up. And their enamel plates and cups kept under the sink. And their children. And and and ...'

Virginia and I keep eye contact for what seems like a long time.

'I haven't written any windows but Virginia visited my home,' says Pinky, 'I'm dying to hear how she sees it. Pleeeeze, can she read it now?'

I look at my watch, 'Steven has two windows to read and it is nearly 12.30.'

'OK Pinky but I've got to go watch the game,' says Steven pointing at his broad-rimmed hat made out of veldskoen leather. Across the band it says 'KAIZER CHIEFS'.

'Today is the big match against Pirates,' he announces gathering his possessions into various plastic bags. Pushing his chair back, with all his things, he limps out the room.

'Virginia, we'll make this the last thing,' I say, 'go for it.'

'I've just called it, "Pinky Tinky's Place",' says Virginia chuckling.

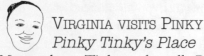

Virginia visits Pinky
Pinky Tinky's Place

My son loves Tinky, as he calls Pinky, and he is also fond of
Moosa, Pinky's 5-year-old son. Moosa can already speak five
languages. He's the only young person who Prince knows who
can speak Venda. I wish I could.

As soon as we alight from the bus in Yeoville, I notice the
streets are free to walk on, that there are real houses, and that
even the high-rise buildings are more homely looking.

We reach the house where Pinky lives with Moosa and
Hlekani, Pinky's sister. The house is very spacious with mini-
mal furniture. To me that means comfort. I like space around
me. What I love most is the big kitchen. It is well equipped
with a sink, cupboards, fridge and some other necessities. Big
windows let in natural light. Maybe it is just a normal kitchen,
but to me it seems the best kitchen I've ever known because of
the space and light it has. At my place, I have no window and
someone next door always turns on the light when I don't want
it on.

There's a toilet separate from the bathroom here in Pinky's
place. As I view those and recall that I share a toilet and bathroom with twenty others, I can't help the self-pity I feel.

What I also like is the one bedroom, which has an African
print curtain and a Shangani skirt for a wall hanging. I find it
very artistic. Even the bed is a work of art in a way. Though
there are settees to sit on, you still have a choice of scatter pillows to use. The whole place and its people are so entertain-
ing, you even forget the radio, the television and the video.
This all reminds me of how much I am missing out of on life.

Moosa and Prince are laughing somewhere outside, so I go
out to look. There is a plum tree laden with ripe plums, which
is also providing shade for our sons as they eat from its fruit.

I've never seen Prince looking so happy and free. I feel guilty as I ask myself – What kind of a useless mother am I if I can hardly provide a home for my kid? Why am I such a failure?

Pinky and Hlekani are good hostesses, but I'm sorry to say that I don't enjoy my visit as much as I should. I am too busy searching my soul for answers to my poverty. WHAT'S WRONG WITH ME?

There is a little cottage among the trees and flowers outside where Nathan, a friend of theirs, resides. I envy him the space with birds chirping happily as they help themselves to the fruit on the trees. Nathan seems to enjoy the main house more than the cottage. I don't blame him, though. His landladies are so friendly and accommodating. As if that's not enough, Pinky is also a good cook. The aroma rising as she stirs the pot is enough to invite anyone to abandon their own home and join the happy household.

❞

Driving home, I catch myself in my rearview mirror. This holding up of mirrors to get views our own eyes cannot see, really works for me. Before I met Kyoko and Masego, I'd stare at myself for ages in shared and rented Yeoville flats, behind locked bathroom doors. I'd walk on the side of the street with the most windows and I even carried a tiny mirror in my wallet. I brush my teeth twice a day now in front of a huge hanging one but I go for months without the need to look.

V
Steven

II

'I learned one thing in the Eastern Cape when eating, or doing anything else which involves looking down, always to face the door,' says Steven as he arrives late for workshop number 5.

He picks up an empty chair from the far side of the table and lifts it over to my side. On his finger is a ring which I notice is actually a watch. It rests behind one of his big knuckles and he cocks it at himself by rotating his wrist.

'Who described Steven's home?' I ask.

I've noticed that he tires and loses concentration before long.

'Me,' says David, holding back respectfully as usual, 'it was easy for me because I live just down the passage.'

He begins clearing his throat.

'Can't I read my description of Steven first?' asks Valentine.

David puts down his pages and holds up two giant thumbs.

 VALENTINE DESCRIBES STEVEN

Steven has an old style balaclava piled on his head, the kind worn by Russians in snow with spaces for the eyes and the mouth. His favourite T-shirt, black and yellow, is getting weaker at the neck level. As he speaks he lisps due to the removal of two of his incisors. Brown pair of shoes, given to him by sympathisers to enable him to teach young kids boxing, is worn out. Nails are untrimmed making him look wild like a

Khoisan. It takes him a minute to clear his throat. He always reminds me of a large schoolboy about to read his homework. He has diagonal initiation scars on both cheeks, and a chest twice as wide as mine.

 DAVID VISITS STEVEN

After a long day, I decide to rest a bit. Then somebody knocks on my door.

'Ja,' I say.

The door opens, 'Steven, it's you bra,' I shout from my bed.

'Hey, wena, m'fana, don't call me bra,' Steve says stepping into the box.

'Are you not my brother?' I ask him.

'A bra is worn by women,' Steven replies.

This is the first time we have seen each other in the New Year. I am wondering why he came back from his home in Transkei later than me, when he said he would be back one week before me.

'Was it a woman that kept you away from Johannesburg?' I ask him.

'No, my eight-roomed house was destroyed by a tornado. It got everything in my town. The walls fell on my furniture, which are only good enough for firewood.'

'I heard about this tornado but I thought it only affected Umtata.'

My room-mate Alex barges in drunk as usual. We leave him and go to Steven's room. As we enter I look at the lamp. There is a towel over it.

'It protects my eyes from being damaged by light and also to cool down my room,' says Steven.

This time Steven is doing what I call straight talk. Usually he

63

would tell a long story before he tells you what he wants.

I look around the room. It is three by three, but it's even better for Steve, as he stays alone, unlike me who has to share with Alex. I see a trolley loaded with his things. He probably took it from Woolworths.

'The trolley makes your room look very untidy,' I tell him.

But his bed is made up nicely and his room, relatively speaking, is more tidy than mine.

I look down and see cockroaches running a marathon, up and down. Who wins, it's nobody's business. I pull at my shirt and pick up a Christian magazine to fan myself.

'If there were windows, David, I would have fresh air coming hourly,' he tells me.

I don't look up but continue fanning and looking at the floor. Next to his locker, where he keeps his clothes, I see some watery stuff.

'Steve, what is this?' I ask.

'It's a glue,' he answers.

'What's a glue doing on the floor?' I ask him.

'A mouse keeps disturbing me while I am asleep, and keeps eating my food from my grocer over there.'

He is pointing at some bags of Ace Mielie Meal and Mabella, and some bottles of Black Cat Peanut Butter, and some cooking oil.

'In the night I hear it stuck in the glue, but I wait till morning till I kill it,' says Steven.

'But why don't you just block the gaps under your door with newspaper, like the rest of us who live here with the same problems?' I ask.

'Because then the mouse just visits all of us and the problem is never solved,' says Steve.

He is a social thinker, I decide about my friend.

We clap. It is a pity David has not got it together to write his windows so far. His sense of dialogue is great.

COWS IN DIFFERENT COLOURS AND SHOES
by Steven

Dlomo, my grandmother, told us this one. Stories about cows and cow thieves were her special. She was a hero to both children and adults. Her hands once poured battery acid and herbs into a young boy's leg after he had been bitten by a snake. He was fetched to his senses. She also kept all her son's *makotis* (daughters-in-law) in line to keep the rondawels clean. This cleanliness campaign was done with an iron fist and she promised us, the goats and the poultry involvement with her stick if we betrayed her wishes.

My father and his brothers were all kept from drinking out and around by her home-made umqombothi beer. During those times there was no Castle and Black Label dominance as there is today. Dlomo was of Madiba's clan but not from the royal family. She smoked the inqawe pipe named mbhekaphe-seya – smoke till you reach overseas – the whole night as she told her stories. Children and adults gathered on her polished cow-dung floor to listen.

One day Madodonke, nicknamed Shorty, found all of his four cows stolen. He reported this and described their colours to the Engcobo police. With the help of the police, who wore khaki and not blue uniforms those times, and the local Chief, and some others, Madodonke tracked the footprints of his cows to a kraal in a nearby valley. Madodonke knew his cows very well and immediately recognised them, but he nearly fainted when he saw all his four cows in different colours.

When he regained his senses, he told the police, no matter what colour, he is going to take his cows. The lawmen refused due to the descriptions on his statement which did not match these cows. Can you imagine his angriness and sorryness leaving his own cows to a thief.

One of the most unusual things that science has never achieved is changing the colour of a cow by washing it with certain milky herbs soaked in milk. The cheek of it is that the milk is most often from the cow's own udder!

Her favourite talking was of her grandfather, my great grandfather, Dumakude (Famous Even Faraway). He was a warrior through and through. His troops were tough guys who were assigned to fight off cow thieves in the rural areas of Engcobo in the ex-Transkei. In one of the fiercest fights between the cow thieves and my great grandfather, on the bushy hills, he was fatally wounded in the leg by a dirty arrow.

The thieves became better organised with guns and some modern ways of stealing. My grandfather, named Phumasilwe, (Come Out We Fight), was very brave indeed, but he didn't want to be a cow protector. He was branded a coward but he made the right move in my estimations. My father, Jim Gxelesha, was born of the first wife on 16 May 1936. He also wanted none of this cow business and left for Cape Town to become a teacher.

Steven stops reading and looks up.

'Are you finished?' I ask.

He nods.

'I like the bits about Steven's family being warriors and the movement to educate themselves,' says Sipho.

'I liked such a clear honouring of your ancestry,' I say.

'I loved the "Smoke Till You Reach Overseas",' says Virginia, 'Steve has a natural talent for translating African idioms into English and improving them.'

I look at Steven who is looking at his ring-watch. He meets my eye and asks, 'can I go on to window 2?'

'Please do,' says Valentine.

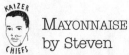

MAYONNAISE
by Steven

Unfortunately my mother and father stayed married for ten years without having any children. She became a laughing stock for being barren. After a decade, she fell pregnant and gave birth to me on the 22 August 1961 in the Cape Town location of Gugulethu. The same women who had teased and insulted her said, 'Sophie this child is gonna bring back all the respect and dignity you did not get as a wife.'

Hearing those words, my mother did not look any further, and named me Mhlonipheki, which means 'Respectable One'.

I don't know when Father started calling me Mayhanasa, Xhosa for mayonnaise. It stuck with me like a dog's hair, 'till I was old enough to fight anyone, except my father.

Even though we were living in a township, it was not so built up and we still had cows. Nothing to write home about happened in my childhood except in the year 1969, which is when I started school. Not because we could not afford shoes (my father had a good job driving a horse and trailer) but to teach me the hardships of life, I was sent to school without any foot coverings. For one whole year I was teased by the others for being shoeless. But my mother also told me shoes is not the important thing at school. She was a lovely lady, and we all inherited her beauty. She told me that she was number one in everything from form studies to athletics.

One thing I won't forget is the time she told me her principal took the whole class to the road to shout at the cars. When us kids used to forget something important she used to tease us and tell that story. She was the only one in the class who had passed the test. This teacher took them all to the main road and ordered them to shout at each and every car which passed.

'We Are Fools, We Are Fools, We Are Fools.'

They stayed out till dark and beyond.

'At least you don't have to do that, Mhlonipheki,' she told me when I complained about the shoes.

Only on December of that year, 12 months later, did my father buy me my first pair. But I was forbidden to wear them until February 1970, which is when my second year of school began.

Whakumusi (You will build our family) was our favourite cow. She produced the most milk and she was the sweetest. Over the holidays, counting the days till school began, my shoe frustration caused me to handle her urgently one morning.

Unlike the other cows, Whakumusi allowed one to milk her without binding her legs with a rope. Beside a smaller enclosure kept for sheep and calves, I sat down on a big stone to begin milking. Birds were doing their best singing in the trees and I was still worrying about my shoes which lay in their box, in tissue paper, under my bed. Like I said, I must have manhandled her teat, because Whakamusi kicked me in the left ankle and I fell forward. Tipped over with my nose in the dirt, she brutally kicked me again on the side of my head and I passed out.

It took all the people who were in my home more than four hours to revive me. What made matters worse, was the fact that we were very far from clinics and hospitals. As I had a big goose on my head I was forced to sleep for two weeks. This made me forget the problem of shoes. What I thought about and missed the most was my teasing friends.

As days went by, I tried to train my leg by walking with the help of tables and chairs. Few people knew first aid but my uncle knew how to bandage the leg of a cow with planks. I was

68

forced to drink PH2 to avoid a crippled leg. A youngster like me could not get out of drinking the very bitter substance. My leg improved and my small mind looked forward to putting on the historic shoes. During the months, I had practised tying the laces – without actually putting them on – countless times.

The day arrived, and my older cousin washed me over and over again to make sure I wasn't a laughing stock because we as youngsters were dirty as pigs. We were used to singing and playing the whole day. When the shoes eventually got on, I put down each foot very lightly in the sand outside the house to prevent any scuffing. It was a shock when my lady teacher smacked me with an open hand for making a noise in class.

Steven looks up proudly. He seems to have forgotten the time.

Clapping is a part I enjoy. Just the slapping of flesh.

'You said your father drove a horse and trailer?' says Virginia,

'Was it a horse and cart or a mechanical one which you need a code 8 for, you know one of those massive trucks?' I butt in.

'A mechanical one,' says Steven, 'he was fired from that job because he worked for the PAC.'

'To get such a position driving a truck in a white man's world is like spearing a fish,' says Sipho.

'I was hit by the way Steven was brutalised from such an early age. It's not surprising he became a boxer,' says Virginia.

'What is PH2?' I ask.

'Zifozonke,' answers Patrick, 'which means "can cure all diseases". It is potassium permanganate, we all know it as very bad tasting crystals that you mix in water to make it purple.'

He is right. Everyone has a story to tell about the bitter stuff. Steven has a way of fitting in ten stories when given a chance to tell one. Cutting him short, we call it a day.

In the passage I bump into Pinky, who works full-time for the *Homeless Talk* newspaper.

'We could do with another woman's voice,' I tell her, 'I really like your piece about Virginia's room, why don't you come regularly and tell your story?'

'I'm busy writing UNISA exams but I'll try,' she tells me.

As I exit the building, Sipho falls into step beside me.

'What you going to do today?' I ask.

He looks down, then stops and stares at the pavement.

'I'm going to Norwood to try and park.' He's talking very softly. 'Some people are good at interacting with people, you check, and they can do it, but I'm not. I'm short, seriously short.'

He turns his jeans pockets inside out and pulls at them till they poke out like ears. They are grey with small flecks of lintel pock.

'Listen Sipho, I want to give you okes something besides money. That's what I'm trying to do.'

'I know, so you don't spoil us.'

I go into the change pocket of my wallet. It's full of five rand and two rand coins. I know this because I recently emptied out all the copper and brass. I take a handful and hold it out. I can't help myself.

He takes them, closing his fist, resisting the impulse to count.

'I'll give you a lift to Braamfontein if you like.'

We end up having lunch together in Nando's. I order us each a lemon and herb, half chicken with chips and leave him at a corner table. I piss into multi-coloured moth ball disinfectant cubes and pyramids. They almost look good enough to eat.

'I don't want to lie to you or make you get the wrong picture,' he says when I return.

I shrug.

'I don't have to live like this. I've got three houses I can live in at Kimberley. My mother's, my father's and my granny's.'

Sort of like my post-matric backpacking in Europe, sleeping in railway stations with travellers cheques in my money pouch. My Kerouac experience.

'Are your parents separated?' I ask.

'Is this confident, confid …?'

'It's completely confidential,' I tell him. 'But I've already begun writing about you, I'm making notes about the group, which I read back, so you must tell me which parts I mustn't. I'll show you what I've written about you before I show it to anyone else.'

He begins, 'I've got Tswana, Xhosa, Bushman and Scottish in me. All the diamonds leave Kimberley and come to Jo'burg. The only way you can get a job is if you have an uncle who retires. They used to call me professor. I began writing a novel when I was twelve. I finished it when I was fourteen. I filled up both sides of each page of a thick hard covered exercise book, tore off the cover, and pushed it into an envelope. Then I sent it to a publisher in Jo'burg.'

'Did you make a copy first?'

He shakes his head. 'Maybe if I'd typed it, they would have accepted it, it was written in bad handwriting.'

The chicken arrives.

'What was it about?' I ask gazing at him over the rectangular plates.

'A married guy who fell in love with his cousin, who turned out to be a ghost. This is my first time in a restaurant,' he says holding his knife and fork very close to the cutting and stabbing ends.

I pick up my half chicken with my hands and take a big bite. I can feel gravy trickling onto my chin but I don't reach for the stack of serviettes with the Nando's cock.

'Tell me about … you must feel free to ask me any questions

71

you like,' I say.

'I'm not a fast thinker,' he says, 'I always remember what to ask later.'

Before we leave, I ask, 'when will you go back to Kimberley?'

'When they die, I'll have three houses. I'm not going back now, how do you say it with my tail here?' he says patting the ochre Nandos upholstery between his jeans.

Maybe the chicken was too rich? Maybe I should have asked them for a doggy bag?

VI
Robert & Patrick

TIPS TO SURVIVE ON THE STREETS
October Tip 1: Now in Winter's grip, you need a drinking hole. That is the
only vaccine of not going street crazy. Indeed it must be a cheap spot.
Regrettably it might be lethal, but what the heck.
October Tip 2: Now to the parks, if you haven't found one by now, where
you rest and gather your thoughts, pity on you, you ain't gonna last.
You need to get down to your knees and pray!
(Sipho Madini, *Homeless Talk*, Johannesburg, October 1998)

'Please could you see Mr Radebe in Section 1,' says the sister,
'he was caught hijacking and was shot to pieces.'

Section 1 in the Reef Clinic, a private hospital in Hillbrow, is
the prisoner's ward. At the entrance a warder in uniform
unlocks the door and signs me in. Ten or so policemen and
warders sit beneath a TV set mounted high on the wall. They
are watching a soccer game. I find Radebe. He is lying in bed
with an oxygen mask over his face, eyes closed.

'You can wake him doctor,' says a voice behind me.

I am tired of explaining I'm not a doctor.

'Thanks.' The sheet over Mr Radebe's legs is half off and I
notice that they are shackled in heavy steel. I lightly shake Mr
Radebe's shoulder. His eyes open one at a time.

'Hello, I'm Jonathan Morgan. I'm a psychologist. Dr
Ngobeni referred you to me. Do you feel like talking?'

My brief, from the hardworking and well-liked physiothera-
pist, is to tell him he will never have sex again.

'I am Ace. I was walking across Jeppe Street and I hear a

73

shot,' he begins in a Zulu accent, 'then I feel pain in my back and fall down. Four minutes later a white man come and stand over me. He shoot me six more times.'

'You mean you were not robbing or hijacking?' I ask.

'No,' says Ace.

'Do you know you are paralysed now and there are lots of things you won't be able to do? Your lungs and your spine have been badly damaged.'

'Please buy me cigarettes?' he asks coughing up blood.

The next day I bring him twenty-four stones. Twelve are tiger's eye, and twelve are rose quartz. I bought them years ago in a Zulu curio shop. As a kid, I used to notice the mlaba-laba boards painted on the man-hole covers on the way to school. The stones came with a vinyl board which I have since lost. I never did figure out how to play. Ace teaches me the difference between Sotho and Zulu mlaba-laba. Over the next few weeks I win only one game.

The day they go to court, I ask, 'tell me honestly now, what happened?'

'I was robbing,' he says smiling.

'But Ace, you made me into a stupid,' I say, 'I told Dr Ngobeni and the prosecutor, I thought you were innocent.'

'I will say the same thing in court,' he says looking me in the eye.

'They won't believe you but they will drop the charges so they won't have to pay for your medical treatment.'

He shrugs, 'thank you Morgan.'

* * *

Peeping up from behind the phone-fax at home, I see some paper sticking out.
Dear Jonathan,

*I can't decide whether to write about my great grandmother on my
father's side, or my grandmother on my mother's side for window 1.
GASP! HELP!*
*I found out we are from a village called Nhlengweni in Mozambique.
My great grandmother and her son, my grandfather, lost all their
family members in the civil war in Mozambique. When their village
was burned down, they crossed the Kruger National Park on foot.
When colouring this story in my own mind I imagined my great
grandmother ducking the lions to protect her child.*

Or

*My grandmother on my mother's side never slept the night before she
used to get her pension which came on the first Thursday of every
month. She would take a bath, put on her best clothes and stockings
and arrange the pillows. The whole night she would just sit comfortably till morning. Then at 4 she would begin walking five kilometres
to arrive three hours early. She never knew her date of birth, but
behind the counter they had a list of world events. The official would
ask, 'When were you born?' If the person said, the time of the locusts,
they would look on the list for locusts, and fill in 1892. If the old person said, 'the time of the guns', they would look at the list for guns
and write, 1914, and so on.*
    WHO DO YOU LIKE BETTER, JONATHAN? ? ? ? ? ?

Dear Pinky,
*Tough choice! Life is so so dense. To story it, we've got to edit out much
more than we edit in. You choose but I think I like the pension one
best!*
Jonathan.

*   *   *

In the evening I go for a ride around the dam. A man, casting
vigorously with a short wooden rod, is on the opposite bank. I

ride around the perimeter, playing with the gears and with gravity. As I shoot down a steep bank through the long grass, I hit my head on some woody fruits hanging in a willow-like tree. As I get closer, I see the man is Robbie, the colourling from Upington.

But he's not fishing. The one metre long line from the branch has a baited hook on it. He's twirling it around over the water. Swallows are diving at the bait. One bird gets jerked out the air. I move closer. Robbie's big fingers slide up over its wings and break the neck. On each of his knuckles is a tattooed letter. He takes the hook out the swallow's beak and puts the body into a yellow Checkers bag.

'Howzit. Long time,' I say. 'Are you going to chow those?'

'Mmm,' he says smiling.

I tell him about the project and ask him if he wants to join.

'Sure,' he says.

'You have a bit of catching up to do. Tomorrow morning, early, I'll come past here and give you a sheet of paper which will help guide your story-telling if you like.'

As I ride away, he shouts, 'Mr Jonathan, can I also have a pen and some sheets to write on?'

* * *

On Saturday, Robbie is waiting under the bus shelter beside the dam.

'Howzit,' I say.

'Morning sir,' he says.

'What's this 'sir' business. Cut it out, OK?'

'Sorry, sir.'

We both smile.

Nearly all the news posters on the street poles are about Viagra, or Clinton and Monica Lewinsky. Nothing about the foreigners who were murdered on the train from Pretoria yesterday. One Mozambican and two Senagalese men were chased onto the roof of a moving train. The Mozambican was thrown out the window and the two Senagalese men, brothers, were electrocuted on the over head wires. Their entangled bodies were on fire and had to be extinguished by firemen.

The only paper who carried the story on the front page was the *Sowetan*. Carriage to carriage, the brothers had been selling leather belts, filofax covers and wallets. 'You are taking South African jobs, go home all makwerekweres,' turned into a lynch mob.

'I just have to go past Kingsley's place,' I tell Robbie, 'he's from Ghana and he has his own pavement barber shop. I think you'll like him.'

We pull up outside the spot but Kingsley isn't there. His friend Michael, who sits at the sewing machine, says, 'You know how it is, mon.'

Just before I park outside the *Homeless Talk* building, I notice a fat mama in a white T-shirt and a pleated skirt shuffling down Bree Street. She has a huge ten-foot plastic bag of Agent Orange chips on her head. 'I Don't Do Crime,' is silk-screened on her bosom.

"

I run up the stairs ahead of Robbie for a piss before I head for the boardroom. Behind the urinal are seventeen neatly arranged empty Castle Lager quarts. In the room we find Virginia, Patrick, Steven and David. One of the tables has gone missing. To close the space we make a triangle.

'Hello,' I say putting down my bag, 'Where is Sipho? I wanted to introduce him to Robbie here. They're sort of homeboys.'

No one has seen him.

'Give me a minute,' I say.

I rush over to the Simota office to call Fresew and to see if Sipho is there.

'Maybe he won't come today. As foreigners, *we* are all standing low,' he tells me. 'This country is not right.' Behind his head is a poster of Haille Selassie.

He wants to talk about the murders but I can't stay. I leave him smoking behind his computer competing for space with squiggly back issues of *Simota* magazine.

'Let's start,' I say back in the boardroom. 'I met Robbie at the dam on Monday and by Friday he had written all five windows! Perhaps he can introduce himself by starting off today's reading.'

Robert smiles at everyone, swallows hard and begins.

 PATRICK DESCRIBES ROBERT

Robbie's untamed moustache, faded jacket and jeans makes him more horrible than some of his stories. His accent is is stone cold, but commanding like that of Robert de Niro, all in the gangster line.

If not for his smart shoes, and his low shaved and neat hair, he could have scared many of the writers. Like Steven, his fingernails have developed to talons. His once handsome face has been tampered with during many of his street fights. As he reads, he stops from time to time to observe people's reactions.

 OOM PAUL
by Robert

Let's take it from me first. My name is Robert Buys. I've heard from the elderly members of my family my surname was written as follows: D-u-B-o-i-s. It is a surname which originates

78

from France because as I've heard it, my great grandfather's full name was Conrad du Bois, which was later changed to B-u-y-s which is pronounced 'boys'.

Conrad du Bois crossed from France to Africa, which was known as 'dark Africa' in those days. He emerged and stopped to put up camp on the northern side of Transvaal. He explored and met a black tribe known as the Venda. These people gave him a warm welcome, and he was later offered the daughter of the clan's chief for marriage.

Two of their four sons married black ladies, and two married white ones. Other family ancestors moved to that part of the continent which was then, and still is, called Mara Buys Dorp. That place, till to this day, is reserved only for my family. As the rumour goes, the late President Paul Kruger, who was simply known as 'Oom Paul', made a written agreement for future reference.

My father was born there but later moved to Upington. I was born in a township called Vergenoeg. Dusty streets, tin shacks, shebeens and tuckshops were my environment. Our shack was six metres by six metres and was divided into two rooms.

Every festive season I went to that place Mara Buys Dorp with our name at the foot of the Soutpansberg, to visit my grandfather. My grandfather had a very vast space. There was a big house and there was a stoep going right around the house. Ten rooms and whenever I visited I had my own. There were three tractors and trailers.

My grandfather was a big man. He was about six-foot tall with tough, broad shoulders. I can say he had a long nose, an English nose, meaning to say he was more on the side of whites. He liked to sit on the stoep and face the view of his mielie fields. He was a dealer in mielie meal. I loved eating mielie meal with warm milk from his cows. He spoke Afrikaans and Venda.

There was a heavily streaming river running through the farm called the Limpopo River. My grandfather used to connect his irrigation to that river. One time, me, my niece, Bianca, and two other cousins of mine, went to the river to swim. I was 7 and my niece was 16 or 19. This is possible if your father has a child with another girl when he is very young. We walked through the mielies, which were very tall at that time, to get to the river. It took us about half an hour to an hour. I remember she told me about life on that side and school and everything. I found her to be very very pretty, especially her face and her legs which were long and shaped just right.

When we got to the river, we swam in our underpants except for Bianca. She didn't swim. I couldn't swim, so I just walked deeper and deeper into the water. In the beginning my feet were in the sand but then they stopped touching it. I nearly drowned in that same river. The current was just sucking me in. Bianca got a branch from a tree and leaned over from a bank and pulled me out.

That same night I got a hiding from my grandfather. I was the one who almost died and the only one to get hit with a willow. He had warned me before about the crocodiles and the heavy river after rain. 'If anything happened to you your mother will say I'm careless,' he shouted as he whipped me.

After hitting me he told me swimming in that river is not an easy game. His brother, who had gone hunting crocodiles in a boat with a rifle, had his boat tilted by a very large crocodile and was eaten.

'Are you finished?' I ask.

Robbie looks up and nods.

'You can write OK,' says David.

'The parts that caught my attention were these,' says

Valentine referring to his notes. 'Paul Kruger, your name, and the fact that you have land.'

'I liked the bit about the four sons who married two whites and two blacks each,' says Virginia, 'Did these families stay in contact?'

'I think but I'm not sure,' answers Robbie, liking the question.

'And your window 2?' I ask, worried about time.

Robbie moves his big body closer to the table, which is at a funny angle because of the triangle.

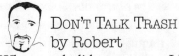

DON'T TALK TRASH
by Robert

When my holiday was over, I had to go back to Vergenoeg to sub A. My father came to fetch me with an uncle of mine. The car belonged to my uncle and it was a Dodge. It was cream in colour with those big backlights, you know Batman and Robin cars, fishtails. It had a dashboard of wood, what they say, walnut or oak. The seats were fabric and there was an armrest that folded out in the middle of the back seat.

I also remember the radio. My uncle and father liked to hear the old songs like Tom Jones and Bob Dylan. I remember one Tom Jones song about the *green green green grass of home*, and one Bob Dylan one about *Jonny's in the basement, mixing up the medicine*, and something about the *government* or something. We used to sing through our noses to sound like him.

On the way back from the farm to Vergenoeg, I can't exactly pin-point which place, maybe about twenty kilos from that farm, my uncle's car broke down. My father and my uncle climbed out, and my uncle opened the car's bonnet to look for the fault. Was it petrol or a flat battery? We didn't know so we had to overnight in the car. My uncle took some blankets out of the boot. Me and my father were in the back and my uncle in the front. We were all sleeping in the sitting position but I could not fall asleep that night. Maybe it was the crocodiles and the hiding I was still feeling.

Then something told me to look out the window into a near-by bush. It was as if something was turning my head towards that bush. What I saw that night, and what my father said was a dream, was something moving in that bush. It was in an upright position and that something had the shape of a human. What I can remember is that it was naked but it was smeared with white ash and it moved silently from the bush. I got cold – cold when I saw it stop and look in my direction. My scream never got further than my breath, and my father and my uncle wouldn't wake up. I even shook them. It was like they were under a spell that I don't understand till this day.

That thing moved towards the car and pressed its face towards the window. It stood there for about three to four minutes and suddenly my screams were heard. That thing just ran into the bush. I could see it was black but whether it was a person or something else, I still don't know 'till today.

'Hey man, don't talk trash with me, you're dreaming,' said my father.

'Maybe your imagination ran away with you or so,' said my uncle.

'You were having a nightmare.'

I still don't agree.

The clapping and the comments tell Robbie he has been accepted. He looks chuffed.

'What about Gert, your Afrikaans friend?' I say.

'I'll try find him,' says Robbie, 'but Clever Trevor may have chased him away. Last night Trevor was dronk and pulled a knife. I told him knife or no knife, I don't want to kill him. Don't take me back to a place and time I'm trying to forget.'

'Clever Trevor?' asks Valentine.

'Ja, he's this other dronkgat I live with,' says Robbie.

'OK, let's keep things moving,' I say.

"Who's next?'

Valentine describes Patrick

Patrick's white takkies are full of brown dust he gathered along the Venda area. One takkie points at the green carpet like a ballerina but he is sitting in a white plastic chair. He has been hustling people along the streets to get to the workshop on time. A meretricious gold watch is clipped on his left wrist closer to his elbow. He scratches his head, adjusts his belt of his tight-fitting green trousers, and starts reading in an accent similar to that of a Zimbabwean.

Wire Bikes
by Patrick

It is dawn in the Venda village of Phadsima. We are sitting behind a mud hut that is only half thatched. Heavy rains have collapsed the one side. Our hands are busy. We usually got the wire from the street, or we cut it from the old poultry farm fence belonging to the whites. There is only one pair of pliers which we share to bend the strong wire.

'Jabs,' called out Mr Thabu to his grandson, 'I want pap, fill the pot with water and make the fire.'

The old man loved phutu pap and milk as a substitute for meat.

I was working on a wire motorbike. It had spokes and on the

handle bars I was going to put thin rubber tubing. Mr Thabu liked my wire things. When the food was ready we ate. Jabu and Fgishiwa were his real grandsons.

Then Mr Thabu stood up holding his back as if in great pain. His other hand balanced him on the stool, which slid back making him fall onto the ground. I jumped up to help him but he refused. Then he got up and sat down again, this time on the stool.

'Your grandfather was a very stubborn man. Your family used to live in the place called Tshamathiana. I knew the place. It was next to Louis Trichardt, an Afrikaner town, in a so-called white area,' he said.

I put down the pliers to listen carefully.

'They lived there before the Afrikaners came. You grandfather and his brother had many cattle. Milk was nothing. They had containers full and anyone could go and scoop at any time. And they regularly slaughtered cattle or sheep. Those times, everything you eat is money,' he said chewing in a rather strange way.

I laughed forgetting he is not silly. He had no teeth except for a few on the lower jaw, which meant he had some leaking problems when he ate.

'Then the Boers came and chased them from their place,' said the old man shaking his head in great pain.

Even though the smoke from the fire was suffocating us, we didn't move although he was much interrupted by continuous coughing.

'That made them flee west like nomads coming here. And many of their livestock were left there because there was no transport to drive them here. The whites had trucks but you couldn't ask them,' he said.

'I was with your family and we travelled on foot. I'm sure the boers knew we would leave the livestock for them. I became a farm labourer here. We would work for three months without pay. Sometimes we would be woken by the sound of a rifle by Baas himself. The first month I would work for my accommodation. The second for my wife's. The third for that of my children. And the fourth for half my wages and packet of mielie meal.

Your grandfather could not farm properly here. There was no rain and the land was no good. The first-born in the family, your father, could not go further with schooling for financial problems. He moved to Johannesburg and became a petrol pump attendant.

That was the last thing I heard before I fell asleep on the rough sack, and something about Baas cannot pronounce your African name so he calls you Jack, and sometimes Bob or Jan, depending on how many you are who work for him.

This is the first time Patrick has read one of his windows. We forget to clap. When I remember, after some comments, I apologise.

'It's like Phillip Trousier, the ex-Bafana coach,' says Steven. 'He said he often forgets to applaud when someone scores a winning goal because he is so stunned.'

'We know you can draw and sketch from the *Homeless Talk* cartoons, but we didn't know you can write so well,' says Pinky.

'I also used to make wire cars and also oxen made of clay,' says David.

'You're a really good writer,' I say meaning it.

He smiles broadly.

'Should I read my other one?'

Chins rock on the top vertebrae.

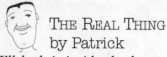

THE REAL THING
by Patrick

'I'll lock it inside the house, if you don't wash first,' said my mother.

She was fed up by my daily routine of waking up early, leaving the blankets unfolded and sneaking out to show it off. When I wheeled it up the sand road I became a centre of attraction.

An old white man had given it to my aunt as a present for fifteen years of hard work with no pay-rise. Then my brother, who was the first-born to my father's second wife, got it. Now it was mine. It made me a superkid in the village even though I could not ride it. The whole thing, except for a bit of silver and rust, was red. Through it, I got to own many privileges. Big boys no longer played tricks on me, except, if others far away from the village met me without my bicycle due to a puncture.

So I jumped quietly, and grabbed the towel on the towel rack used to hang washed clothes in the mud hut. It wasn't a rack like those stainless steel ones in bathrooms, but more of a wardrobe. It was a rope fastened from one pole to another, and it allowed the clothes, which ranged from children's to my grandparent's, to hang freely. Taking care to be less noisy, I poured warm water inside the enamel basin and grabbed a bar of Lifebouy soap. My face, my arms, and halfway my feet got washed.

The sun was only half out, but Elias was already waiting outside. As voluntary work his job was to teach me how to ride it. Seventy-something percent of him was muscle and he was three years older than me. Even boys in bigger classes were respectful of his power. It was not only my bike which kept Elias coming over to our house so often. My mother had talents for being the best vetkoek and dakbrood baker. The vetkoeks never had a chance to pile up in the plastic bowl, and the smell from them was exceptional.

As we moved away from my parents' house, he held the seat while I sat and he balanced me from falling. After a short distance, round the corner and away from family members, nicely but firmly he would make me get off. For a long long time, measured either in distance or minutes, with the pretext of giving me the lesson, he would ride standing up, sitting down, holding the handle bars and letting go.

'You are robbing me of my bike, which is mine and not yours,' I would shout, 'give it back, I am taking it home.'

Then we would both get on, him pedalling, but me in the seat. This is how it went nearly every day. Up to two or three on a bicycle was normal up to the age of 12. The tyres would look as if they were punctured but would keep on going. Elias did his job every morning until he found me gone because I could do it myself.

All of us started with wire bicycles, but by the time we were in high school, we were mechanics. His bike had a steering wheel of a car to make him and the bike look manly. Lots of hours were spent wrapping black and white tape around the bars, putting reflectors on his pedals and making the spokes click with playing cards.

As I was carefully riding on the bumpy road full of holes, this big guy called Jonnah came from behind me and forced me off till I fell down. Elias found me bleeding and even though I had discarded him, and he spent lots of time hunting for me, he found Jonnah and fought for me.

'Ee! Ee! Mula ndu,' said my granny, when I got home. She was the first person to notice the scabs and blood on top of my eye and cheek and palms.

'He will know me better!' she shouted, not believing I just

fell from the bicycle.

I soon came to the idea to charge five cents a ride, a ride being more or less the distance of a playing field. During sunset I'd come with a green ten rand. Unlike a wire car, which sometimes gets mangled or stolen by your bully big opponents, we soon realised there is plenty of money there. Sometimes when I'd go fishing with my friends, Elias would sneak away from our sight. I learned from others, that he'd fetch my bike to rob people of their five cents each to buy bread and artificial sweeteners with his profits. One such evening, a boy came running to me on side of the river.

'Your bicycle is fucked up!' he shouted again and again.

I found it mangled along the road. The other idiot Elias had loaned it to had run away when the truck hooted at him. He just left it lying half in the road and the front wheel was damaged beyond repair. I hated him I was that angry.

Back to square one where I belong, I'd go hunting the birds and fishing with half a heart. The other boys would give me the last small fishes left in the mielie bag. I'd angrily toss them back to the river for crabs to dine on. Back home, I would take the ladder and nicely climb the roof of my zinc house. The footprints of my bare feet would follow every line and track made by the wire car across the warm and dusty zinc.

'I'm working on an interview with Fresew from Ethiopia,' says Valentine before we disperse.

'How's it going?' I ask.

'He's told me about his grandfather who was a district traditional chief, tax collector and cattle rearer. This was about a century ago when King Menelik was ruler of Ethiopia.'

The Great African Spider is beginning to creep.

'What about you?' says Virginia.

'You don't read anything,' says Valentine.

'I spend all my time getting your stuff onto my computer,' I tell them, 'I'm sorry but as much as I don't like it, I've come to accept my role as different to yours.'

'Remember I said I have no interest in any money made from the book? Will you cut me in for an equal share?' I ask.

In order to begin attracting publishers, I hack out a story about the project, for the *Mail and Guardian* keeping Sipho's instructions in mind: 'Take out the bit where you appeal for computers and money; you make us seem like beggars.' Dozens of encouraging e-mails, faxes and phone calls pour in. From Pretoria, Cape Town, Grahamstown and New York. 'Send me a one page proposal by yesterday, and I'll see if I can't get you some funding,' says Roger from the Southern Metropolitan Local Council.

VII
Jonathan & Gert

TIPS TO SURVIVE ON THE STREETS
October Tip 1: Make friends; they may have the know-how of street survival and prove to be valuable assets. But remember and be careful, a friend might build you up and pull you down. Maybe it is better for now, to settle for acquaintances.
October Tip 2: Doing crime might seem like a viable prospect. Everybody is doing it and some appear to have the luck of the devil. But don't. If you had luck, you wouldn't be here in the first place.
(Sipho Madini, *Homeless Talk*, Johannesburg 1998)

It is 7 o'clock in the morning. Kyoko and I are chanting. The doorbell rings. It's Robbie and Gert.

'Hi, guys,' I say thinking 'it's not a good time'.

'Next time you see Gert, make sure you catch him,' kicks Virginia's voice.

I invite them in for coffee, make a phonecall and cancel my only morning appointment. We go down to the therapy room. Chairs are still out from a family session last night.

'Jonjibum, you better finish up,' says Kyoko four hours later, 'you've got a 12.30 at the Reef Clinic.'

'Have you got any old shoes and pants,' asks Gert as I see them out, 'my shoes are really klaar.'

'I can't look now,' I say closing the green door, 'but I'll see what I can find. Meet me at the dam tomorrow at just after 5.'

*   *   *

90

From the turnstile on the pavement, over the merry-go-round, and through the jungle gym, I can see Gert and Robbie. They are standing under a willow tree. It is the Jo'burg version of an Impressionist painting, Millé or Renoir.

A Disneyland-fat tannie, and her skinny husband in khaki shorts, lie on a bank of green kikuyu grass. They are tending a flock of five rat puppies and three very hefty kids, lazily orbiting on the merry-go-round.

'Pasop die hondjies, moenie hulle squash nie,' says the woman, not looking up from *You* magazine.

Behind them, the oldest and hugest willow tree standing in the middle of the island, fills up with sacred ibis. Gert has a line wrapped around a long tom of Black Label. Next thing the sinker is flying out over the water, the beer can is spinning.

'Fok, I don't think I can cast that far with a rod!' I say not sounding quite like myself.

'I learned to fish right here as a lightie, and in the army we also had to learn to survive with less than four fifths of five eighths of fokall,' Gert tells me winding up some slack.

'Clever Trevor schemes he can fish,' says Robbie, standing to one side, 'but he can't, not like Gert.'

I hand over the footwear.

'Shoes for us is like cars for you,' says Gert, putting his on.

'I already typed up your interview into stories,' I say, 'I'm really pleased with how they came out. Will you come on Saturday to read them yourself?'

'Ja, do,' says Robbie.

* * *

First I go to the Spar and buy a kilo of sugar, one hundred Joko tea bags, a box of Ouma rusks and ten Chelsea buns. Maybe if there's something to eat, people like Sipho will be less inclined to miss. I've resisted this line but I want to get this book out.

I pull up in front of the bus-stop by the dam. An Egyptian goose sits on the lamp-post which bends over the road. When I open the car door, it takes off squawking before landing in the water.

"

'Gert couldn't make it,' says Robbie, 'he had to go to Turffontein.'

'At least I've got his stories in my file in here,' I say patting my backpack, 'I'll read them today.'

Robbie helps me carry all the food up to the boardroom. The huge security guard in his very smart uniform no longer asks me to sign in.

'Anyone seen Sipho?' I ask.

'He wasn't at the *Homeless Talk* meeting,' says Valentine.

'Help yourselves,' I say spreading out the grub.

Fresew goes to the Simota office to boil a kettle and to fetch cups. When he comes back, Steven does the honours. An eighth of a half kilo bag at a time, the sugar is poured into the plastic cups. He uses a mangled red marker pen, with a black lid, to stir the tea.

'I got it together to write windows 1 and 2,' I say, 'and I met Gert at the dam and interviewed him at my house, covering nearly all his windows.'

Everyone claps.

'I was hoping he'd come today,' I say, 'can I read you his windows one and two?'

'No, read yours,' says Virginia.

'Yes, yours first,' says Valentine, 'but first let me read you this.'

Valentine describes Jonathan

Jonathan is always the first to arrive. His thin dark hair is short but untidy and his brown eyes always look tired but never miss a thing at all. The army khaki trouser is the one you'd expect on a teenager. A green watch on an aluminium strap, used by deep sea divers, and which is always facing down with gravity, makes the only ticking sound in the graveyard silenced room. Jonathan's once Jewish accent has been overshadowed by conventional Anglo-Japanese. His white T-shirt, having drawings of various African hair-styles, takes me backwards. It is a Ghanaian street barber advertisement on mustard background: 'Salon of Good Time'. A black comb design like the hand of a man, and a rectangular non-safety old fashion razor blade is in the centre of the styles. As usual, Jonathan's face always looks a little discomposed.

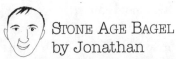

Stone Age Bagel
by Jonathan

My father, Issy, tells me this story at eighty kilometres an hour on the way to the farmhouse he used to live in. I am sitting beside him holding a tape recorder. My mother, my brother and my two sisters are in the back.

'Grandpa Ben was a tinker in Lithuania. A tinker is someone who repairs pots and pans. He and your Granny Ethel were born in 1901 in a village called Seta. In 1921, Ben served in the Lithuanian Army. Ethel loved reading and writing and all the young women in the village came to her to compose and write love letters to their absent soldier boyfriends. She had no boyfriend of her own. Ben received a batch of her letters. After his military service, he came back to Seta, found out that his girlfriend was illiterate and married Ethel.

In 1928 we sailed from Libau to London to Cape Town. With the Czar and the Holocaust around the corner, it was a good place for Jews to leave. We still have the ship's ticket and lots of other photos and documents and stuff.

Grandpa Ben who could only speak Yiddish, knew almost nothing about farming, never mind farming in Africa. He was put in charge of a group of Zulu labourers on a relative's farm. They couldn't understand a word he said. Every time he opened his mouth, all the workers heard was 'Hom Hom' which became his nickname.'

We pass the school in Bethal where my father regularly broke his knuckles on anti-Semitic Afrikaner schoolboy heads. He takes his right hand off the steering wheel to show us.

The farmworkers called my dad 'Umchecha' – One Who Hurries. On the next-door farm, lived a bad Jew called Jack, who killed a worker. This worker allegedly took a few swigs from Jack's liquor cabinet. The Jews in the neighbourhood of Leslie and Bethal are notorious. In about 1950, they were suffering from labour shortages so they clubbed together to build a prison according to government specifications. Around that time there was a wave of African rioting and resistance to apartheid. A rash of arrests followed and, in partnership, the farmers and the government stocked and staffed their prisons.

We are ashamed to admit it but our family, the Morgans, owned and paid for one unit of the Leslie prison. Our return on our investment was thirty prisoners we could call our own, plus an armed guard who watched them work in the mielie fields.

Jack owned more than one share. One day, this Jack dropped dead in a pharmacy for no apparent reason. Sometimes God does pay attention.

The *Haggadah* is the prayer book for the Passover Seder

(celebratory meal). It's a great festival. We, the extended family, sit around a huge ping-pong table, sagging with food and symbols. The table is covered with a white table cloth, wine for forgetting, unleavened bread for leaving in a hurry, bitter herbs for tough times, apples and honey for a sweet new year, chicken soup, kneidlach and teiglach.

Seated like this with one chair left empty for Elijah the prophet, we take turns to read from the *Haggadah*. It is full of stories from the Jews' times in Egypt under the Pharaohs, their wanderings in the desert, and their arrival in Palestine. There are also some songs that have crept in reflecting times in the Diaspora, and reflecting life in the shtetls of Eastern Europe. There is one favourite song called 'Chad Gadya' ('An Only Kid'). It's about a goat that someone's father buys for only two zuzim:

An only kid, an only kid, my father bought for two zuzim, an only kid, an only kid.

Then came the cat, that ate the kid, my father bought for two zuzim, an only kid, an only kid.

Then came the dog, that bit the cat, that ate the kid, my father bought for two zuzim, an only kid, an only kid.

Enter more characters/animals/perpetrators/objects/supernatural beings. Sticks to beat dogs, fire to burn sticks, water to quench fire, an ox to drink the water, a butcher to kill the ox, the Angel of Death to slew the butcher and finally the Holy One Blessed be He, to destroy the Angel of Death. The sentences get really long and it has become a perverse kind of unofficial tradition to read 'Chad Gadya' very very fast without pausing for breath and without cheating by skipping words.

Nu? (So what?) What has this to do with my Dad and Jack?

This Jack, the killer of Black farm labourers, always used to turn up on my grandparents' farm, Bankpan, looking for his fox-terrier. An only dog, an only dog.

It came to fight with their cat, an only cat, an only cat.

Then came my father Yisroel Avram who tried to separate this dog from his cat. He was only a kid. An only dog, an only cat.

The cat sunk its teeth into Yisroel Avram's leg. It wouldn't let go and the dog killed the cat still attached to his leg. An only leg, only a leg.

Then came the country doctor, who was also a vet and also a dentist, to sort them out. Chad Gadya, Chad Gadya.

Sixty-five years later my Dad still has the scars.

'This feels good,' says Virginia.

It does for me too. I can feel warmth coming from her brown skin and from beyond and around her. Prince, who usually plays in the corner, is sitting on her lap. The circle feels rounder.

'When you write, it's like I'm there in places I didn't even think I would go or not go to,' says Valentine.

'I heard about Bethal from my uncle who was a farm labourer in Leslie, eishhh,' says Patrick. 'They used to call it Betalie.'

'You are a writer like your Gogo,' says Steven, who I remember was so proud of his Gogo who smoked a pipe called 'Till you Reach Overseas'.

'Did you get into fights at school?' asks Valentine.

'Actually I did,' I say, 'but not around anti-semitism. 'I went to a Jewish school, it was more about standing up to bullying.'

'And window 2?' asks Virginia, 'I can't wait to hear it.'

'I'll read it at the end of the morning,' I say. 'Now I'll read Gert's stories.'

'When will we get to meet him?' asks Steven.

'Ja, why doesn't he come?' asks Patrick.

Looking over at Robbie, I begin making excuses.

'Never mind,' says Valentine. 'I realised the other day this project is going to push us all to unprecedented heights. Let's work with who is here, read us your window 2.'

POWER SHIT
by Jonathan

I am 10. We live on a busy intersection. I lie in my room, which is closest to the street, under one sheet and one pink Waverly blanket. The headlights sweep through the burglar bars making the knot holes and the evil eyes in the pine ceiling glow. On the pavement just outside my bed is a bus-stop for black people and green buses. Across the road is one for white people and for red buses. There is also a Greek café, an Italian barber, a Portuguese vegetable shop, a black newspaper boy and a black mielie man. He arrives and leaves on his bicycle balancing the biggest hugest sack of green cobs.

The kitchen looks into the yard from one side. Emma's and Phineas's rooms open onto it from the other. A dark concrete sink with long bars of marbled blue and white sunlight soap and a drain always clogged with old mielie pap stands near the kitchen door. The view is mostly obscured by sheets and clothes. They hang from wooden pegs on the lines, suspended from crossbars on solid steel poles. It is the Third World part of the home, where things happen. There is also soil erosion and music.

A shongololo crawls into our giant female tortoise, Oldie. A hole has been drilled into her shell. She pulls us on a little sledge down the hill in the front garden. With my bum higher than my head, I watch this hundred-legged-black-little-creature march and disappear across her scaly skin. It goes in the space between her front leg and her neck. Oldie is over 100 years old. We can tell from the patterns on her shell when we turn her upside-down. The day after the shungu crawls in, she dies.

I watch Phineas hollow out her shell in the yard with a bread-knife. He has a big afro which is unusual for a garden boy. He once showed me a little red tin with a dragon on it, pointed to his pipi, and told me when I'm big, I must rub it in to make me strong. As he told me this, his one fist went into the crook of his other arm, his forearm sloping up at the oak tree. Then he wiped imaginary sweat from his brow and flicked it off.

When the tortoise is dry and stops smelling, I walk to school holding it in both arms and give it to Mr Tisdal for the science museum. Emma cuts a chicken's head off and it runs round and round the yard, spurting blood through its neck till it drops. Power shit.

I'm sitting in this kitchen on the tiled window ledge drinking hot chocolate. A man runs into the yard shouting, 'Ek sal jou doodsteek!'

Then he stabs Phineas in the shoulder. I'm called to court to give evidence. The defendant's lawyer tries to show that I can't understand Afrikaans but the judge says, 'Your Afrikaans is very good for a 10-year-old English boy.'

Long before that I used to sit on the floor in Emma's room when my mom was at work. Emma wouldn't let me sit on her bed, which was made up with heavily starched and elaborately laced linen. She'd iron and arrange it into fans every single day. When she took a nap at lunch time, she'd sleep on the floor. That way, things wouldn't get messed up. The bed stood with three bricks under each leg, so the ugly dangerous dwarf with the long penis, Tokoloshi, wouldn't make her pregnant at night.

Tomorrow is Thursday. The day the dustbin truck comes. I love watching the dogs. Roger, an Alsation, and Ambrose, a labrador, chase the dustbin boys in the driveway. Emma says it's not funny. How can so much fit into one corner?

I am playing two-a-side with my younger brother Barak,

against Gavin and David from next-door. I call David, Dipede or Dipe. He's nippy. There is a hole in the hedge. Today is a home game. They and their house are weird. Totally different fauna and flora. Another planet wouldn't be putting it too strongly. They have red hair and freckles and their swimming pool is acid clean. Their dogs double up as cats. Our pool is always green, full of leaves and water skates. They have fine grass and cacti. We have kikuyu and flowers.

Today we are killing them. The score is 32–14. I dribble past Gavin, feint to the left and score with the outside of my right foot. Dipede is fetching the ball, which is the yellow Lion, from the hedge full of mousebirds. Sometimes even now, I like to hold that ball under my chin when I sleep. Emma screams. Dipede stops with his hands in the green leaves.

I run towards the yard. There's this man I recognise from shul who is a part-time police reservist. Behind him are four other policemen in blue uniforms.

'Good afternoon,' I say.

They ignore me and kick in Emma's door. They hit her with a baton on the back.

Gavin and Dipede run home and Barak runs inside. Emma ducks into her room. The reservist, and one in uniform, drag her out and handcuff her. They lead her to their yellow police van.

'Why? Why?' I cry.

'She's running a shebeen. Selling alcohol illegally,' says the reservist.

That night, Dad bails Emma out of the Fort Prison in Hillbrow.

Two days later her friends are back sitting around drinking Lions and Castles.

'Aren't you scared the police will come again?'

Emma shows me her gums and clicks, 'I have paid them for

this month and next.'

I slip out to make a catapult from the forked branches in the hedge. Even though flies are harder to hit than birds or butterflies, I prefer them.

'Well there's it, I've caught up with the rest of you,' I say, 'we don't have much time, so let's move on to Gert.'

'Hold it,' says Valentine, 'let's take five minutes.'

*   *   *

'Ready?' I ask when everyone is back.

'Just let me set the scene. Robbie and Gert came to my house. Robbie was sitting to one side in my therapy room. Gert's shoes were really fucked. Robbie was free to interrupt but mostly I was interviewing Gert. Sometimes Robbie explained stuff and sometimes he asked Gert questions. After they left, I typed up these stories from my notes. This is Gert's window 1.'

It's a white boy day.

 SMACK SHOT LOUIS
by Gert

My mother was 16 when she came into South Africa from Buenos Aires, Argentina. It was the time of the Boer War. When her family landed in Durban, they put her in a bomb factory. That's where she met my father who was in the South African army. I have never visited his side of the family who were heavy lanies (posh whites). Mostly my father talked about war times. I grew up with my mother's parents who lived in Ararat street right here near the Westdene Dam, close to Jonathan.

The only one of my father's family I knew was his brother, Louis. Sometimes I used to stay by him in Mayfair but he was taking main lines, you know heroine with a syringe. Before he used to spike himself he used to hide the key to his room to stop himself going outside. Then when he was lekker on, all he wanted to do was get out to the street so with his pistol, he'd shoot the whole door into splinters to get out.

'I'll race yous round the back,' Uncle Louis shouted at me one day when he was tripping. 'Go, I'll give yous a head start.'

I just stood there, my barefoot stuck to the pavement.

'Go, jou fokken lightie,' he screamed.

'But you're old Oom, and I'm fris, I should give *you* a head start,' I said.

'Nooit, fokken go until that tree and run before I lose my temper,' shouted Oom Louis.

The trees were planted evenly up the road.

Walking backwards and facing him, I walked to the next tree. He jerked forward so I turned and began running again. I looked over my shoulder but he just kept the same distance behind me, not trying to catch me, but not letting me get too far ahead. Every time I stopped, he'd make like he was going to come and catch me.

I came to the corner near the Jan Hofmeyer café and he was about two trees behind. When I took the corner, he took out his gun, and PHEWW he shot me right through the leg. It came in here and came out here.'

[Gert leans forward in the chair, rolls up his brown trouser leg, and points to the holes below his knee.]

Even though I have just read it, I join the clapping.

'This is sad sad but good,' says Virginia. 'Imagine an uncle shooting his own nephew like that.'

101

'I want to know what happened to Louis. The reader will also want not to be left in the balance. Did he get arrested or shoot himself?' David adds.

'Uncle Louis reminds me of a ghost,' says Robbie. 'They follow you but every time you stop they stop.'

'I know that area Jan Hofmeyer,' says Valentine, 'it is behind the SABC. The people there are poor whites. They are always on their stoeps, or lying under cars fixing them with their feet in the street.'

'This is the one I've been boasting to you about,' I say going on to Gert's Window 2, 'it's about the horses.'

HORSE DIEFS
by Gert

Me and Koelietjie – we used to call him that because he was like brown in colour even though he was white you check, he just looked coloured. After school we used to join our ties together and walk from Crosby Primary to that Claremont Location there. That time it was still wild man, all the coloureds had their horses in this big field. We'd go into the sloot, this big river drain thing, running through the veld, and one of us would jump up and grip the horse that was nearest the edge. We'd gooi a knot from our ties, around its mouth and under its tongue, jump on, and fokken ride away. The other ou would stay in the sloot, and run in there so as not to get seen and caught. We'd meet him later by the dam.

There by the dam some others would be waiting. Like Piet who now owns a huge panel beating plek in Booysens, and Sarel who is a security guard in Florida. We'd take turns to ride the horse around, wherever we wanted, even into the Melville Koppies, as long as we didn't take too long.

One day Koelietjie was you know stealing this lekker spotted horse from the veld. He was already on it and suddenly this coloured oke came galloping on another horse and started sjambokking him. You check this coloured oke, a toppie, could ride good. Koelietjie kept on moving it. He knew if he fell off this coloured toppie would bliksim him. From the sloet, I checked them going like this, neck-by-neck, all the time the coloured ou swearing and sjambokking Koelietjie.

Then Koelietjie made his horse jump into the sloet, and the other horse, a big brown one, wouldn't follow. We escaped and came down to Westdene Dam. We don't know where that oke went to because we never saw him again.

Those days, there were three and not two dams, before the University drained and covered the middle one for the rugby stadium. Koelietjie and me took this horse down to the middle dam, and we rode that horse *sat* because we were like pumped up from that toppie chasing us. Taking turns, we rode it all the way to the koppies, and up some fokken steep slopes. There was white foam and sweat coming out its mouth and all over its neck and chest. We schemed we had better cool it off, so we took it to the top dam and rode it in the water. I was on it that time. When the water was up to its chest, this horse just fell over. I got off quick and we waited but it didn't come up.

Our ties were all stretched and fokked up so we had to go home and wash and iron them for school the next day. When we came back to check the horse, it was just lying there all blown up.

Our ties were also taking wear and tear from benzine. In our suitcases, or in those school desks which you could fold up, we kept a jar. We'd fold the end of our tie in our hand, dip it into the jar and suck till everything zinged.

One time Onnies, the teacher, was writing on the board making that squeaking noise and we were full of benzine. In our heads we heard, 'Squeak, Squeak, Squeak,' and started laughing.

Onnies turned around and asked, 'What's so funny?'

We just kept on laughing. You check lots of us were doing it. Nobody knows what's funny so he keeps asking and in the end he also laughs along but he doesn't know what for. Then this oke Attie, pimped us. He fokken told Onnies what we were sniffing. Attie had a pair of big fucking ears and a fat face, and he wanted to be class prefect.

Onnies came and looked in all our bags. He found nineteen jars out of thirty boys. We were taken to the head's office and had to bend over a desk holding the legs from the other side. Our toes were hanging in the air. He gave us six of the best. After the first one, your gat went dead, and you went to the back of the queue to wait for your second one. On this second one, the life came back into your arse and it hurt even more. Three, four, five and six were into the wound. After six we would run past the other classes to the toilet and check out the marks. They were blue like big lips. One ou Dirkie rubbed onion into his to make it swell up and he showed it to his mom and got Onnies into shit.

To tell someone's story without them there is a responsibility.

'That piece is fascinating,' says David. 'Do you have your scrapbook here Jonathan? I want to have another look at Gert's picture.'

'He looks more like a coloured than a white guy,' says Valentine.

'It is from all the meths and hard outdoor living, your skin becomes like leather. But what makes me laugh is that his friend is called Koelietjie, normally reserved for Indian chaps,' says Steven.

'This onion thing,' says Valentine, 'we usually do it in Cameroon but in another way. We would take the teacher's cane and rub it with newspaper. Then we put the handle in the heap of a black ant, down a tunnel for one night. Next time the teacher picks it up his hands will start swelling.'

VIII

A fax comes through the machine in my lounge.

'What's this? Is it for you?' I say to Kyoko, squinting at the thing from across the room to see if it's in Japanese or English.

'No, it's not for me,' she says, standing over the thing.

It's from the Southern Metropolitan Council. Something about a ceremony in Soweto. I phone the number.

'Will you be attending to collect your cheque?' asks the African voice.

The master of ceremonies is a fat cat wearing lizard skin boots and a cowboy hat. After the speeches he pisses the mayor of Soweto off by counting and feeding back to her the number of times she says 'and in conclusion'. Before the cheques are handed out, we have to endure Sasko Sam, a huge orange dinosaur thing doing aerobics and chanting, 'I'm Special, Your'e Special, We're All Special' to a kwaito rhythm.

When I get my hands on the envelope, I rip it open – R35 000. I'm not asked to sign for it. Half the recipient organisations are not there to collect their donations.

I manage to get Fresew, Valentine, Patrick and David on the phone. We go out to celebrate in an Ethiopian restaurant, the one Pinky described. From the street, you'd never know there was a restaurant inside. Over huge plates of spongy fermented bread, spicy food and sweetened avocado drinks, I tell the group that I want to take time out as the main point of view character.

'Like how?' says Valentine.

'Seeing you asked,' I say, 'from the first time we meet in the New Year, I'd like you to pay attention and take detailed notes, capturing what goes on in the room and what is happening in your life between sessions.'

We raise our glasses filled with the green juice. We drink to the project and to Sipho.

*   *   *

Going through passport control helps create the illusion of far-away. I'm glad to be away from the book and the group. Mbabane, Swaziland is only four hours drive from Jo'burg. The borrowed mansion has a fine collection of cds. Careful not to get mango onto the pages, I work through the owner's collection of *Granta* magazines.

On the second day, we spend most of the morning outside a bank in a four-wheel drive. Roxanne, the woman whose friend lives in the mansion, pops into Standard Bank to withdraw some money. After two and a half hours I go look for her and find the bank locked. Inside I can here people chanting, 'Break the Glass, Break the Glass.'

When she finally gets out she tells us she was told she has no signing power on her own account. That her husband has to co-sign. That she has been signing by herself for four months, no problem. The riot started when a Taiwanese man was told that none of his R100 000 is currently available. From his briefcase he took out a hammer.

*   *   *

We've only been home a few hours and the phone rings.

'Hello, this is Virginia.'

Loud music in the background.

'Where are you?' I shout.

'In a horrible tavern, I just came to phone you.'

'Is something wrong?' I ask.

'I heard Sipho is dead. Another street kid told me he tried to steal a cell phone and was shot in the back.'

Straight away I get Valentine.

'Some other *Homeless Talk* writers,' he says, 'already looked at the mortuary but they are not exceptionally reliable.'

* * *

At a high wooden counter stand a group of men paging through a photo album. It is difficult to determine who works here and who is visiting. I take out a photo I have in my diary. Holding Masego's hand, Sipho stands ankle deep in my uncut grass, his eyes looking out for puppy shit. Behind him are rows of mielies and sunflowers.

'Malini, iphoto?' a woman wearing a colourful doek asks us.

She plucks the photo from my fingers and examines the grain of the print making approving noises.

'Sorry, I don't speak Zulu,' says Valentine.

'We're not selling photos,' I say, 'we have come to look for this man.'

She looks me up and down.

'Do you work here?' I ask.

'I help, my name is Maria.'

She is not wearing a uniform.

A man in front of us squints through thick glasses at a tattered black and white photocopy of an ID photo. It takes up only a fraction of the page and his eyes move from it to the colour photos of corpses in a big book. After a minute, Maria takes the book from him and slides it across the scratched wooden counter towards us.

DEATH REGISTRATIONS, STERFGEVALLE, GOVERNMENT MORTUARY.

Ledger pages with red columns have been divided into eight.

108

Each space has a photo of a person lying on an aluminium cot. Down the chest is a rough line where you are sawed open and stitched shut. The final effect is a platted thong. On each photograph is a green sticker which corresponds to the number tagged to each body. Some bodies have more than one tag. One photograph is of a pile of bones and a pair of boots. A tag is threaded through the skull's eye-socket, and another through the boot's eyelet. Nearly everyone is black and there are more men than women.

'Ons het een,' says an Afrikaans white male voice.

I look up. He is behind the counter. A gun is under his belt. His finger points outside to his vehicle. On the wall behind him is a calendar advertising Rand Funerals. On it are photos chronicling the annual improvements in hearse technology.

'Keep looking,' says Valentine flipping the pages.

Some photos say 'ONBEKEND' and others say 'ID'.

There is a strong smell of formalin and I'm trying to act matter-of-factly.

'If you see him, tell us and you can look in the fridges,' says Maria, cheerful as ever.

When we let ourselves out, everyone is out to lunch. The only other live person is a woman sitting on a twenty-foot long wooden bench at the back of the waiting room.

IX

In the boardroom and in the men's toilet there are posters of Sipho, one of which I remove.

By noon no one has arrived.

On my way home I take a turn past Sipho's drain. I leave the car idling in the alley and squat down beside the covered trench.

'Excuse me, is there anyone here?' I ask.

A head pops out at the other end.

'I'm looking for someone who used to live here,' I say.

'Sipho?' says the young man hoisting himself out the drain.

He looks about 15 and has an alert calmness about him. I take out the photo of Sipho and Masego and hand it to him, saying, 'I'm a friend of his from his writing group.'

'I'm Foster,' he tells me in an accent with a trace of Portuguese. 'Sipho was arrested last year. Before he told me he was planning a hit to get money to rent a flat. One night he got drunk with that other Rasta who also lives here. They broke into a Spoornet near Park Station. Only Sipho never got away. I think he's in Sun City.'

* * *

Masego is pretending she's making a fire in the sandpit. Some boys, with scooter tyres around their waists, join in.

'We pay this Montessori Pre-School, three hundred and fifty rand a month so our kids can learn to play necklace-necklace,' I say to Vivian, a mother, as we sneak out.

At Prontaprint, I make one hundred copies of the poster. Valentine is waiting outside his flat. He's brought nothing except for a little wire bound notebook and a pen. I'm never sure which Soweto turn-off to take. Near South Gate Shopping Mall, I stop beside two Shangaan women sitting next to piles of mangoes. Valentine gets out to ask directions.

'Sawubona Mama, iphi Sun City – Diepkloof Prison?' he asks in pidgin Zulu.

'Sitengisa amamangos,' replies the one woman.

He turns to me, 'They don't know. They are from Thembisa.'

I laugh at his translation. Further on, a worker in the back of a bakkie tells us it is just a little further on.

The prison stands on the right side of the road. A huge concrete edifice behind two tiers of fifty-foot wire fences. The signs read, 'DANGER, GEVAAR, INGAZI'.

On the back of a hand-torn scrap of paper, stamped with Head of Prisons – Johannesburg, a warder asks me to write down Sipho's name.

The same turnstile both admits and discharges visitors. We enter another room in which a woman, who seems disturbingly computer illiterate, searches for Sipho in front of a monitor.

'He's not here,' she says after a minute.

I take out a copy of the poster. A name search is useless anyway. He carries no ID and why would he want a criminal record against his real name?

'Go to Medium A, awaiting trial prisoners, and ask in there with the picture,' says a voice.

When we get off, I notice that the firecracker things on the fence, joining the spirals of razor wire, are fuses. They look like those red and black armoured locusts that hit Jo'burg in September.

A pretty warder with bleached hair, in an outfit that is more cream than khaki, frisks us. She admits us into a courtyard full of visitors under umbrellas. Three hundred bodies at least.

They look ready for a long-long wait. I push to the front of the crowd. I tell the warder we are looking for someone. Mr Madini. Mr Sipho Mandini. And I tell him our story.

'You can't go in, you must wait till they call the prisoner,' he says.

'But he's not using his real name,' Valentine begins to explain.

The man shrugs.

We turn around and begin marching to the admin buildings, outside the perimeter of the prison.

Soon we are lost and turn around. We take a short cut back through patchy fields of yellow daisies. A pole, almost as thick and tall as the Hillbrow tower, looms above us. I look up. At the very top, mounted on a giant ring, are sixteen spot lights.

We find an office with a sign 'Chief Social Worker' opposite another one that says 'Chief of Security'.

'Kom binne,' says a voice.

'Where did you study?' says Piet Jeppe. Quite young to be a chief, I think to myself. A tin of green paint sits at his feet beside a copy of *South African Journal of Social Work*.

'Eddy is who you want,' he says after hearing us out.

A heavily tattooed guy in prison pants, a scarlet waistcoat and a back-to-front cap, comes into the office.

'E53,' he says taking off with the poster.

'Can't we go in there with him?' I ask. 'To tell you the truth, I've always been very curious about what it's like in prison.'

'We do this fundraising thing called Breakfast Behind Bars,' says Piet. 'The best I can do is invite you to that.'

'A lot of guys in here look like this,' says Eddie when he comes back.

We get luckier with the Chief of Prisons.

I slide the poster across the desk, past a box of two hundred Panado. He has a green platted rope disappearing into his armpit. We are sent out under escort. Behind Ivan Meyer, a sharp short warden in uniform, we enter the bowels of the prison.

'Wat soek jy kortbroek?' says the giant armed warden at the front gate. He is brandishing a twenty-centimetre key which is attached to his wrist by a type of dog leash.

'Poephol,' says Ivan.

The key is punched into the lock, and CLINK we are in. To our right is a row of very small cells. Each one has a white toilet bowl at the far end but no bunks. Prisoners sit with their heads in their hands or sprawled across the concrete.

'For court today,' says Ivan.

We pass through another gate, into a in a long alley-way teeming with men.

'Ken jy hierdie ou?' asks Ivan flashing the poster.

'He's in 31,' says this one.

'In 39B,' says another.

Up a flight of stairs, the poster is passed through the bars. Jeans and trousers hang out to dry. I peep through. The interior of the cell is poorly lit. I can see steel bunk beds and slow movements.

'Hey, give it back, it's not for zol paper,' shouts Ivan calling for the poster.

'Don't look at it like it's a woman,' he tells another guy who keeps it too long.

Some of the cells are locked and others are not. The entrance is through the ablution space. Two urinals, two showers and two toilets. A curtain made from blankets separates the final section into a private bedroom.

We pass two guys with shaved heads. Their shirts are unbuttoned to the waist. I look twice. They both have exceptionally flabby but shapely breasts.

'Jonathan,' shouts Ivan motioning with is head.

113

In the sea of black and brown, bobs the occasional whitey. Many of them look like they've just fallen out of a rave, and can't understand why the drum and bass has been turned off. Someone who looks remarkably like Boris Becker in skateboard takkies and a Diesel shirt asks me for a cigarette.

'Why are you in here?' I ask.

'I was caught with a stolen credit card but I didn't steal it.'

I don't mean to raise my eyebrows but I must because he laughs and says, 'Ja really'.

The cook doesn't know Sipho, but points us to cell 31 anyway.

'Ja, he sleeps here, he comes from Kimberley, with some Xhosa and Tswana in him, don't say much.'

On the floor is a man curled up in a foetal position. The back of his head is shaved and his face is buried in a balaclava.

I kneel down and move my face right into his. The lighting is very poor. Carefully cut toilet paper has been hung around the fluorescent lights which flicker epileptically. A breeze blows through the bars, and the bog roll flutters around the long tubes. I stay down waiting for a bright flash to illuminate his face.

It is not Sipho.

'No, I'm telling you, not this one,' says a prisoner, 'this ou is Sonny. The one you want moved yesterday to B, he said they give more food there.'

'I'd better get going,' I tell Ivan.

'Don't give up so easily,' he says.

It's true I need to fetch Masego from créche but I'm also beginning to feel locked in. My eyes keep going up at the blue sky and at koppies rising up beyond the concrete walls.

Diep Kloof, Diep Kloof. Diep Kloof. Diep Kloof.

I leave the pile of posters with Ivan.

'Hand them out for zol paper. His face and his name may get

seen. My home number is handwritten here at the bottom, 447-1682.'

Valentine and I don't talk as we leg it back along the perimeter fence. A bishop bird and four chicks sit under their untidy nest on a segment of razor wire.

A loud whistling from behind us pitches in urgency. We stop, turn, and look up. Through the wire, I mind-fuck-hurdle the terraces, and the next fence and the next. The castle's concrete walls are scaled, and in the highest turret, in the darkest shadow, someone is staring down at us. He has two fingers in his mouth, whistling only like black and brown boys can. When my eyes meet his, he jumps back.

'You have exceptional powers of clairvoyance like me,' says Valentine, 'I know he is in there and he didn't want us to find him.'

PART 2

10
Virginia & Patrick

THE NOMAD I AM
Do not feel pity for me
I have no need for it
For I am a wandering stranger

The open trail my home
Like people of old
Here today, gone tomorrow

I am the forever adventurer
A pilgrim of probabilities

Like a cowboy I roll my zol
Keeping out the race for humanity

No tax man to dread
No landlord to dodge
No family to deject

Free
But am I coming or going
I live by my honest hands

As long as it's not pity
I'll take it
Do not look for me
I am a wandering stranger

Let me feel pity for you
(Sipho Madini, *Homeless Talk*, Johannesburg, June 1998)

119

It is 17 January 1999. This is the voice of Valentine. No need introducing myself to you because Jonathan has written about me and I have told you my stories beginning with the mermaid in the village in Cameroon. Remember my grandfather looked at my palm and said something about the luck I am having? My girlfriend Anna in Canada has sent me $1375, enough money to come and visit her, but I have already spent most of that money. (I paid Mr Zulberg, the landlord, rent for the next six months.) I refuse to give Anna my home address in case she comes. I don't want her to see me living like this.

This morning I felt very lazy to come to the workshop. In fact, I even contemplated twice before saying my rosary, the one my grandmother gave me before I left for Canada.

'You are wanting to become more Christy than Christ,' said Morris my Nigerian flatmate.

He and Sultan, the other flatmate, read the Bible before they go out to sell cell phones. Sultan is a Catholic like me but Morris attends Rhema.

'There are beautiful ladies and plushy cars at Rhema, you should both try,' Morris always publicises. Sultan has tried them and is in the process of moving over.

I bang the door of the apartment and call the lift to the second floor. When I'm sound I take the steps. Harley Street is in its summer finery. An Indian guy leans and yawns on his gate, admiring nature. A City Golf speeds past me, its sound at full blast. I step back on the pavement. At the Harrow Road intersection it screeches to a halt.

'Never trust those robots,' says the Indian, talking with his hands on the gate, 'you've got plus or minus eight seconds to cross. From that balcony up there, I've watched many pedestrians somersault and toast.'

His house is the old kind, built like a post office. I move swiftly along Bree Street. I want to read the *Saturday Star* before the subscriber in one of the offices in Longsbank Building collects it. Today one of my pieces should be appearing on page two. It is about two blind people who got assaulted for complaining about loud music to their neighbour. The blind man is a rally driver. He reads maps made of braille.

A beggar is drifting toward me. My dressing is deceiving him. I spin a fifty cent to his cup, like Michael Jackson in 'Billie Jean'.

I take the elastic off the paper. My piece is in! On page seven. There is huge picture of the two blind people facing the general direction of the camera. By Valentine Eboh Cascarino. Their faces are all bruised. I take out the page for Jonathan, fold the paper neatly and take the stairs up to the second floor.

''

Usually Jonathan is the only one before me. When I enter he is not there. I sit down. Virginia comes next. Her hair is drawn behind. A pink smile hangs on her lips. Her son Prince follows her in, scrambling with a bananna and beating his foot on the ground in merriment. Soon the others come. Everybody is well-dressed today. Even Jonathan is wearing shady green glasses from Roccoborocco perhaps. He looks more responsible. His pacific nature is pristine from the first time I saw him.

'Won't you repeat the title?' I ask Virginia, once we are settled and most of the chairs are filled. She is to kick in today. After ensuring Prince is content by the window, she begins reading. She has an actress's voice so people can just relax in their seats.

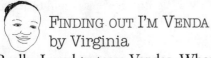

FINDING OUT I'M VENDA
by Virginia

Really, I used to tease Vendas. When the time came for me to

121

start school, I was taken to live in Soweto. I wasn't allowed to go to Boetie's school, Kensington Primary. It was for whites only. Gogo's sister had a two-roomed house in White City, Jabavu. Can you imagine how confusing this was for me? Why call it White City when only blacks were allowed to live there?

Soon after I arrived, Soweto kids would come and ask me to speak the white language for them. I never knew what to say because they expected me just to talk without asking me any questions.

'Jou hemp is blou en daardie hond is bruin,' is the kind of thing I said. Sometimes if I was lazy, I'd just count to ten, 'een, twee, drie, vier …'

Being able to speak Afrikaans was a great help to me because everyone wanted to be my friend. With my new friends one of the things we did was to tease Vendas. It was part of Soweto culture. Everyone knew they were backward and simple. Is it not clear enough looking at our neighbours next-door? Which other tribe has such black kids and still loves them as if they are just fine? Nnditsheni and Nnditsheni were pitch black like midnight in the homeland. Nnditsheni and Nnditsheni! Who else would have two children, a boy and a girl, sharing one name? And the most stupid part was that they never played out their yard.

'U wena mampara, your mouth is dry because you are so hungry!' we would shout, but they never fought back. They were weird.

Just as I was becoming a heroine, Gogo came to visit and told me Mrs Stein wanted me back. I don't know what I meant in her life. So I moved back to Kensington and began to travel to Soweto by train every day. It was a strain because I had to leave Kensington by 6.30 to be at school on time.

'Virginia uya travul,' whispered the others.

Everything has two sides and my travelling became the third

way in which I was special. The first two were that I could talk boer language and that I wasn't a Venda.

On holidays, if Baas was home, I'd go to White City. He needed lots of rest because of his lung cancer, which was in the terminal stages.

One time, I was standing in the kitchen. 'Virginia, this is Shadrack Maubane, your father,' said Mamkhulu, my mother's sister. She looked both happy and sorry at the same time.

The man's small black eyes filled with tears. He lifted his arms for an embrace and I cautiously went over to him trying to read his face. He bent down and put my face against his scratchy chin, enfolding me in his strong arms.

I had no feeling whatsoever. All I could think was how different he looked from my mental picture. It took me some time to understand him as he spoke in a language I hadn't expected. Venda! From our surname and those of our relatives, I'd always assumed him to be Xhosa. Who could blame me for being surprised at how he spoke, and a surname different from mine or anyone else that I know? He must have understood this or maybe I said something.

'Your real name is Mudau,' he began, 'your clan is that of a Lion. We can pass anywhere where there are lions and nothing happens to us. Never kill one and it will protect you. The Vendas are a noble people.'

To me this sounded like crazy crap. Why was he now talking about Vendas in Sesotho? There are enough mad people in my family.

'I have come to fetch you,' is the main thing that stung my ears.

I was angry as he lovingly led me to his car. It was a blood red E20 minibus that looked brand new with white-walled tyres. The inside smelt fresh and the seats were covered in transparent plastic to keep them new. Along the drive, which was very long, I did not even admire the sights. I refused to eat and there and then I decided never to talk, ever.

When we arrived at his place at dawn, I hated the sight. All I could see was mist, silhouettes of mountain and sharp pointed huts. We fumbled into one of them. There stood a good-looking woman in a long beautiful dressing gown and slippers, holding a candle.

'This is your new daughter,' said my new father to my new mother, in Venda.

We all clap. In a nanosecond the room becomes deadly quiet. Adjusting his reading glasses, brown rectangular ones, an improvement on his last Woody Allen styles, Jonathan breaks the silence: 'Comments?'

No one says anything so I kick in, 'This White City thing has struck me a lot. Many places in South Africa have English names and when I go there for the first time I am expecting whites only, only to find they are infested with blacks.'

'That thing comes from when the National Party government,' says Steven, 'when they put people in settlements they did not let them name them and they even named them with insults like Kaffirfontein.'

'It is interesting the you could speak Afrikaans but not Venda,' says David.

Steven licks his lower lip while staring at his finger. 'How do you spell "Stein"?' he asks.

He always comments if one mentions something that has an Afrikaans affiliation. It surprises me how proud of his Kannetjie side he is.

As usual Jonathan always has the last word, like a shepherd guarding his flock, 'Did you really stop talking altogether?' he asks.

'I only talked at school, but never ever to him, or my new mom, for over four years,' says Virginia, looking up without smiling.

It is my job to move things on. Jonathan is no longer the chairman.

'Window 4, Virginia,' I say going straight to the point.

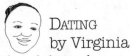

DATING
by Virginia

I hated dating because to me it represented suffering. Was it not through dating that people fell in love, married, made children, then divorced leaving their children to grow up confused? Dating was not for me, thank you. I had my own plan in life. I was going to work, buy a house, and invite relatives or friends who needed a home. I would adopt a little girl when I felt ready for parenthood.

In my teens, many boys tried to date me, but I would be so aggressive and violent that eventually they got tired and stopped. A few days before I wrote this piece, a man who I recognised very faintly, stopped me in the street. After exchanging greetings he asked, 'Don't you remember me, I'm Caephus? I still have the scar where you hit with me a paraffin bottle just because I said I love you years ago when we were teenagers.'

He bowed his head. Right there was a shiny scar.

'Me? I did that? Remind me what happened. Are you sure?' I asked. I'd forgotten how I used to react to boy's advances those days.

When I was in high school in Venda, my peers started to apply for IDs, so I also did likewise. But my name did not appear in the computers.

'Go to Johannesburg,' I was told in the Pietersburg office. I went there with my aunt. We travelled by bus and I remember that there were lots of women in ZCC outfits on the bus. Along the way they sang non-stop. They always sing something decent and don't jump up and down like men. After a while I also got in the mood. Reaching the offices in Johannesburg, I was asked to produce my birth certificate. Somehow my aunt pulled it out from her bag which I still think is a miracle.

She took it out, unfolded it and spread it out on the wooden counter.

'Go to Transkei, you were not born here,' said a voice through a hole in the glass.

I could not go there because I knew no one and Gogo was too ill with complications from sugar diabetes. At the time I was not dating anyone and I had no ID. These things made me feel different from other girls. The fact that other parents used me as an example of a good child, when scolding their kids, made me feel worse. I was praised by my teachers in front of everyone. A nerd who hated herself.

Freddie was a neighbour of ours. He used to greet me and make conversation. I neither liked nor disliked him. He was not good looking as such but he dressed in the latest fashion. A lot of girls were crazy about him because he travelled to and from Jo'burg.

Somehow Freddie got to hear that I was having a hard time getting an ID. I was already 20 years old when one day he said, 'Virgie, I will introduce you to a friend of mine who works at Home Affairs in Pretoria. He will help you with your document problem.'

Since Freddie's home was one of the few with telephones, he made contacts from his phone with his friend Basil at Home Affairs. When I got to Home Affairs, my fingerprints were taken. Basil, a white guy with lots of Brylcream in his hair, said, 'Go home and wait for your ID. It will be posted to you in about three months.'

My problem was solved but naturally I could not refuse when Freddie started asking to date me and we became a regular couple. Everyone, except me and his mother, was happy about our relationship. I was unhappy because I'm afraid of marriage and his mom was unhappy because I am not circumcised.

How can I describe her? A typical traditional Venda woman. She wears nothing but muthvhela, which is the traditional Venda dress. Powder blue or pink of light material wrapped into a skirt and another piece over one shoulder, all decorated with zig-zag binding. And lots of bangles on the legs and arms. She is a traditional healer and knows which girls are mashu-uhuru (uncircumcised) and which are ready to be women. She is one of the oldies who are always in the middle of such things. To her the worst thing a son could do to his parents is bring home a shuuhuru for a bride.

Luckily for me, Freddie understood about my obsession of wanting to buy my own house before marriage. For years he waited patiently for me. Sometimes I looked at magazines and photos of weddings with him but I was not rushing it. After three years, I was ready to marry him, if only to shock his mother. He had taxis that his elder brother registered in his name as a gift for having helped him run his business. When a taxi feud started in Venda, he was one of the first owners to be shot. I grieve for him even now. He was my best friend.

An atmosphere of grief fills the room. Patrick breaks the silence. We turn to him away from Virginia, who has tears in her eyes.

'It is better to have love and lost than not at all,' he says.

'Virginia's philosophical way she sees dating fits exactly with Hollywood. You date from a long way back but the marriage only lasts two to three days,' I offer.

'Yes,' says Steven, 'by the time they get inside a church to get married, they have already lived as man and wife and it is time to be discharged, but the main thing your story reminds me of was when I went home this last Christmas and my son struggled to realise I am his father. I forced him to sleep in the bed with me to get to know me.'

Jonathan's face looks discomposed. He wipes his face and asks, 'What is this shuhuru circumcision thing?'

I don't know myself but I like to keep things on track so I look around for others to comment,

'I can answer that with my story,' says Patrick.

'One time in Transkei, I was …' Steven tries to interrupt so I urge Patrick to start reading before Steven seizes the microphone again. He can destabilise a discussion with his breadth of interest and memory. Patrick opens an old exercise book and turns from page 18 to page 3 to page 6, like he always does. I'm sure Jonathan will have to cut and paste a lot to make his story flow.

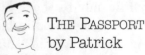

THE PASSPORT
by Patrick

The bush I am under is so dense that light can hardly get in. The ground looks like it was a soccer field that has never seen grass and it is very dusty. The traps I have set are nearby and I'm waiting for some birds.

What makes the cold worse is my khaki shirt, which is torn at the back, and my short pants and bare feet. All of these make my shivering worse. Every time I breathe, it as if I am smoking and blowing out fumes. My skin also flakes and cracks – I looked for vaseline but could not find it. Damn the hell. Vaseline is only applied when going to town, school or a bit far.

A noise causes me to look up and I see some birds flying into my trap. My palms are pushed down and my elbows out.

Before I can be upright, I am confronted by two young men.

'Ro liwana,' they cheer, 'we have got you uncircumcised.'

In our tradition, if you are not circumcised, you usually suffer rebuke and are called a coward. I look to escape, but in this place the entrance is also the exit. They both grab me. One tackles me heavily as I try to run and I fall on my face.

'Today you'll know us better you scum,' says the leader.

Another runs away and comes back holding my traps full of two birds, 'Eat them now you coward,' says the leader through his teeth.

As I chew feathers, they watch smiling. Then they leave me but from a distance shoot me with their catapults. One stone hits me on the jaw, which is the most painful of all of them. I'm so dirty, I force myself to the river to wash so as not to be ridiculed on the streets. The shirt is so tattered it gives me a hard time washing it. I lie in the grass waiting for my shirt to dry.

I see a group of men coming towards the river. The two who had beat me are not with them. These ones now are the boys from the circumcision school. They have no shoes and are covered with mud and have an animal skin to cover their penis wounds. Even their hair is covered with mud. I grab my shirt and run like a hare. They begin to chase me. I know if they catch me it could mean the end of my era.

Screaming and shouting they pursue me like wild cats herding for prey. In a short time I am down and they are around me. I have lost my shirt and neither they nor I will ever know where it is.

'Show us your passport!' demands the tallest one.

They know I can't show them what they want to see.

Huelele ele hogo
Huelele ele hogo

With songs and screaming cries, I am beaten until I am dizzy and can't feel anything anymore.

'You can leave him now,' says the leader's voice.

Happy with songs of warriors, and their whips tipped with blood, they go.

I lay there flat like a pancake bleeding from the lashings. Everything was quiet and I was feeling very very cold, as if I was dead, but I was able to cry 'till I was dry.

'Come finish me off … Come finish me off … Come finish me off …'

Along the way back home it was only me and the darkness sending me on.

'What?' asked my grandma at the gate by the low mud wall around the hut.

My mother just stood, not knowing what to say. She just burst into tears. The blankets were already down by my young brother. I'll be dead by the following day I thought.

The following day I spent the whole day under my grandmother's care as she soothed me with traditional herbs and rubbing ointments into my skin. It had already been arranged that I would go to hospital to be circumcised in a Western way.

I am happy although I know I'll still be treated only as a half man. But one thing is for sure, for sure. If they come again, I will show them my passport.

We all cheer Patrick. It is the first time to see every one putting up fingers to start comments. I notice Virginia has come back to herself and I signal for her to begin.

'I don't know why grandmums are so crazy for their grandchildren to be circumcised, be it by a Western or African method,' she says, 'at least my grandmum warned me against these things.'

Pinky who hardly comes, is adjusting herself. It seems this is the moment she has been waiting for.

'I think for men, this certificate thing, it is reasonable, but not for women. I don't know if I'm right, but for you guys, it improves hygiene and it even improves the look.'

'Certificates?' asks Jonathan looking perplexed in his whole body.

'A burn and two cuts on the left upper thigh,' says Virginia slashing and poking at her trousers.

'When you go to wash at the river, if you have no certificate, these young girls call you shiburau and laugh at you,' says Pinky.

'What is there to tease about?' asks David.

'They imply that they, the circumcised, are very skilled in love making, and that you are backward and stupid. They also say that if they want, they can steal your boyfriend like this,' says Pinky snapping her fingers.

'My granny went to such a school,' says Virginia, 'and she said she learned nothing of value and told me to go get a real certificate.'

By now I am curious. When I left Cameroon, I was too young to know of these things.

'What actually happens there?' I ask joining in.

'When these girls come back they don't say much,' answers Pinky, 'they say if you talk about it you'll go mad. I hate them.'

'They don't look as happy as they make out,' says Virginia. 'When you look at them they look and sound traumatic and they just talk about how nice it was and what nice presents they got.'

'Presents?' asks Jonathan.

'Pathetic things like safety pins to put in their hair,' scorns Pinky.

Jonathan seems to like this conversation and is not signalling

131

me to move things on.

'As far you know, what does happen there?' he asks, unable to hide his intense enthusiasm.

Virginia takes a deep breath, 'there are three versions. One, they just introduce sex education to girls. Two, they stretch the lips of vagina by pulling them so they get very long. And three, the most mutilation, comes from a group of Venda called Balemba, who say they are Jews from somewhere in upper Africa. Lips from the vagina are cut off, and the rest is then sewn up so there is just enough room to pass water.'

I think Steven, Jonathan, Patrick and me, are a bomb-shell-shocked.

Pinky's smile is grinning and she is nudging Virginia, who is giggling.

'I also heard about a beautiful flower with one single pink bloom,' says Pinky ending the silence, 'girls get taught how to use this to shrink their vagina. One thing I know, men say these girls can perform like crazy.'

'There are many stories about rich men,' says Virginia, 'even whites and traffic cops and inspectors, who leave their families to go live in mud huts of Shangaan women.'

'Did you know,' asks Pinky looking around at us, 'that the ones who wear those big skirts that stick out, don't wear panties? They are very very sexy.'

I don't know what expression I have on my face because Pinky's eyes rest on me.

'I hope we are not traumatising you Valentine.'

'No, not in the least,' I shoot back to her, 'black women are not in my calendar.'

This was not the right thing to say. Even Jonathan got in the fight and had to defend why he didn't marry a Jew.

Only when Patrick reminded us he still has another story to read, did we get back on track. Coughing is Patrick's way of starting and stopping others.

'Are you sure you've arranged your story properly this time?' I ask.

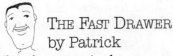

THE FAST DRAWER
by Patrick

The classroom is the structure made of planks and the roof sheet metal. The floor is soil mixed with water, smeared and left to dry and then polished with cow dung. The windows are just the opening of wooden frames that let the coldness inside the class and leave us shivering. Sometimes in winter they, the teachers will make a fire inside the class and we all feel warm.

'Where are the chalks?' says Mr Mufamadi holding a very short piece, and looking at the empty chalk tray.

No one answers. He walks to the middle of the board, looks over his shoulder and scrapes the board with his nails. We push our fingers into our ears and just wait. The other teacher, Mrs Baloyi, would come in the second period. The subjects would be Afrikaans and Health Education, which was to do with eating healthy food, wearing clean clothes and brushing teeth.

I became the chalkboard cleaner after many dusters went missing. To be in charge of that area, to keep the duster under my desk shelf and to bring it out at times when it was needed, was my job description.

'Everyone take out their homework books and you clean the board,' shouts Mr Mufamadi, still cross about the missing chalk.

While I am rubbing, Mr Mufamadi is searching his pockets for a short piece. I keep glancing in his direction. He finds it on his desk, looks at it and angrily throws it at the bin behind the classroom door. Then out of the torn pocket of my grey shorts, fall two brand new long pieces of chalk. I just stand there not sure whether it will be worse to pick them up or not.

Actually, I use these chalks to draw on the board, during study time in the late afternoons when I know the teachers have left

'What are you doing with chalks?' he screams.

'I thought I had to keep them also,' I defend myself for some silly reason.

Mr Mufamadi walks up to me, his right hand held palm up in front of him, and he picks up the chalks. He puts one in his pocket, and then he rolls up his sleeves.

'You are like this guy,' he says while drawing a young boy – me with a baboon face – sitting on a rock.

The whole class is hooting and hackling with laughter. I know my teacher very well. His teeth are very white unlike any pupil in our class, or perhaps in the whole school. He is black, but not just black, but pitch-black. He is a joke maker and can make fun of you with chalk anytime he likes. I really liked the way he drew. I stole the chalks to be like him.

My classmates ask me to decorate their poetry books and some Bible verses. I would use mostly coloured pencils and they would score high marks. Mr Mufamadi realised my talent and encouraged me by asking me to design things like posters and time-tables.

'But don't be funny and forget to do my work or you will see yourself.'

My creativity grew till I could draw a creature with brains that cares for homeless people.

'Why did people steal the dusters?' asks Jonathan.

'As boys we would do the same thing in Uitenhage and make busses by putting wheels on them,' says David, 'and the girls stole them to play school at home.'

'It struck me how Mr Mufamadi trusted Patrick,' says Virginia, 'he chose him to look after the dusters and to train him in drawing.'

No one has anything more to say so I take a turn. 'In West Africa they do the same thing but they take a tall dry tree and let it burn from the inside like a cigarette for five months.'

"

I'm at home eating curry and rice when the phone rings.

'Cascarino, how can I help you?' I say taking care to keep gravy off the portable hand-set.

'Valentine,' says the unmistakable voice.

'Jonathan, how are you? What's up?' I ask, 'can you wait a minute while I turn down the music a little.'

'Listen,' he says like always before talking, 'on Saturday we never got a chance to talk about Sipho. You understand his writing and you're an investigative journalist right?'

'Right,' I say not sure where he is going.

'Listen, do you think you could try and dig up any poems and stories he submitted which didn't make it into the paper?'

'I could do that,' I say.

'I've got to go,' he says as Masego's shrieking washes him away.

Jonathan is right. Whether Sipho wants to be found or not, all the clues are there, in his writing.

11
Jonathan & Robert

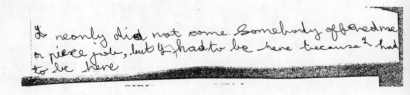

I neonly did not come. Somebody offered me
a piece job, but I had to be here because I had
to be here

It's Wednesday. Brendon Serry, the managing editor of the *Saturday Star*, has asked me to submit my article before noon. I go through the story again like a pupil preparing for an exam. I don't wish him to ask me to go out and get any more information. One sentence can take more than five days to get.

On the third floor of the newspaper building, I hand my typed pages to him. I typed them at *Homeless Talk* even though most of the computers are broken. Brendon squints at it, shaking his leg, reading the first line out loud, in his polished Afrikaans accent: 'Why do prostitutes apply locally brewed charms to their private parts? Customers will keep on coming.'

The rest he reads to himself.

'OK, it's a good investigative piece,' he eventually tells me, looking me up and down.

I've never seen him smile. Most freelancers say he's the best they've ever come across.

'Give me a shout on Thursday, Cascarino. Since Thabo Mbeki will be talking to the nation about AIDS, I think this article will tell people what is going on in the sex industry,' he says in a paternalistic manner, also telling me my time with him is over.

136

* * *

I'm walking along Pritchard Street. Along the side of the Sanlam Building made of mirrors, someone has stuck a line of about one hundred posters. Each one is only A4 size, which is why they probably put so many of them. Advertising is causing more pollution than two years ago. Three black cleaners in smart blue overalls are removing them one by one. Their manager stands close by, supervising them and hurrying them up. People stop to read the posters before they are taken down. I cross the road wondering what sort of bargain can be so compulsive to so many.

'A writer works and sleeps with open eyes,' Jonathan had recently said to me acting as my mentor.

When I get closer, I am more than surprised. The poster is of Sipho. The same one Jonathan and I left at the prison. I was the first one to see it on Helen's computer when she designed it on Quark. I was the one who handed her the photo of him. The way I always seem to be close to my best missing friend Sipho is not surprising, but it is shock to see him multiplied. Like a head in a mirrored lift. I wonder who put them up. Maybe Cassius Plaatjies, Sipho's poet friend, who is also a Rasta and an urban terrorist.

'Please move over, you are obstructing my men,' says the manager, addressing me.

I move along down the row of posters, shaking my head.

Seeing his portrait torn down like that, smacks me hard. I remove from my pocket the handkerchief which my boer girlfriend in Pretoria, Sandra de Beer, gave me. The poster is black and white, and not so clear, but I know from memory that the tsotsi cap Sipho is wearing is green. The scar on his cheek is visible. A thin smile hangs off his lip.

137

'Bro, I'm ugly here,' is what he said when Bongani, a photographer from *Homeless Talk*, showed us that photo.

'No, Sipho, when you start making money, your body structure will improve,' I told him.

I move down the line and stand in front of an unpeeled photo.

'Sipho, if you are lost, I will find you, I don't care what it takes,' I say aloud.

The manager and his workers are looking at me. With my dreadlocks, they must think I am mad. If I can investigate for people I don't know, it is the least I can do for him.

*   *   *

Friday is always my best day. In the evening, obeying Grandma's advice, I go to church to attend Exposition and Benediction. It is always at the Cathedral of Christ the King, which lies on the left side of the T-junction between Saratoga Avenue and End Street in Hillbrow. Inside, there are two little chapels, sandwiching the main alter. The local priest told me that there used to be three statues of the Virgin Mary inside the main hall. A large real statue of Christ hangs on the cross.

Most people inside the cathedral are above 60. An old priest comes forward and places a large gold crucifix on another gold globe. There is a red light beside the cross. I have never seen it off. Incense is lit and we start singing, 'O Salutaris Hostia'.

As smoke fills the small chapel, my memory drifts to Cameroon where we would gather natural incense in the forest for our parish. We would find it covered by thick grass and thorns. With our cutlasses we cut the grass and chopped down the incense plant. Since we didn't like going into the mosquito infested forest too often, we'd fetch as many as possible to last nine months to a year.

A car backfires, bringing me back to the old priest leading us into 'Tantum Ergo Sacramentum' and we end with 'Adoremus Sanctissimum Sacramentum'. I can easily distinguish a gunshot from a backfire.

At 7 p.m. I leave the chapel and I walk home. There I find my Nigerian flat brothers, in the lounge, listening to music and installing sim cards into a fresh batch of cell phones. I no longer enquire about their beginnings and histories. We all do things here we would never have dreamed of and that we will grow out of.

'Good night Sultan, Morris,' I say going to my room.

*   *   *

Saturday morning is quite chilly. On the street is a game. Two men stand over a cardboard box on the pavement with three bottle tops covering a piece of twisted paper. They try to get pedestrians to choose. Choose the right one and you win a one hundred note. I want to take a photo for a story on street gamblers, but these guys are criminals and dangerous. I am standing behind a pillar with my camera. Jonathan comes around the corner with his blue backpack and his strange step, 'Howzit Valentine.'

I just look at him shaking my head to push him on. A dozen fake gamblers, including some women, keep drawing passers-by into the game. The leader of the racket, dressed in a blue overall, will manipulate the covers and ask people to stake. At times he will move the covers so slowly, that a new player will easily identify the cover with the paper hiding inside. A tactic to get you addicted! They are quite brilliant. A young girl in hipster jeans has been persuaded into playing by some of the ladies.

I don't want to use a flash, which will reveal me, but I know the photo will not come out without light. The weather is dark.

Still behind the pillar, I press the button and a green light indicates the camera is ready. As I step out and aim my camera, one looks up and shouts, 'Hey wena, voetsek!'

Just then Patrick comes out and says, 'No he just wants to take me a street picture.'

He poses in front of them.

'No, go take it on another street, not here,' shouts the leader.

We walk away and come back from the other side. As we pass them, I shoot the scene holding my camera low, and without looking through it. Some of my best photos have been taken from this angle.

"

When we get to the boardroom, Jonathan, Steven and David are already there. Jonathan is wearing a heavy cotton jersey with stripes on the sleeves. He is reading through a typed manuscript. Minutes later Virginia enters.

'I left Prince with Pinky's son,' she tells us as if apologising.

'Let's start with you Jonathan,' I say pointing my smile at him. He is sometimes too courteous.

'Me?' he says trying to slip out. 'Mmm, OK, but can we first talk about Sipho for a minute, did you manage to find some of his poems and stories?'

'Yes', I say, 'I'm still busy but you know that column he used to write about survival tips for street living?'

Everyone knows it well.

'Well,' I continue, 'he was following it up with one called "How to get off the street" and he handed these three pages into Ted.'

Hungrily, Jonathan takes them from me and the others insist he begins reading his window. In a radio announcer's voice, he starts.

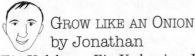

GROW LIKE AN ONION
by Jonathan

'Ein Kolahenu, Ein Kadeneinu, Ein Komosh ee Einu,' chants my dad along with all the men downstairs. I prefer looking up at the girls and mothers. Every year the girls get a little bigger but I never get the ones I am most in love with. I learn to be a looker.

It is Yom Kippur. The highest holy day in the Jewish calendar. I am in shul sitting beside my dad. The rabbi's sermon is about Atonement and the Book of Life. I stare at the back of a velvet yarmulke. Black hairs escape from under the collar and touch the gold embroidery on the tallis. It belongs to the reservist who came into our yard and hit Emma on the back with a baton twelve years ago. Is he still on her payroll? Will God write his name in the Book of Life so that he may live one more year?

This is my first year at university. On Republic Day we boycott lectures and we chant, 'NO CAUSE TO CELEBRATE! NO CAUSE TO CELEBRATE!'

I steal Mao's complete works and a set of I-Ching cards, from a second hand bookshop in Braamfontien. Granny Dena dies and leaves me her grey '52 Volvo. The gear lever is over three feet long, and the speedometer needle is like a snake's tongue that only comes out and hisses when I drive too fast.

The afternoon sun is gone and we're all wearing jerseys. My mother has a big antique table. There is a big enamel plated pot of minestrone soup boiling on the stove and there is no one in the kitchen. It is the main chance I've been waiting for. I run to my room. I reach to the inside pocket of my old barmitzvah suit jacket, and I pull out a bank packet of excellent Maritzburg dagga, already depipped and crushed. Emma comes back into the kitchen just as I sprinkle the last of it into the soup.

She cries, 'Hey wena, what are you doing?'

I run past her out into the yard, but she catches me a shot on the bum with her dish cloth, 'Awu u stout wena, stout, stout.'

My mother reaches past the tiny gold saccharin holder and rings the stainless steel bell. Emma opens the door from the kitchen. She enters the dining room balancing a silverware soup tureen on a pale wooden tray, the underside of which has black concentric rings from the time it was left on a hot stove. Our eyes almost meet but don't. By the time the main course comes we are all so happy. My parents are even holding hands under the table.

Barak, my younger brother, who is in on this little piece of social engineering, makes eye contact. He grins widely and he asks me the Youngest Son Passover Question, '*Manishtana halaila haze, micol halelot?*' (Why is this night different to other nights?)

Suddenly my father gets up and goes off to bed with a splitting headache. I begin to feel bummed out and guilty. I'm white and I'm Jewish.

Lastly let me tell you about Innocentia. I am in the kitchen making a veg curry after university. She runs into the yard and stands right there on the other side of the window crying, 'Help me please help me!'

I step into the yard holding a big spoon. The police are doing a pass raid at the bus-stop.

'Please hide me in your house!'

Granny Ethel who has lived with us since Grandpa Ben died, walks into the kitchen wearing a powder blue nightgown. She sees us talking at the door near the outside sink.

'Jon-Jon, vots going on, so much noise?'

I'm not sure whether I should consult her. She refers to Black people as 'schwartzes' but through pogroms and the holocaust she has known suffering.

'Gran, the police want too throw this girl in jail just because she has no papers.'

Ethel looks at Innocentia for a few seconds and then at me without saying anything.

'You stay here,' she orders, addressing me.

'Come vit me,' she tells Innocentia.

I watch them disappear down the passage and then into Ethel's room. Two cops run into the yard and right into the kitchen. Breathing very hard and without greeting me, one asks. 'Where's the kaffir girl?'

'Who?'

'We saw her run in here, where are your parents?'

I tell them they're at work but they just push past me. They look in all the rooms, even under my parents' bed. They both take off their caps and put their arses in the air to lift the huge bed spread made of thousands of flowers, bordered in brown, that my other Granny crocheted.

When they get up, I notice the one with the thick neck and the moustache has grey eyes. In front of Ethel's door they stop.

'Who's in here?' says the other one with a rash on his hairy arms.

'My Gran, she's not well, you mustn't disturb her.'

The short one smiles and opens the door. I push in front of them, 'Don't worry Gran, it's just the police looking for some-one, everything's all-right.'

She's in bed with her teeth in a glass of water, and all her pills in front of her on a special bed-tray, like the ones you see in hospitals. We bought it at Dions for her birthday.

The same short one says, 'Scuse us ma'am but have you seen a kaffir girl, about this high, we have reason to believe she's in this house?'

'Vel she's certainly not here, this gyel, vot has she done, is she dangerous?'

143

The cops look at each other. The same one starts to answer but Gran isn't finished, 'if she vas here, I certainly vood ef seen her, my eyes are still gut Baruch Hashem.'

The other one says, 'we're sorry to have troubled you ma'm.'

'Vot trouble, did Jon-Jon offer you some tea?'

As they leave her room, in the same voice, she says, 'Zol er waksenwie a tsibele mit die kop in drerd.'

The taller one nods and forces a smile. I see them out the front door and return to find Gran letting Innocentia out the cupboard. Two bigger smiles you couldn't find.

'You were fantastic Gran, really a-mazing.'

'Fantastic shmantastic, leave me to finish reading my book.'

As Innocentia and I are leaving her room, I turn around and ask, 'Gran, what was it you said to them in Yiddish?'

'May you grow like an onion with head in the ground,' she says without looking up from her book.

Innocentia slaps her thighs and screams with delight, her little breasts shaking beneath her dress. 'Shhhhh, the Boere will hear you!' I say, but she carries on laughing.

That night, on a revolving dance floor at the top of the Hillbrow Tower full of German men and black prostitutes, she tells me she's from the Ciskei and that she's looking for a job as a domestic.

'I know all about Nelson Mandela and Walter Sisulu and Thabo Mbeki, you're Xhosa like them aren't you?'

The click in Xhosa comes out of sort of all right.

'Hesh, Jo, it is like what we see on action cinemas every Saturday,' begins David once Jonathan stops reading, 'were you panicking when you saw the police in your house?'

'Your Grandma could have made a great Hollywood star,' says Pinky.

144

'What did she mean by the onion thing, you know, may you grow like an onion?' asks Patrick.

'Parables don't need to be explained to Africans,' I butt in, 'Achebe once told me, in African writing every reference is symbolic.'

'You met him?' asks Jonathan.

'Many many times – the first was in 1992 when he was a guest lecturer at the University of Calabar in Nigeria – but let's move on to your next window.'

While Jonathan slips what he has just read into his black file made of shoe-sole rubber, Virginia asks, 'How old was Innocentia?'

'A few years younger than me,' says Jonathan.

'Did you meet her again?' asks Virginia.

'Can I answer that with this story? I'll tie the one to the other.'

Jonathan begins reading but my mind is on Virginia's question.

'Sorry,' I interrupt him, 'please will you begin again?'

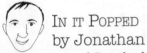 In it Popped
by Jonathan

Innocentia and I make love for the first time on my granny's bedspread. Now I nearly have my BA. Her breasts have small hard nipples like the acorns on our oak-tree. I look down and see a dark and a light body joined at the pelvis. Gran's flowers seem to be alive and I think of onions growing. I teach her how to swim in our swimming pool and we sit with our legs in the water eating black katauba grapes you can squeeze out of their skins. They grow on a vine, which weighs down the pool fence. Then one day she is gone.

'How much do you earn?' I ask Nimrod who I think is also in

love with her.

'Three hundred a month,' he replies.

He pumps petrol at the Mobil station and sells me the Durban poisons. I have a job as an apprentice in Soweto, learning and teaching people how to grow vegetables on plots the size of a door. Nimrod resigns from the garage and joins me for the same money.

When the project merges with Operation Hunger we both emigrate to Bophutatswana. Our boss orders us to make a garden outside the Chief's house.

'But it's meant to be a community vegetable garden,' I say.

'It sounds like a god-forsaken place,' says Raymond.

I am sitting around Raymond's brother's starched white table-cloth. On it are two silver candlesticks just like Granny Ethel's, and a platted chala loaf sprinkled with poppy and sesame seeds.

Every Friday morning I begin the 300km drive back to Raymond's house in Orchards, Johannesburg, to attend shul and to sit around that table. He says Kiddish, we break bread, and we sit down to eat.

One box on my temple, one on my forearm. I begin criss-crossing my forearms with leather straps attached to black boxes. Each is filled with ancient Hebraic script. In shul, the men in black and white penguin suits with tails don't pay too much attention to my sun-tan and my ear-ring.

'Don't worry, see that guy over there with the long beard praying,' says Raymond, rocking on the balls of his feet in the aisle, 'yes, the Rabbi used to be an acid head, totally out of it.'

During the week, while I grow vegetables in one of South Africa's driest areas, these guys deal in diamonds. They drive mini-busses full of their own kids. For them everything is prescribed. I glimpse a way to narrow my margin for error.

'Why Israel? Why are you running again? Rather go for

therapy,' says my mother at the airport.

'I want to learn how to drive a tractor,' is all I tell her.

I land in Tel Aviv, catch a bus to Jerusalem and another to Safed. Pronounced 'Sfat', it sits on a hill, an ancient Galilean village, the capital of Jewish mysticism. Cobbled streets spiral up the hill. From the market you can see the Sea of Galilee. Every third building is a synagogue. The Chasids all dress in black. I find a yeshiva, a house of learning that suits my ignorance. During he day we do physical labour, reconstructing a sixteenth century synagogue. In the afternoon we study Hebrew and Torah.

Meals are had with different families. European Jews. Middle Eastern Jews. Americans. Ex-beatniks. Ex-Hari Krishnas. Been to Tibet. Knew Tim Leary. Now we have found the deepest truths in the simple truths of the Baal Shem Tov.

I rise before sunset. I time my first prayer so the first word flies at the horizon, the moment the sun appears. Ritual baths are taken in dark cold rooms, in deep stone mikvahs, filled with natural springs, along with fantastically holy looking chasids. On a wooden bench, I unlace my boots and take off my jeans. Opposite me a few of them begin an elaborate strip-tease. Black outer and white under garments are hung on wooden pegs above the bench. First the black hat. Then the suit jacket. The waistcoat. The trousers. Tsitsit. Black socks. White collared shirt. Underpants. Thick-rimmed glasses. Skull cap.

Naked they look less impressive and intimidating. My body is lean and firm. My skin berry brown. They are white and flabby and pimply, and their breasts hang, and they squint with pink eyes at the streaming sunlight.

1 – 2 – 3 – 4 – 5 – 6 – 7 – 8 – 9 – 10. Dunk – Dunk – Dunk in the freezing water. Screams are sucked in. Bump. Noses touch. God forbid, no smiles. Soaked and drenched, their beautifully spiralling earlocks and their beards almost touch

the ground. Naked penguins. Wet shivering male angels. I fetch my things from the yeshiva.

'It's not for me,' I tell Aaron the main dude.

Down the hill is a vegetarian Moshav. An old poor-sighted man with a sack over his shoulder welcomes me.

'Shmuel, shalom,' he says.

'Shalom, I'm Jonathan.'

We walk very slowly and from the path I look down on the Sea of Galilee. Shmuel was active in the Palestinian underground against he British in the 1930s. His farm is only the size of my parent's house and it is run-down. First I clean up inside. The handles on the aluminium pots and pans are repaired with odd rivets and pieces of wire. A tinker like my grandfather. The house is surrounded by tall cedar trees, planted by Shmuel as saplings. The vegetable garden is over-run by weeds. The orchard needs pruning.

'You can have my farm if you stay and look after me.'

I make a dent in the neglect but I won't take money from Shmuel. Sarah, another moshavnik, offers me work as well. One afternoon, she presents me a mole in a shoe box.

'Kill it, it has been eating my lettuce,' she says in her thick Israeli accent.

I lift the lid of the box. His eyes are covered by a permanent lid that won't come up, and his nose quivers at the light. Making sure the lid is secured tightly with string, the box is placed into my backpack. I release it five kilometres away and return to work.

Still panting, I only notice the two-inch thorn on the pomegranate branch after it has been in and out of my eye.

PLUPP, through my cornea, and my iris, into my lens, and HLUPP, back out again. No pain and no blood, but in that instant, it all came rushing in, the glare, the sky, the past. Everything.

Sarah turns out to be a nurse. Peeling my eyelid down, she peers in, 'Don't worry, there's no damage.'

Next morning I wake up but I can't see.

I bum a lift, to Safed with Philip, a Brit, with a kombi, to Safed. He is married to an Israeli woman.

'Six years ago there was a fire here, on the moshav,' he says as we hit the bumps, 'we all came out to beat it with sacks, and I fell and I lost this one. Now it is glass.'

He points at his left eye, taking one hand off the steering wheel of the old Volkswagen. At the bus-stop in Safed, I'm let out. I catch a blue bus to the hospital, where I wait in a queue full of soldiers, Arabs and chasids. All of us either have eye patches or are holding one eye.

'We have to operate, you may lose your eye,' says Dr Abulafia, as I allow my head to collapse onto the chin rest of his laser instrument.

He tells me that he got all his best experience at St Johns Eye Hospital, next to Baragwanath, in 1976.

'Drom Afrika is a beautiful place. Why you come here?'

The little piece of silence after a story, is frequently better than comments.

One moment we're in Venda, the next in Cameroon, and the next in Israel, this is what I love.

'You had a BA, what made you become a garden boy?' asks Steven.

'It is like a Biblical story,' I add, 'like seven years and seven plagues, the blind old man, the mole you wouldn't just kill, your injury and the guy with the marble eye. Fate.'

'Yah, my knowledge of Jewish custom is bare,' says Robbie. He wets his index finger and starts turning a twisted exercise book.

'I love the strip-tease thing and your berry brown skin,' says Pinky, 'I can just imagine you.'

Jonathan blushes and we all burst into laughter.

'So you know what it is like to have suffered, and to lose a body part that worked,' says Steven with a serious face.

'That was just the start of it,' says Jonathan, 'I lost my mind next.'

'Can we take a break first, just five minutes?' asks Virginia.

We do. I am the only one left in the boardroom to look after people's things. Fresew's computer was stolen in a five minute gap from the Simota Office on Thursday. He told me he thinks they're professional assassins. They are hired by the Ethiopian Government to hunt down political activists and recently killed two in Nairobi. Fresew also showed me his name and photo in a red covered book which told how he was tortured. This country is reducing him fast.

Everyone comes back. Robbie wipes his mouth and dives into his window number 3.

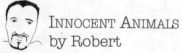

Innocent Animals
by Robert

I attended school till standard six. I dropped out because of the environment I was living in.

As jy meng met semels dan gaan die varke jou opeet.

It means if you mix with those King Corn brews that farmers feed to pigs, you'll get eaten by pigs. Kind of, if you live by the knife, you'll die by the knife. I left because I felt school was for kids and sissies but my marks weren't so bad.

What actually blocked me from learning was my teacher. His name was Vermaak and he was stout with serious type little moustache. We were always having arguments, like for instance he said the word 'kleurling' means 'coloured', and I

150

said no, it means colourling in a direct translation. I've never liked being called a coloured.

'Jy moet fok uit my klas uit,' he would say whenever I argued and won a point.

I became his focus. He hit me till he became scared. Through his investigations he found out that I belonged to the Bad Boys. When he stopped picking on me it was too late. I'd already left school full-time. I only came when I was bored and when the streets didn't have much to offer.

The other well-known gang that time was the Spaldings. In the beginning, the smaller guys like me were sent to approach someone walking in the street for money or cigarettes. If this guy refused, the older Bad Boys stepped in and assaulted the guy for everything he was carrying. We learned to challenge everyone we passed just like this.

'Why you look at me like that? Do I owe you something?'

'No sorry you look like someone I know,' the guy would usually say.

'Then why didn't you greet me?'

Once he had said sorry, I would take advantage and put my hands in his pocket.

To prove myself I had to stab someone. I remember the first guy well. He lived near us and had kids I knew.

'Fuck you, if you want money, go work for it, or ask your own father. I'm not giving you any, you're a fokken lightie.'

The other guys were watching me but they were not there to help. I had to stab him so I took out my knife, fast like we practised, and flicked it open.

This guy whose name was Roland, was already picking up a brick. I stabbed him maybe two or three holes. I never went to the extent of killing. He was just an ordinary guy.

'Any action you take against us will be fatal,' we told them after stabbing them.

By the age of 13 I was becoming the leader of the Bad Boys. Zakie who was 21, didn't take this kindly. I began plotting our hits and telling the others what to do. He knew he was losing control of the gang.

One day, when I was talking to a girl over her fence, Zakie came from behind and stabbed me in the back. Right here on this side check. The knife was still in but I picked up a brick and hit him against the head. He opened a case of assault against me but I went to the other gang members, and we all went to him in hospital. We told him the same thing he had taught us to say, 'If you proceed with this case we will kill you.'

The cops tore up the docket in front of us. They told us we were wasting their time.

I watched Zakie's every move for revenge, until I came to visit my aunt and my sisters in Pretoria. There I met some gangsters.

'We can organise guns for you,' they said. When I left I had four guns in a bag. I took them in the train in books. Big thick books, you just cut a space for the guns to fit into.

When I came back to Upington, I called the other guys except for Zakie, and handed out the guns. This made us the only gang with guns.

Two days later we went to the shebeens to threaten the owners to give us drinks. It was my first encounter with alcohol. The owner was a big big guy and we asked for two quarts each without showing our guns.

'Gents, you have to pay,' he said when we ordered more.

Elwyn, who was the shortest and the most aggressive, said, 'no, you must pay us, this is protection fee, why are you asking money when you still owe us lots of cases?'

We were still lighties and this ou was groot. We were wearing big shirts and big trousers to play big. We all had to turn up our trousers six or seven times so that they didn't drag in the road. We even wore our father's shoes, and put newspaper in front. As we were threatening him, his wife entered, 'What's this about protection and not paying?' she asked.

'It's very good of you to be listening and overhear so we don't have to repeat,' said Elwyn.

All three of them pulled out their guns at the same time.

'Ok, gents,' said the shebeen owner trying to pull himself out from the complicated situation.

Guns were at his head and his wife was ordered to get more cases and seven hundred rand.

She came back and put it on the table. We left, each taking a case. We carried them like briefcases hanging and swinging.

The next day we woke up sick but we got up and shot cats and dogs. These things I regret because they are innocent animals.

Virginia, who is sitting next to Robbie, drifts away a little bit.

'Is it the Robbie that I'm seeing now who was doing all those things?' she asks.

'Yes, it is me,' he says 'who do you think killers are? The people who eat with you every day.'

'What happened to Zakie?' asks Patrick.

'He became a police informer who spied on our activities,' says Robbie.

I already told Jonathan this book will be rocketing us to unprecedented heights. I sometimes get frustrated how long it is taking, and how slow the others are.

'The beginning of a good road looks bad,' says Robbie, 'and the beginning of a bad one looks good, but if we don't finish we will never get anywhere, good or bad.'

He looks at me and I nod him forwards. He is a quick mover like myself.

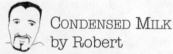

Condensed Milk
by Robert

There were these other rich kids who wanted to be gangsters. We called them moffies. They didn't even have the guts to cut a chicken's throat.

By being scared of us, and wanting to be like us, we allowed them to buy us beers with money they stole from their parents. Sometimes they even asked us to help push their father's cars out in the yard so we could drive to the shebeens. They also used us to threaten people. If one of us got jailed or arrested, they had to steal money from their fathers to bail us out.

There was a street fight against the Scorpions. I was 16. There were fifteen Bad Boys and thirty Scorpions but we had guns. That night in a wide street with no lights, I stabbed their leader Gys in the spine and to this day he is paralysed.

After the fight, the cops arrested us one by one in our homes. The rich kids got all my bail money, which was one thousand rand. I visited Gys in hospital, not to threaten him but to bring him fruit and cooldrink.

'It happened in a street fight and it could go both ways,' he said from his hospital bed when I handed him the fruit.

I lost the case and went to jail in Upington. Medium B, twelve months with a suspended sentence, five years for three years. The other two Bad Boys all went, except for Zakie who pimped on us.

The walls were so big you get a feeling you are cut off from a lot of things very fast. Mostly freedom of movement. That time it was still under the old regime. There were no sports. Nothing much to do.

Tattoos kept us busy. They were also a way of marking you for others to know where you stood. The Twenty Sixes were the robbers, the Twenty Sevens were the stabbers and the

Twenty Eights the leaders of gangsters for serious crimes. The Big Fives were pimps and spies, and the Airforce and the Board Members were those who had done more than two years. I joined the Twenty Eights who specialised in punishing warders for mistakes.

This is how we tattoo ourselves: You take a wrist band made from a rubber washer for a cylinder, you know those black bangles, and mix it with water to make it a bit thick like. Then you draw on your bodies with an ink pen. You take a needle and a matchstick, let the needle stick out a little, and you wrap cotton around them both. Then you begin pricking and dipping the needle into the rubber.

My first one, was this one on my forearm of the Bad Boys. This oke with a scarf. My second, was one of a skull. My next one was a big one on my chest. It's of a man with ear-rings, and behind him is this book which is the rules of the gangs. Down my calf, it just says 'Spalding' our rivals, and on my other calf, which is faded, is a sword.

Here in Brixton, near Jonathan's place and near the dam, I've met a girl who is a maid. She knows how to take them out with condensed milk. You just do the same pricking you did with the rubber in each and every hole with a needle also.

Now I know why Jonathan brought Robbie to join the group. He brings in the rough side, which is there but hidden.

As if everybody's hand is tied to a fifty kilogram bag of cement, the clap is not as solid as usual. Softly come sighs of relief as everyone starts exchanging glances.

'Jonathan, will you open the comment bowl?' I say asking him to unhook us.

He shakes his head.

'I really feel sorry for the life you have led,' says Virginia staring at Robbie with wide eyes as if she's swallowed a bee.

'It is sort of interesting to me,' says David, 'that rich kids want to go a level down and be gangsters.'

'It was Gysie who had such a big heart. That is very rare,' says Steven. 'Most families and victims are praying for revenge.'

'It will make many people readers think twice about becoming gangsters,' says Patrick.

'I'm not sure about that,' says Jonathan, 'do you know that programme Yizo Yizo? It showed the situation in schools and tried to portray gangsters in a bad light, but parents are saying that their children are imitating these gangsters and hero-worshipping them more than ever.'

'Time up!' I call.

Well I have forgotten that I have an appointment with another Canadian lady called Colleen who I met at Kippies. I never told any of our group, not even Jonathan, who is almost like my mentor. They all feel for Anna. Jonathan has offered to e-mail Anna for me but I refused, just playing with words.

'OK, we need to publish this thing before 2000. Please put in all your effort,' I say to end the meeting.

12
Steven & Gert

TIPS TO GET OFF THE STREET
Tip 1: Go to the refurbished Old Turkish Baths for a free bath, or if you
know someone with a tub, go soak there. Even a rag and bar of soap and
any water anywhere will do.
Tip 2: Before your shine rubs off, borrow some clean clothes, make a CV,
and be prepared for diasappointment. Let's face it who wants you?
(Sipho Madini, Unpublished)

I should have revealed my love to him. He is the one of the few people I love. I know how traumatic it is living the kind of life he was living.

'I saw him last night drinking at Jabula Ebusuku,' says Themba Mathe, a writer with *Homeless Talk*, near the newspaper photocopy machine which is still out of order.

Jabula Ebusuku means 'Celebrate Tonight'. It is along Soper Road in Hillbrow. I know not to go early. Nicely dressed drug peddlers, mostly Nigerians, are piled up along the way waiting for customers. Leaning helplessly along a wall, is a white lady I once knew, when I first came to South Africa. Her eyes are as red as the traffic light when it asks cars to stop. When I knew her it was adventure that brought her here from her big house. I heard she sold everything to get enough crack. Now she has sex with druggies in exchange for crumbs. A nasty pair of takkies hangs in her one hand.

The music coming from Ebusuku is earblasting. They say very loud music relieves drunkenness. Two thin guards fumble my body trying to search me. One doesn't have a belt.

Everytime he gropes me, his Castle breath fumes me, and his threadbare trousers try to get away.

The two guards slur in Zulu. I throw searching eyes past them into the room. At the far end is a teenager passing beer out of the side of his mouth. On the bar counter are six empties. Three more unopened ones are waiting for him.

'That guy is drinking himself to his death,' I cry.

'No,' chuckles an old woman, 'he is standing the taste of time.'

"

Steven is to read first today. He is wearing a brown cowboy hat. On it are tags of Kaizer Chiefs and a sticker advertising shock absorbers. He squints against his paper as he reads.

'Be fast since you have to watch the Chief and Pirates game today,' I tell him and the group. He never misses a game. It is my job to make sure he is on time today.

Without preambling, unlike his well-known usual style, he just looks down and reads.

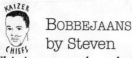

BOBBEJAANS
by Steven

This is a story about bobbejaans (baboons) and BDF 774B, the number plate of an actual bakkie, which followed me and my family around. The owner of the bakkie, called Nozinja (dog) by my family, assaulted me and my father at different times.

'Bobbejaan, hoekom drink jy daardie brandewyn, het julle nie bobbejaanbier op die berg nie?' (Baboon, why are you drinking brandy; don't you have baboon beer on the mountain?)

They told my father this, when they found him drinking alone, parked in his car.

Our town, Queenstown, was one of the most conservative towns you could find at that time. It became worse after 1976. One day I was in a park minding my own business. It was forbidden then for blacks to be in a park. But I was young and I saw white children playing. Sitting on a piece of concrete in the park, reading some comics with photos of Kid Colt and a guy with a beard called Beau, I heard CLICK-CLICK ladies shoes behind me. There, when I looked up, was a lady in a yellow mini-skirt. I kept my eyes there and before long a police van stopped.

'Hey, Bobbejaan, hoekom kyk jy na die baas se vroumens, is daar nie kaffir vrouens by die bobbejaan se berge nie?' (Baboon, why are you looking at the master's woman, aren't there kaffir women on the mountain?)

I was made to get in the bakkie and these teenagers beat me up. What lingers in my small mind is that I know baboons live in the mountains. Father, who knew all the hatred whites held against us, told me that every black man is a baboon to them. He had been called one many times.

During those days it was not permitted to stroll on the street in groups of more than two. The police would say you are planning something to overthrow the government. The penalty was either to be beaten to a pulp or clean the police cells. Some of my friends still speak about the brutal days in that town.

It was not long before a white man called me a baboon again.

'Waar gaan jy bobbejaan, is daar nie busse vir die bobbejaan nie?' (Where are you going baboon, aren't there buses for baboons?)

I was in a club rugby team with some white boys. We were getting on the bus after a match. I felt dizzy not knowing what to do when he brought out that baboon talk again. My friend, Du Plessis, pleaded with the driver, telling him I can speak

Afrikaans like any white lad. I just looked at the driver savage-ly, got off his huge bus and walked away.

I gave up rugby and school as well. I became a full-time activist full of bitter poison. Still I could not get the bus driver and the baboon out of my head. They stayed there like the police dogs sent to bark and bite the lights out of us.

We applaud Steven. He smiles licking his tongue as his won-dering eyes search our faces.

'Steven, was that the actual number plate?' asks Jonathan.

'There are certain whites who still think blacks are baboons,' says Virginia.

'I can understand why these things remained in his head,' says David, 'a white boy came up to me about one years ago and called me a kaffir. He was only 5 or 6 so I could do noth-ing to him and I kept my cool.'

'I bumped into a white woman on the pavement once,' says Pinky, 'and she brushed herself off like I was going to leave my colour on her.'

'I just remembered,' interrupts Steven, 'when my friend said to the bus driver that I could speak Afrikaans, he said, "I'm not worried that the baboon can go *boggom boggom*, I don't want him on my bus."'

'I don't like to think about the past,' says Patrick, 'it can make one want to get an AK47 and start spraying every white thing one comes across.'

'I can't understand why you are so anxious to have a white girlfriend, Valentine,' says Pinky. She knows about Anna and the others and that I show no interest in her friends. Everyone looks at me expecting me to defend my stance.

'OK Steve, wrap your next window quickly,' I remind him.

He goes straight into it.

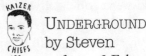

Underground
by Steven

I will never forget 2 February 1981 as it took from me the most precious thing I adored with all my heart. In that same year, my father got tired of the apartheid at work in Cape Town, and came home to the Transkei to work as a driver in a bakery near us.

The job at the bakery was not enough to support us, and he decided to move to town with his family. That black day, although he had a bad dream, he told Mommy to fetch his friend's big truck to take us all into town. My mother made us all work very hard that day to collect all my father's cows and sheep, and put poultry into cages. We were all happy, as children, to be going into town and more important to see the lights at night. We packed everything nicely and waited for father to arrive in a truck to fetch us. When mother was beginning to get nervous, father's bakkie arrived but he was not in it. His friend got out and spoke with Mommy for few minutes before she came and told me Father is seriously ill.

'Look after your brothers and sisters till I come back,' she told me.

I repeated these words over and over till she returned to tell us that we were going to stay with family in town. Young as I was, and though it was the first time I saw people walking slowly and speaking in low voices, I became suspicious that something terrible had happened to my father. Nobody told me anything, although as a first-born, I thought I had the right to know. It was only early the next day the elders called me and told me he had passed away during the night. I stood for about five minutes before falling down.

My small mind wondered how a healthy man could die so quickly within eight hours? I remembered him wishing for me to become a lawyer. All those dreams were gone as I watched old family members preparing for the funeral, which was going to take place after the post-mortem. My mind was dull thinking about how life without father would be.

It was on that day I made a vow that when I leave the world, I must be buried without a casket and a wedding-like funeral. When the day arrives many will be shocked. I painfully told my grandmother what had prompted me to take such a difficult decision.

'You see, Gogo, as a guy, I didn't cry when Daddy passed away. I thought that job was for women. But alas, the family of ladies accused me of being happy that father had passed away. They thought that as a first-born I would inherit everything my Daddy had. Maybe Gogo, they even accused me of being the one to poison him with arsenic.'

This is what the ladies said about my not crying as they attacked the meat and the food like locusts on green crops. I angrily shaked my head for all to see that I was disgraced of their actions. But life doesn't move on by holding on to small things. Our family quickly regrouped after the funeral and waited for mother's mourning time to be over. I decided to go look for work in Cape Town.

I got my first job with the ugliest guy you ever saw on a dairy farm in Malmesbury. After a few nights we escaped because the farmer gave us only food and no money.

We took only a small portion of food and clothes but no blankets, which would make our trip more difficult. We walked and ran until we reached town about 22km away. This was a tough journey but nothing compared to what we were running from.

When we arrived in town we decided to split as we were afraid that we would get caught. The Cape hadn't treated me properly so I went to stay with a family member in the

Transvaal. This was to follow my dream of being a well fed, good looking and tough shirtless miner. With a helmet and a shining light, I wanted to help my family by digging for our country's richest gold.

I soon got a job in the mines. It was so festive on the bus there and guys were joking about how they'll save money before going home in December. Back home I had seen so many coming from the mines with lots of money. Even ladies loved those guys. Our first stop was Wenela, a big place where all men were thoroughly checked for injuries and disease. We were also weighed and we had to stand naked nearly two hours when they were checking us. We blacks were the only ones who suffered that treatment because whites just passed through. They just went to a separate room to fill in forms. I again made people to laugh when I refused to sign the form.

'Oh no, I don't want to sign my death warrant,' I said very loudly.

On the form, I had to write who would get my money if I died. Even the strict officials laughed and explained their rules. After finger printing, and all other stuff, we were called outside and put in different lines, waiting for buses to take us to our mines.

How can a young guy like me stay where there are thousands of men, I cursed myself as I looked around. I had never seen so many people in one place. Trying to look around for some-thing softer, I could see no women in sight. We were herded to our Xhosa Induna, elected by the management to oversee the people inside the compound. In this way we were separated from other tribes and given rooms. There were over five Indunas for each and every tribe inside the hostel.

I couldn't believe that a man could be a bird sleeping in a nest, which was a cement-made bed three up. It worried me to sleep on the top bed. As a makhwenke (uncircumcised boy) you sleep on top and do all the jobs, like fetching mageu and raw meat from the kitchen on weekends, and you cook it.

When I was still dreaming early the next morning, there was a noise screaming so loudly from outside. It was a siren to wake you up for the daily bread. As soon as we were up, as newcomers we were taken to Maziso personnel assistant. It was his job to help in problems both underground and surface.

'How can you make such a young guy like this work underground with Mtaliana, the cruel Italian foreman?' asked the man behind me to the assistant.

'Do you not want to work with him?' the clerk asked me.

'Yes, I want to,' I said not wanting to be a coward.

I was to meet Mtaliana the following day but in the next fourty hours, I was to hear many many stories about him. I still carry visions of that cruel man shouting at us like we were nobodies.

When we were woken up by the same machine the next day, we went to the kitchen for the miner's famous imbunyane – a very hard brown bread that you can knock someone cold with it. We also got phuzamandla, brown sweetened powder mixed with water.

In the cage going underground, I sized up Mtaliana, trying to find his weak points, hoping he'll try beat me. He was tall with a crippled leg and walked like a monkey with his arms low. Underground he had a hard hat called a makaraba so I couldn't see his hair. The only thing I noticed were the tattoos on his shirtless upper body. There were snakes and girl tattoos, but even they did not have legs but more snakes underneath. Mtaliana's face was always looking down at us but his eyes looked up.

Within two minutes of being underground, we were sweating like pigs and couldn't breathe easily while a team leader told us of the job of the day. Then we went to the hottest place

164

I ever came across. The place they call amaside, where people work to take out gold rock. As one of the tough-looking guys amongst them, they chose me to be on the tip breaking big stones. The hammer that I was using was a fourteen pound one.

After ten minutes, I could take it no more. While I was still resting on a rock, Mtaliana came from behind and kicked me in the ribs.

'Wena pikinini yini indab wena lale laphakalo job?' (Boy, why you sleep on the job?)

My reaction was something that caught him unawares. I moved across the rock to a standing position and kicked him hard and high on the chin. This was followed by a fast punch on the mouth. Seeing that he was dizzy, I kicked his legs under him and he fell like a sack of potatoes. At that time all the workers were shouting for me to kill him if necessary.

The communication between underground and surface was quick. When I took a cage up, mine security men were waiting and took me to the underground manager. The good manager said he can't believe a young man like me beat one of the cruellest underground foremen. Even the management was so tired of him but couldn't discharge him as he was a white. Because of Mtaliana's bad record I was let off the hook but I was warned, 'Don't come again in my office with the same case.'

From underground fighting, I soon moved into the ring and received professional coaching. Just when my career was taking off, I was suspended from boxing and working at mines for organising a strike. There was nothing to do but to go home and get drunk too much.

Steven puts his dog-eared papers into an antique airway travel agent bag, which has a broken zip. His face carries a heavy expression.

'This room is full of actors, actresses and escapees,' says Fresew. He has spent a week in the Oxford Dictionary.

'Steven, I think it was wonderful and touching,' says Jonathan. He always says 'moving' and 'touching', but when he doesn't like something he can be straight and sting you.

'Steven, your story was remorseful and euphemistic,' I elucidate.

He bows and leaves.

'Is it OK if I read some of Gert's windows?' asks Jonathan.

I nod.

Some pages are held up for us to inspect. I recognise Jonathan's untidy handwriting on the side of typing. It seems doctors and psychologists both scrawl in unreadable manners.

'Remember, the "I" here is Gert and not me,' Jonathan adds moving his fingers into inverted commas, after looking down once.

 GAS STOVES
by Gert

I was always the first to get home because all my brothers were at high school. Helpmekaar. We were staying in Jan Hofmeyer. All the houses had those gas stoves and sometimes the pipes would burst and give off this smell. One day I came home and there was this strong strong smell coming out the gutter of my house. Fok, Gerrit, I told myself, you'd better do something. I tried to open the front door but it was locked, so I ran to the back but it was also locked. So I ran to the front again. Then I looked for the kaffir girl, Lena. She wasn't in her room. Yurr that's funny, I thought and tried the front door again. I pushed and it moved. It was not locked but there was something in front of it. I bumped it open and there, next to the burning coal stove, was my father lying on the floor.

Lena had made the fire before he gave her money to just go away. The pipe from the coal stove was red hot and it was stuffed with dishcloths which were nearly on fire. A towel was rolled up like a sausage on the floor in front of the door.

My father didn't live with us so I was surprised to see him. We all used to live in Horizon with him but my mom ran away to Jan Hofmeyer. Pa always came there to look for us. He always noticed the flower pots on the stoep that we took when we left him. Then he just hanged around at our new plek till we came home from school and because I was the first, it was me who let him in.

Some nights, I would find him sleeping in the outside toilet we had on our balcony. When I went in the night or early in the morning, he'd be kipping there. My brothers and my mom didn't want him in the house or in their beds, but I would let him in the kitchen door. I'd make my bed on the floor and share it with him.

So there he was lying on the floor by this burning stove and the gas oven on. The whole place was just waiting to explode. There was a shit in his pants and he had pissed all over the wooden floor. Lanies pay good money now for those old houses with those floors but not in Jan Hofmeyer. I opened the back door and dragged him into the yard. When I had him out the house, I started pumping him and rubbing my toppies wrist for a pulse.

I scheme I was also screaming for help because an ambulance came and took him to hospital. The oke in a white sort of army uniform told me if I'd been one minute later, my toppie would have been dead. He reckoned they were going to give me a medal. Lots of people told me this but I'm still waiting.

It took them over two months in the JG Strijdom to get him right. When he got out, he came back to fetch me to take me to Soppies. Soppies was a tearoom bioscope. You'd get a glass of cooldrink or tea on a saucer, which was your ticket. As long as you had a saucer you could get in. His plan was to get dronk, take me there, fok off and leave me to get lost. If I got lost he would not have to pay my mom support. But I always found my way home. He must have schemed I was stupid or something because it was not so far to get home to Jan Hofmeyer.

Clapping, without having Gert to hear us, is unique. So I clap louder. We all look around for him but end up looking at each other's faces.

'What causes his father to come to his wife's house to gas himself?' asks Steve.

'Maybe he missed his family and his wife didn't want him back because he was a drinker but it felt the most like where he belonged,' says Patrick.

'Actually his dad reminds me of mine except Gert's dad executed these things,' I say. 'In Marseilles and the few times I lived with him he usually talked of terrible things like the easiest way to kill yourself. One time he sent me along the beach to look for an Indian trader selling cobra poison. Another thing, the medal he was promised but never received, reminds me of a black and white goat called Pedie. She was beautiful and everyone in the village loved her. One day she got one of her legs stuck in a hole from an uprooted fence pole and my grandmother said we must slaughter her. I said no, let me try some of my grandfather's tricks on Pedie. I took two sticks from a tree and some plantain ropes and some chillies and other herbs and wrapped her leg in newspaper. Every five days for one month I changed these dressings and she got healed. My grandmom said no matter where you are, when we do slaughter her, we will send you the heart and liver which are the symbols of heroism. Like Gert I am also waiting for that

168

medal till today.'

'Did Gert say "kaffir" when he told you that story?' asks Pinky.

Jonathan nods, 'I wrote it down just like he said it.'

'It seems his upbringing had brought him a lot of damage to call us kaffirs and to be so loose with words,' says David.

We must finish it up. Seeing Jonathan shaking another set of papers, I know there is much to get to.

'Will you read us his next window?' I ask.

'Actually,' says Jonathan, 'I've made some notes here about the time he spent in the army in Angola, but it is not a real story yet. I'll have to try find him to fill in the gaps.'

'What will people not read in this book?' asks Virginia. 'Just by sitting wherever they are they can learn about life in the army in Angola, the apartheid years and Cameroon and and and …'

Robbie is shaking his head in wondering contemplation. Maybe he is comparing gangster life to all the other kinds.

Jonathan passes Gert's picture around. He is squatting with Robbie outside Jonathan's green garage door. Masego has just handed them little purple flowers they are putting behind their ears. Gert doesn't look white due to hygiene and spirits.

Once everyone is out, I switch off all the office lights, close the door and leave the keys with Fresew. He is the last to leave the building and sometimes he is here before it is light. I wonder about this. Does he sleep here?

On the street I run after Jonathan who gives me a lift to Yeoville.

"

13
Pinky & Valentine

No Santa Clause
Hi, ho, hi, ho
Who has been a bad little boy or girl?
Hi, ho, hi, ho
Come to me you sweet little things
I've got presents for everyone.

A bag full of pain and tears
Loadsful of hate and strife
Pocketsful of pride and discontent
Gum to put in Mary's hair
A catapult to shoot poor boring Joe.

But be careful my little pals
Next time when I come you little ones
I leave with your soul my little friends
For I am no Santa Claus
Hi, ho, hi, ho-ho-ho.
(Sipho Madini, Unpublished)

It is 4 p.m. on Monday morning. I'm going back to the office to attend Clive's journalist workshop. I spot Armstrong, a former writer who now distributes *Homeless Talk* to all the sellers from St George's Church. Armstrong was writing before my time, but they say he used to be the best. He used to 'own and manage' this park in City Centre and charge people a story to sleep there. It was a popular place. He still knows what is what.

'They tell me you're looking for Sipho Madini,' he says when

I greet him.

'I am,' I say.

'Maybe you want talk to Diane Wicks,' says the old man with comets of white hair and a heroic homeless reputation.

The next morning there is no breakfast at home. I say my morning prayer, swing my black bag across my shoulder and take the steps two at a time. At the bottom, I contemplate the shortest road leading to St George's Church. Past Jabulani Ebusuku in Abel Road, past the Checkers, into Twist, and to the five big wood doors of the church. Armstrong is handing piles of *Homeless Talk* through a security door to sellers who buy with small notes and coins.

'Diane is in there,' he says pointing.

I knock on the huge wooden door. Diane Wicks, the legendary female American reverend, known especially to the homeless, lets me in. Her nose is running.

'I'm looking for Sipho,' I tell her, 'he often used to talk about you.'

'So you're Valentine,' she says gazing into me, 'he talked to me about you too.'

She leads me into the church itself. We sit down in the back pew, in a beam of coloured light refracting our heads by the stained glass window.

'Hold on a minute,' she says in her Kentucky Fried accent.

She returns with an envelope. In front of me she counts out exactly five hundred rand in soily notes.

'This is all Sipho's,' she says once she has counted.

I wonder how he earned it.

'Every now and then he'd deposit a note with me,' Diane continues as if clairvoyant, 'this is how they came. We'd sometimes talk a bit but not too much. He was depressed. The last time he came he asked me to send the money on to his mother in Kimberley, the address is here.'

171

I recognise his inimitable handwriting on a page of Jonathan's exam pad that he often hands out.

'Weren't you worried about suicide?' I ask voluminously, not succeeding in hiding my anger.

'I was,' says Diane, 'but we spoke about this and he promised me, in fact he took an oath on the Bible, that he wasn't contemplating that at all. He also promised me he would contact me before doing anything rash.'

I look into her very clear eyes, then away to the church cavern in front of us and say goodbye.

Outside, in front of the big window, standing on a flat bridge over a drain, is a woman who I have seen around *Homeless Talk*. She is wearing a very faded, nearly white overall. Long summers ago it may have been green. She has no teeth on the left side of her mouth. The skin around her eyes is as dark as a forest doe.

'I saw him in that abandoned building opposite the Market Theatre,' says the gogo.

I don't even know how she knew I was looking for him. Diane and I were talking in hushed tones.

*   *   *

It looks like a five-story building that caught fire and the top two stories fell off. Even level one, two and three are scorched. Everything was consumed by the fire except for the heavy foundation metals. What window panes hang in the wide and tall louvres look like they have been sprayed with bullets from a high-calibre machine gun. With the panes, it would be much hotter.

A shack village, within the building, surprises me as I step inside. Cardboard and some corrugated shanties run in rows with streets in between. I walk to the edge of a huge crater in the floor. A mountain of cardboard boxes and plastic rises up from the bottom. Suddenly I hear shouts and turn away from the edge. About ten guys with batons and traditional weapons are closing in on me.

'Nobody enters Parliament without permission. Give me that fucking camera,' says someone behind me.

The guy is wearing nothing except old River Trader jeans. He pulls the bag from my shoulder and slams it into the ground.

'You rich people eat and drink and when you want fun you come here to ridicule us,' shouts another metallic voice stepping closer.

I look down into the pit, touch my grandmother's rosary in my pocket, and make my last prayer.

'Call Mulambo,' orders the guy who has seized my bag.

'He has gone to help fetch some new cardboards from outside Joshua Doore,' says one of a new group of younger boys who have popped in.

'Who is Mulambo?' I ask tremoring.

'He is in charge of discipline.'

'Never mind, Mulambo,' says the guy who is holding my trousers by the belt, 'I can handle this one.'

'Ah Deus,' I say in Latin.

'Comprendo la lingua Español?' asks the same one holding me.

'Si Señor,' I reply.

His mouth is wide open. He takes his fingers out and barks something in Zulu. The others lower their sticks.

'Adon de to va?' asks the leader.

In English I explain to him the mysterious disappearance of Sipho. While we are talking he holds my hand amicably.

'Commo te yammos?' he says going back to Spanish.

'Mi yammos Cascarino Valentino,' I say.

'Adon de to vivas?' he asks smiling.

'Yeoville,' I reply.

The others are amazed and start laughing.

'Commo te yammos, Amigo?'

'Ah! Ndiki Señor, Ndiki.'

I laugh too.

'Don't laugh,' he says smiling, 'I speak all South African languages, Portuguese, French and some Chinese.'

'Si, I can see you are elastical in your speech,' I say.

We are talking on the doorstep of someone's shack. Señor Ndiki asks me to greet the old man, who invites us in to his home. A black pot of mielie meal cooks on a paraffin burner, and a bush lamp hangs from the ceiling. The walls are all made from various materials and each one has its own picture: Mandela, Bafana Bafana, Bob Marley and Martin Luther King. His bed is made up of old foam and cartons, roughly placed on an antique hospital stretcher.

Away from the farrago of nonsense, Señor Ndiki pointing downward tells me that Sipho slept in Lusaka for one night only in early December.

'What is Parliament, Lusaka and Union Buildings?' I ask.

'You're standing on Parliament, first floor. It is the most decent as you can see. Union is the second floor up there. It is made up of intermediate drop-outs. Lusaka is that hole in the floor. It is the basement and the poorest live there,' says Mr Ndiki.

The old man is stirring his meal.

'Take him around, Ndiki,' he says without looking up from his cooking, in a voice of command that surprises me.

Lusaka is filled with flies and malodorous smell. Women sit sorting cardboard wearing Checkers bags as gloves. The wet and rotten cardboards are piled to one side. The good ones are tied into bundles with orange and yellow twine. Locally brewed beer is between everybody's legs.

I hear a thump behind me and turn fast.

'Hey wena, we know this place is dirty, but don't try to add more dirt,' shouts a woman to a man who is emptying a pot of mielie meal from the first floor. She walks over to a square refuse bin on wheels. It is the kind recently issued to the rich suburbs by the Council. She lifts the lid and takes out a quart of Castle. A fly lands on her finger, rests and then spreads its wings.

'Some prosperous people in Parliament can afford that stuff,' says Ndiki. 'The rest of us make do with home brew.'

'Muchos gracias Señor Ndiki,' I say.

'Un momento,' he calls as I'm leaving. 'Expedicione al mundo animale, and next time, let me know if you coming.'

'Ah, no problemo, buenos tardes, hasta la vista,' I say, dashing out the doorless building.

▌▌

Bringing Pinky to the workshop, especially with something she has written, has always been a bullfight. She always uses her son Moosa or her exams as an excuse. Today, she is sitting next to Steven, coy as a lioness, dressed like a West African. A protruding head-tie points to the roof.

'Give us a taste of what you've got,' I say.

She covers her mouth with her left hand, just like my girlfriend Anna, and smiles with her eyes.

1976
by Pinky

My younger sister was born on 2 May 1976. When my mother was pregnant it was torture because my friends and I used to laugh at pregnant people. I did not even understand how people got pregnant.

That time, I was attending the school in Orlando where my mother was a teacher. When they started shooting school children, she was already off on pregnant leave, so there was no one to fetch and take me home. I had to run with my brothers Charlie and Temba, and my sister Ethel.

I was only 8 years old when everything stopped, including school most of the time. We could not even play on the streets because the police would shoot anyone, especially if you were in a group. We would climb on the roof and spot a Hippo or Casper from far away. Camouflaged soldiers invaded our streets. Delivery trucks were called targets and were overturned and burned. Black smoke covered Soweto. One thing I remember is taking Cadbury sweets and chocolates from an overturned van in Kliptown. The police came and some children were beaten but at least we were not shot and buried like so many others.

At that time, missing school was not a worry. The reason for this riot was clear to me. Why would I want to go to school to learn everything in Afrikaans? Actually, my brother Themba explained everything. I just couldn't understand what made those whites so superior and cruel? Why did they hate us so much? Most coloureds and Indians also did not like us. Why? Why? Why?

Soon, with all the rioting, the schools closed altogether. My home was not far from the road to Avalon. Ask anyone in Soweto about Avalon and they will know you are talking about the famous graveyard, Avalon Cemetery. Our house was in Naledi street which actually leads right into its main entrance.

When schools closed, we were asked to help the comrades but what could an 8-year-old do? We could stay at home and wait for the older children to finish the struggle. We could throw stones at Hippos. We could toyi-toyi at the funerals of friends who were shot. My sister Ethel, who was only 13, would tell our mother that she was going to study at school. Even though schools were closed some stayed open just as places to go even though there was no teaching. She would dress up in her school uniform over other clothes. I followed her and we would toyi-toyi at each and every funeral we could.

Police would chase us when they saw us singing and dancing in the streets and then we would run into other houses near the cemetery. Quickly we would take off our outer school uniform and pretend to be someone else cleaning the house.

'Have you seen some students?' the panting police would say.

'No, no,' we would say and we would carry on cleaning having made them into stupids.

Most of the time my job was different. Me and others would carry buckets of water and face-cloths as the police used to spray tear-gas all over the comrades. So that they could keep fighting back, or run away and not be arrested, we washed their faces to get the tear-gas out their eyes. I felt like a nurse in a war. But we could not just stand there under a tent with a red cross on it, we had to hide in the hedge and run when the police came out with guns. Others were shot and arrested, even children of our age. Tear-gas bullets, guns and blood, it never stopped, it went on and on and on. It was pathetic and fascinating.

But at every funeral, I felt I was facing change. I don't remember a peaceful one without soldiers shooting the mourners, except after the election when Joe Slovo was buried in Avalon. Comrades were riding on Hippos and police cars. The tears that fell onto Avalon were not caused by gas canisters thrown by an enemy.

There was an article and a photo of such helpers in one of the newspapers. I don't know which one. I was not that well informed so I don't know if the 8-year-old Pinky was in it. As I have said before, nothing stays the same.

'There is no single black soul that apartheid didn't touch,' says Patrick. 'Everywhere was the same story, toyi-toyi, tear-gas, shots. I'm glad those horrendous days are over. Even though I was only 2, our neighbour who was an assistant to a veterinary surgeon in Johannesburg, told me about those times.

'What stories did he tell?' asks Jonathan.

'He told us all about Hector Peterson, the first black child to be shot,' answers Patrick. 'This man even named his first-born son, Strike, after those times.'

'I was 2 months old, still in a sling under my mother's arm on a coffee plantation,' I say, sorry not to have more to add, 'suckling my mother's breast in Victoria, Cameroon.'

'It reminds me of the famous Kennedy and then the John Lennon question,' says Jonathan, 'where were you on June 16, 1976? I was 16, in a white Jewish private school which didn't even know what was happening,' he says, answering his own query.

'My story about that day also has a cemetery in it. I was in Jabulani, Soweto,' says Virginia, 'at one of my aunts. I was 11 years old. There comes this crazy day when no one knows what is happening. When all the shootings and shouting started, we rushed home from school and she put her baby on her back and rushed us into the Doornkop Cemetery around the corner from our place. She took a primus stove and pots with her, but we didn't need to do that because we just sat there between the graves and then went home. There were lots of aeroplanes and helicopters, but they just flew over, the riots were not coming to our side.'

'I was 15,' says Steven calculating it with a pen and paper, 'I was here in Johannesburg visiting my uncle who was in CID.'

'CID?' asks Patrick.

'I only know the *investigating* part,' says Pinky.

'Criminal Investigative Department,' says Robbie.

'I was still young,' continues Steven, 'but I had that feeling of knowing what was going on in South Africa and I had been protesting Bantu Education in the Cape. But I was just here on holiday. Then my three friends and I noticed lots of police in the streets even though nothing was happening in City Centre. One policeman came up to us and asked, "Waar vanaf kom julle?" We told him we come from Transkei and he arrested us and put us in a kwela mala.'

'A kwela what?' asks Jonathan.

'It means ride for free,' says Pinky laughing her unique laugh.

'From there they took us to Park Station,' Steven carries on, 'and they put us on a train for Queenstown. Only when I arrived did I phone my uncle to tell him what happened.'

Everyone is putting up their hand to say where they were on that historic day. Next is Robbie. I love this eruptive aspect of the group.

'I, like bra Steve, was visiting Jozi,' says Robbie. 'Actually Alexander, all the way from Upington. People were starting to loot shops and were taking money from Putco bus drivers. I remember some people were trying to make a hole in a bottle-store's wall but they didn't have the right tools.

Then one guy called Penny-Penny, who is in for life at Leeukop Prison now, did this terrible thing. He climbed into a parked Putco bus, which was parked up the road. He pulled off the handbrake and he reversed it back fast, rolling it into the bottlestore's wall. The wall fell down, but he didn't see a little girl and that's how he crushed her. She died instantly.

All these people then were trampling on the legs of a dead child to get boxes of J&B and high-class whiskies and brandies, but they were mostly after the whiskies.'

'Where were you in all of this?' asks Jonathan.

'I was still carrying my grandma's parcel of meat,' says Robbie.

'Your window sparked off a lot of other memories, Pinky,' says Jonathan, 'thanks, that in itself is a hallmark of a great story.'

'It reminded me of one more,' says Pinky, 'can I tell it?'

The stories have all been of exceptional quality and she has not delivered much, so I say yes.

Her 1976 story makes me look at her more carefully. She has a little cowrie shell in her dreadlocks, which are almost as long as mine. Actually, she is quite beautiful I think to myself as she tells her second story.

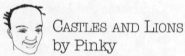

CASTLES AND LIONS
by Pinky

Every location had beer halls owned by the government. They sold traditional Bantu beer in cartons and other beers like Castle and Lion too. My sister who was 13, took part in the looting of the beer hall in Tshawelo. She came home swinging two cases from her short arms. That is 48 bottles. One case of Lion and one of Castle.

'You cannot bring those in the house, we will be arrested,' said my mother at the door. So my sister took a spade and buried them one by one in the garden.

When my dad came home from work, she dug some up and said, 'look what I've got here!'

He took one look and drank them without any questions.

Then, in 1984, my parents wanted to build a stoep in front of the house. The builder was digging and something spurted and foamed out from the ground under his spade.

He thought it was a burst pipe and began to swear. Then he pulled up is trousers and kneeled down to look more carefully. He saw it was a broken beer bottle from 1976. We found six others.

'They belong to Papa,' insisted my sister.

When he came home from the electric factory where he worked he drank them all and he only got to sleep very early the next day, just before work was supposed to start.

'Like an old vintage champagne found in a cellar,' says Jonathan.

We take a short break and I go to the toilet. Standing there I wonder where this book is going. Will the rest of the world be interested?

'Perhaps you should remind us where you got to with windows 1 and 2,' Jonathan says when we get back, 'it was so long ago.'

'Window 1, I caught a mermaid with my grandfather in Cameroon. Window 2, I seduced the headmaster's daughter. I was caned and burned down the school fence.'

He winks at me and trying to sound clear, I start reading.

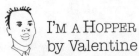

I'M A HOPPER
by Valentine

Since childhood I had learnt to become almost a loner. When my mom got her first job as a pharmacist, I had very little time to spend with her. Before I got up from bed, she had already gone to work in her white overall. Most times, she left a couple of assignments for me to do after school. In the evening, she would correct them. She would also check my school-books, and shout and beat me whenever necessary.

At times, after hitting me, she would comfort me again, saying, 'I don't want you to be like your father, or like your older brother and sister, who have no interest in studying.'

My father was hardly to be seen at home or anywhere. He just lived but in an omnipresent manner. I was lucky if I spoke to him four or five times a year. I heard that he was in France and in Botswana and all over a lot.

Most of the time when he arrived home, he and my mother would quarrel. Our neighbours would share the duties of whose turn it was to separate fights. And when they were fighting, my grandmum would carry me to the kitchen and ask me to help her pound palm nut or cassava.

'Ask him what he is doing, why can't he settle down and show you the light?' my mother shouts at me crying as she burst into the kitchen.

I would turn, with tearful eyes, to my recently returned Dad, and repeat to him what she said.

'I'm a hopper,' he would reply smiling his handsome face.

'And both of you will end up against a windscreen,' yelled my mother in our faces.

Nobody ever asked me what job my father did. They just knew he was very rich. Even ministers were driving cars inferior to his. They drove Peugeot 504s but he drove a Citroën. The hydraulic kind, that goes up off the ground when you push a button. He also pronounced Paris, 'Pari'. But that car was mostly parked, because he was away so often. He promised me a bike but even up to today I can't ride a bike.

During some of the summers, I went to France for holidays, and my Dad's mum would complain of my dad's mystical ways of living and of our resemblances.

'You are as tall as your Grandfather, as handsome as your Dad, and as short tempered as your Mum. Study hard and become a reporter, don't be like your Father, a thief,' she said.

It's a blistering sunny afternoon, I can't comprehend the cacophony, made by boisterous school students as they sweat while talking. My red Walkman, whose patched up earphones hang on both sides of my head, is my escape and my plug. My school bag is falling off my left shoulder, and my right hand holds my newly bought pair of shoes. I am trying to imitate barefoot poor children. They tell tales of how hot the tar is. It's my first time trying it. Yes it is absolutely hot. How do they make it in this condition for years?

Some students are trying to borrow my Walkman. I have saved my breakfast money to buy this Walkman. It is made up of assorted colours of cables, and it has a radio and a cassette. Another one, a black Sanyo, has been taken away by my Mom. This was when I dropped from a regular third position in class to ninth place. At 7 a.m., 3 p.m., 7 p.m. and 10 p.m., I tune it to listen to foreign correspondents in war zones.

The children keep asking to listen, 'NOT NOW!' I shout.

I refuse because it is approaching 3.00. Newstime. A cool palm tree is in the corner of the school-yard. I make my way carefully, remembering basking green mambas.

My fingers are crossed for it to be Burt Reynolds reporting. From the way he paints pictures during his report, I imagine soldiers at war, in mud, shooting and wearing helmets. I curse at times when he doesn't report. Catching me sighing in anger, my grandmother asks, 'What is the matter Cascarino?'

'There is no good news today,' I reply.

She was the one keeping my new Walkman so that Mum could not find it. When it approaches 7 p.m., my grandmum would shout for me as if she wanted to send me on an errand. At this time my mother would be helping me with my lessons. Grandma's shout was the signal that it was getting close to newstime. I would get up and follow her into the coffee trees. From her basket, she would hand me my Walkman.

183

But it was making me lazy. I didn't like farmwork, or even my environment. I think my grandmum noticed this because she began taking me deep into the forest. I got to know the time by the sounds of certain birds, or little bush flies that parade sweating eyes. Even by the exact heat of the sun, I could tell the time to her approval. When my Walkman finally got spoiled, I felt my inspiration of being a reporter shrinking, but my friend Elvis Destin was never short of ideas.

'Let us go spy on those big girls and boys in the garden,' he would say. The next day at school we would blackmail the girls who were cheating on full-time boyfriends, and make them cry.

'Your writing is getting better and better and better and better,' says Virginia whilst clapping.

'For one so small and young, you've been around,' comments Pinky.

The praises heaped on me must make my teeth and ear-ring shine double wattage.

'Next window, next window!' says Steven, looking at his watch. He's always got somewhere to go.

Not until there is complete silence, do I begin.

 ### HIGH OCTANE RELATIONSHIP
by Valentine

My dad informed her of bringing in a third wife, even when the divorce papers of the second wife had not yet been signed.

'Rather let me divorce you,' said my Mum.

I told him plainly that I would go with her in case of any divorce. According to him I was rude and he stopped paying for my studies. Mum was doing further studies at New Era College in 1983 in Cameroon. When he informed her that she

184

was no longer his wife, she got a job, and swore she would do all she could to send me overseas. I was to study at Universitat Compultense de Madrid but I was reluctant to study Spanish for six months as the university required. Universitiet de Montreal was what we decided on after spreading out all the brochures.

It was a hot Wednesday afternoon. In my suitcase were lots of African foodstuffs. We agreed not to tell our neighbours of my departure for my mom was afraid they might bewitch me. Only two of my closest friends knew. Elvis, my blackmail friend and Gabriel, my fence burning friend. At the airport they brought Wuke, a lady I had admired very much at school. Before this, my mum had suggested we consult a witchdoctor to predict my travel.

'My grandson is a Christian, you can do that when I'm dead,' said my grandmother.

When my Mum cried, my gran said to her, 'he is the first in our family to study abroad, be happy.'

She thrust her hand into her breast, and popped out a white rosary, as bright as the egg laid by a cuckoo bird.

'This is all I have for you. Let it be on your neck for eternity, may God bless you.'

An immigration officer tried to demand 1000 francs for cooldrink. When I landed in Ontario, it reminded me of Paris. I lived at Steelcase Road in Markham West. I registered for the Humanities. School life was interesting.

Soon I made friends and we were known as a crowd who liked to talk into the morning. In fact we shared the same dream: to travel to Jamaica during our summer holidays. And we did. When we came back, I became infatuated with some of the beauties I met on campus. Jennifer was one. Each weekend I would travel with gifts to International Boulevard in Rexdale in search of her. Melanie was another who lived in Acorn

Avenue, Toronto. I ran into difficulties keeping one oblivious of the other. They met in my flat and furniture was destroyed till I lost them both.

Luck stayed my companion because Stan, a friend of mine, introduced me to Anna who came all the way from Halifax. After disclosing my history to her, she fell for me. She loved listening to my childhood adventures in Cameroon. The only aspect in me which created a fuss in our relationship, was my superstitious manner. At times in the evening, both of us all dressed up in tux and long dress, I'd refuse to go to a ball.

'My left leg is kicking or my left eye lid is shivering,' is all I would say as an excuse.

Anna would scream. A few days before my world turned downside up, I had wounded my left thumb when cutting a fish. We were about to go to Halifax to meet her parents. A fat mailman brought two letters. One from a friend we had met at St Anne Bay, Jamaica and the other from Cameroon. I slit the one from Cameroon open. It was from my grandmother. Anna said she saw me shivering and then collapse.

'Your mother has died from breast cancer,' said my grand-mother's ancient script.

I was rushed to the hospital. I knew my education had come to an end.

'I'm more than impressed,' says Jonathan to me.

'Is it true?' David asks me, 'have you really been to Canada and back?'

'Every word happened,' I reply and reach into my black wallet. Out comes a photo of Anna sitting bundled beside a fountain.

'This is Anna,' I tell them. They can see the statue is nowhere in Johannesburg or any place they have been to.

186

Then I take off my rosary. It is a pearly colour. I slip it over my neck and put it down for all to see. Jonathan is the most curious. Maybe because he is Jewish. He questions me as if I had stolen it and we were in court.

'These oval ones, there are fifty not counting these three down here, and they are Hail Mary's. These perfectly round ones are Our Father's and there are only five,' I explain.

'And these pictures?' asks Jonathan, holding them gently.

'That is Jesus of Nazareth King of the Jews, and his mother Mary, and behind is Jesus's foster father, St Joseph.'

'How long does it take to do fifty Hail Mary's and five Our Father's?' he asks.

'That depends if you are praying or meditating,' I tell him. 'Meditating takes one hour and praying twenty minutes.'

'Thanks for carrying the point of view for the last few weeks,' he says, 'you did a great job, from next week Virginia takes over.'

He is cubist in his approach. Through him I have learned that power in literature rests in many angles.

PART THREE

Fourteen

Tips to Get Off the Street

Tip 1: You are a man now, you must start picking up a vice, like drinking …
It's the way to be and everyone is doing it. Sure as hell, it's a good way to
have fun. Don't worry, later on you'll be drinking to forget why you started
drinking in the first place.

Tip 2: Marry for all the wrong reasons, like loving the dimple on a
woman's cheek, or the way she smiles. That is all alright, but it doesn't
mean you have to take the whole package, just doing it because she's the
boss's daughter, with your eyes on all the future prospects.

(Sipho Madini, Unpublished)

Hello, my name is Virginia. This morning I woke up at 5.00
because my son Prince wanted to go to the toilet. It is down the
passage from my room, the one Pinky described in Cornelius
House. Prince is very scared to go alone. I took him, then I
went to the communal kitchen and cooked some mielie meal.
Steven's tuckshop was closed so first I went to Steven's room
and got him to open the tuckshop. He looks very funny in the
morning. His hair stands. His body still has a very wiry boxer
appearance.

You've heard about my immunisation scars, my white friend
Boetie, and my Venda-ness. I'm not used to ordering people
around but I look forward to this new role of mine.

''

We are in the boardroom, which is where I feel more at home
than at home. Prince is eating a banana next to the window.

'Virginia, remember your job begins now,' says Jonathan

191

'record who says, does and wears what over the last two windows, and keep things moving.'

He is wearing a lime green jacket with a black stripe down the sleeves. Valentine is sitting nearest me. In the passage he told me I must start with him. Him and Jonathan are still a bit bossy even though I'm the boss now.

'You can go now,' I say to Valentine.

He seems to have two sets of papers in front of him. The one, which looks very old, he picks up.

'I was looking for Sipho at the place in Braamfontein where he used to sleep,' he says. 'A street kid called Jewel or Joel, was outside their drain. I asked him if he could look under the cardboards on which Sipho slept.'

There is a silence. I love Sipho and I miss him but I think we should forget about him. I believe he will turn up. Jonathan and Valentine have done all they can.

'We found this,' says Valentine holding up scruffed pages, 'it's one of his windows.'

There is a shocked silence.

'Which one?' asks Jonathan. 'Is it the one about when he sent his book as a teenager to a publisher in Jo'burg? I kept asking him to write that story up and I knew he was working on it.'

'Did he know more about where Sipho may be?' asks David.

Valentine shakes his head.

Now I understand why Valentine wanted to go first.

'I think you should just read it to us,' I say.

Valentine starts to read.

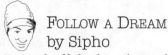 FOLLOW A DREAM
by Sipho

I jumped off the big elevated truck, returned to the passenger seat and heaved my luggage off. It was the early in the morning.

I turned to the driver and smiled at him, at his fattish frame and at his easygoing manner. I did not know how to thank him, he had been my longest lift. When he picked me up just outside Klerksdorp, I thought my destination had been just over the hill, but the ride had shown me wrong.

Thanking him profusely when he dropped me off five hours later did not seem enough. I took off my wristwatch and offered it to him. It was not expensive but dear to me. He refused but I pressed on because it was not a payment but a token. At last he accepted it, and without me the truck moved on to the highway to Pretoria.

'Over there is Soweto, here to the left is Eldorado Park. Just take that road and you'll get a taxi to town,' he told me before he rumbled away. My eyes could already see the mine dumps and the tower of Hillbrow.

For a moment I digressed from the direction he gave me. I entered into the big tall green trees near the road that reminded me of a forest. It was green green-green and I could believe I was in another country. Gone was the golden hue grass and the scrub thorn trees which had always surrounded me.

In the mini forest I started looking for a suitable place to bury my bag. I didn't want to appear conspicuous and attract the attention of thugs. After all that was Soweto just over there.

I looked up and I could hardly see the sky through the tree-tops. Looking down at the thick leaves, my skin crawled and I began imagining a newspaper story of a rotting corpse in just such a place not far from the location. The voice of my great grand uncle and the stories of his escapades to Jo'burg long time ago had to take a back burner. So did ideas of living on the fringes of the location until you found a far off relative or a good Samaritan. I beat a retreat out of the forest which had become menacing.

Three days before, a Monday as usual, I had woken up in

Kimberley, my home, with no prodding or outside interference. The decision to hit the road was not the fruit of long deliberation and forethought, nor was it a spur of the moment thing. It had always been there floating in and out of my ideas, waiting to become decision.

The night before, I had been looking at my mother trying to keep a house of seven. There were nephews and nieces and sisters and me and her. It was an extensive family house. The poverty was not screaming and we had never had to go to sleep on an empty stomach, but the torn curtains flapped in my mind. I never got comfortable stepping over all my cousins to get to my sleeping place under the eating table.

The main factor was that I was no more a child, and a man had to do what he had to do. As I fell asleep that night, I knew that I was leaving a now or never situation.

With everyone else dead to the world, I washed and stole my own clothes, just enough to travel lightly. But what about being presentable for a job interview? The bag ended up heavier than planned. I put it outside. I did not want an early riser to stumble over it, forcing me to answer awkward questions. In my pocket, I put a photo of my uncle who had disappeared into Jo'burg ten years ago. The red bricks of the houses in the photo were calling me.

'Hello mom,' I said as she woke up. I was standing on her side of the double bed she shared with her niece. 'I'm leaving now.'

'OK, go alright,' she answered me.

I looked at her hesitantly. The words 'I love you' stucked to my throat but care came out of somewhere and I said them.

'Yes,' she instantly agreed and smiled.

'I only wanted you to know,' I shrugged, facing her with a drawn-in look. She propped herself up on the pillow.

'I'm going now,' I said again, 'goodbye Mom, I just woke up early and I feel happy to see you.'

She still looked sleepy and no doubt wondered what I was saying. Outside I collected up my bags and strode down the dusty street past a few early birds on their way to work. After an hour's walk I reached Transvaal Road, the road to my destination. Occasionally, but without slackening my pace, I flicked my thumb to the passing vehicles. The litre Coke bottle full of water kept stabbing me in my back as the sun was rising fast behind me.

Without any success, my city became smaller with every step. Under a small tree, I mixed myself juice with artificial sweetener, and nibbled on the dry loaf I had packed. I chose this dry one specially because it is better to learn early. With something in my stomach, I put out my thumb again and instantly got my first ride. The white wreckish bakkie came to a spluttering halt and I ran to meet it.

'Thank you, sir,' I said out of breath as I slid in near to him and swayed my bag near my legs.

He was a big man, more or less my father's age.

'Where are you going to?' he asked.

'To Johannesburg,' I replied concedingly.

'Johannesburg, I am not going far, but I'll drop you a little further and maybe you'll go on from there,' he said.

We spoke for a bit and then he said, 'Hey, I know your father, you are his son?'

He tried to dissuade me from going, telling me how hard it is in Jo'burg, how people are suffering on the streets and of his son in that situation.

I listened but I told him, 'I know what I am letting myself into, it is a chance I must take.'

When we came to his turn-off, he stopped and smiled at me understandingly. 'Have a good journey,' was all he said. I walked away but then he called me back and took out from his pocket a lot of silver coins.

For hours the bag hung draggingly, and the sun drew my water, stinging my neck. A mile further out of the bushes along the side, a black snake rustled out onto the tar road. I jumped back, my neck felt needly, my throat deserty and the world became even hotter. For a hundred metres, I sprinted. Never had I been scared so stiff. That was the closest I came to turning round.

A couple of lifts took me past Christiana to Potchefstroom. In-between lifts, I could not stop but walked on, and my ligaments were worn thin and sore. On the other side of Potchefstroom, I slept near the road not far from a lonely garage.

Before the day was through, I had several lifts past Klerksdorp, and I walked on to the next town. In its centre, a removal truck offered me the job of unloading heavy video and money games. I smiled as I pocketed the ten rand, little money but perhaps a good omen of what was to come.

I rested most of the day till night when I caught the ride that brought me here, to this mini forest in-between Eldorado Park and Soweto. The place was abuzz with people hurrying for transport, children in school uniforms and the road full of cars and buses and anxious taxis. A feeling of *déjà vu* struck me as I stared at the houses of the coloured area. Everything was like I had expected it to be, even the stream which ran near the road into a swamp filled with reeds. It was just like the photo my uncle had sent long ago. The oldish red brick houses were just there across the way.

I thought of asking if people could identify him from the photo but accepted its futility. Was it in my name I asked myself? The few girls called Matlakda (rubbish) had accompanying morals and the Leratos (love) always gave credit to the name. My father called me Loet, 'The Walk' in Tswana.

I walked over the road anyway, with my photo, into one of the red brick houses and asked, 'do you know my uncle?'

No one had ever seen him or heard of him. In a taxi rank, which was in a market, the Indian influence was strong. I took a bite into my pocket and caught a taxi to the city. From the taxi, as it leaned over a bend on an intricate criss-cross of highways, the skyscrapers and towers rose into view. Elation, plus a kind of bitterness, rose to my throat. How could it be so big and the place I come from so small? What happens to all the diamonds we have found all these decades? Do they all come here? Compared to what I saw, Kimberley was a farm. With my first class matric in my pocket, it had taken me less than a day there to walk the town to no avail. No wonder the youth had gone despondent and recklessly suicidal. No wonder the only way to hero status was speed with a knife. Kimberley was a retrenched man dying.

In the overfull taxi, hearing nothing of the conversations, I disembarked onto a street lined by towers, glass mirror buildings and vendors. The place was soundtracked by so many droning engines and shouting voices. The blast of a hooter got me going. Soon I was in a place where the buildings were shorter and more dilapidated. Then, suddenly, I came to a stop right in front of the Market Theatre. I looked at the billboard. It advertised a play by John Kani. I kicked the golden ground.

Then I noticed an old man sitting as still as Father Time. I straightened half ashamed and went over to him, 'Hello, my name is Sipho.'

He motioned to a tin bucket and we sat and talked. He wanted to know all about me and he showed me where he slept – under the steps that lead up the wall. I went to the shop and bought a small packet of mielie meal. We cooked pap in an open tin and I knew for the first time I was home.

'Shit, that boy really could write,' says Jonathan. 'The way he started with the middle, and came back to the beginning and then the end!'

'*Can* write,' I correct him.

'I wish I knew that for sure, Virginia' says Jonathan, 'sometimes I lose hope.'

'He was sitting on diamonds. Heaps of diamonds were under his legs,' says Valentine in an emotional tone, 'and what did he find in Johannesburg? Greed. Greed has always been man's falldown. With all the riches they took from Kimberly, Sipho could not even have a grain of a peanut.'

'One thing that touches me,' says Steven, 'was that food was never his problem at home in Kimberley, but that here in Jo'burg he sometimes went for days without both a morsel or a roof. Like the title says, he was following the dream of being a writer.'

'It will leave an "if" on most readers minds,' says Valentine, 'him vanishing into thin air but not being a magician. I totally don't blame him for being forced to commit an act here in this city.'

'Let's end the workshop for the day,' I say. The mood is very heavy and no one knows what to say.

On our way out, the security guard, Mike, who is seven feet tall, and who always wears a blue double-breasted blazer, is coming out the toilet. A roll of toilet paper is clutched in his big hand. Embarrassment gets the better of him and he looks away. He is always calling me to ask me if there are enough chairs and if everything is alright. During the session this morning he interrupted us again.

'Virginia, what was it he wanted when he came in today?' Jonathan asks me.

'He told me he is going to fill his car with petrol, that is to say he has a car.'

'He called you out to tell you that?' says Jonathan looking confused.

'Yes, and he told it to me in very bad Venda. He also wants me to know he is a Venda.'

Fifteen
Valentine

DEATH
Watching the father proud in joy
The mother in elated labour
Death stepped out the shadow
And the baby cried no more

A young man made his plans
By the candlelight
Confident in his dreams
Books on the one hand
A maiden in his heart
Death swung the sickle
And the flickering flame burned no more

The middle age sweat and strived
Amassing as much fortune as he can
Death creeped onto him and pounced
You ain't gonna enjoy your gold

Old man gritted and grunt
Hearing the battle of approaching bones
Horror in his eyes indescribable
You ain't gonna see the rising sun

Satisfied and swaggered
Death leaves his trail
He ain't pickey or choosey
Just another day's good work
(Sipho Madini, *Homeless Talk*, April 1999)

It's Tuesday night. We are in the Hillbrow Theatre doing physical exercises, which is what we always do before rehearsals. Most of the cast are happy because I am leading the exercises. Since I hate exercises, I make us do the easiest ones.

Tonight we must rehearse Scene Three. That is the one where I dress as Ma Khumalo used to dress when she was young. Ma Khumalo is an old homeless woman who used to be a beauty queen in her young days. Now she is dirty and dresses in rags, always drunk. She also takes snuff, which she keeps under her tongue, and it makes her talk as if it is tucked in her bottom lip. Both in name and type, Ma Khumalo exists out there and we have her permission to use her real name. Tonight is dress rehearsal so I have to put on her tight-fitting evening suit and afro wig. I hate a lot of lipstick.

In the scene Ma Khumalo is showing her friends her old album that she has managed to hold on to. I step out and pose as if I am the photos. When it comes to the one of her wedding, a loud wedding song plays, and Mandla comes out to march with me as my groom. At 10, after rehearsing this several times, we call it a day. I fetch Prince, who has been playing amongst the empty seats, and we go home.

* * *

Saturday at last. Prince is excited as I prepare him for the walk to *Homeless Talk*. We often get in each other's hair in such a small room and I sometimes shout at him. Being an active intelligent child, he shouts back or ignores me. He is a bit colour blind. I have a red and white striped T-shirt and he has a blue and white one. When I wear mine, he complains that it is his, but I have no other clean clothes to wear today.

'Mama, will Jonathanee be there?' he asks in Venda, 'will Masego be there with her dolls?'

201

I reassure him that Jonathan will be there but that I'm not sure about his daughter Masego. Last time she shared Prince's rice crispies and milk that I made in a tupperware. We walk to the *Homeless Talk* offices. It takes us half an hour.

"

Jonathan and Valentine have arrived before me. They both have their bags with them. I always wonder what they carry in those big bags. David and Steven come in just as I'm taking my seat. They complain that I always leave them behind because we come from the same place. I don't like to walk and talk with them because I like to be with Prince. It gives me a chance to be closer to him. I just ignore their comments.

I ask every body to get ready for listening to Valentine's window 5. He starts with his slow smile as he always does.

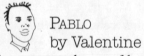

PABLO
by Valentine

Just one week out of hospital, staying at Anna's parents, after hearing my mother had passed away, I decided to stroll along the beach. I had just finished dry-cleaning and splitting wood with Anna's father. Anna was shopping with her mom.

'I notice you have a passion for detection,' said a man as I tried to trace a crab from its prints, 'your facial features also tell me you are depressed.'

'You're absolutely right, Sherlock Holmes,' I replied, looking up into the face of Pablo. He was Chilean. He said he had been watching me for quite some time.

'If you explain your situation to me I may be able to help you,' he continued.

I don't know why I did but I did. I told him that my high life

202

of being a student had been snapped like a razor on cotton.

'Meet me at the beach at 1.00 tomorrow and don't be late. If you can't keep time, you will always find your business drowning,' he said after listening.

He walked away but I tailed him to see the kind of car he was driving. After a few metres, he turned and stared at me for a very long time. I continued to stand there watching his Corvette Stingray pull away. Then a hand covered my face from behind. From the fragrance I knew it was Anna.

'Who was that?' she asked.

'A friend I met today.'

'You just met him today and already he's a friend? Be careful,' she said.

The next day I arrived an hour early. With my last fiver, I bought juice to relax. At exactly 1 p.m. Pablo appeared but he wasn't the man I met the day before.

'Give me your student card,' he ordered. I gave it to him and he studied it. 'You've passed your first test Valentine Eboh Cascarino. Come on, we're leaving town for a few days.'

'But, but ...' I began. I needed to tell Anna and her parents.

'Soon those things will be of no interest to you. Consider yourself a knight who is about to fame his people,' he said seriously.

Out of his boot he fetched a suitcase. He opened it in front of me. It was full of dresses. 'Take this to Montreal by train. I will meet you there.'

Six hundred dollars were held up. I needed five thousand before school reopened in July. My fist closed.

On the train I wondered about Pablo. Why wouldn't he travel with me? He smiles and speaks only when necessary. His eyes ... a policeman cut me off from my thoughts. Ten more in uniform were coming down the aisle with many dogs. A chill moved down my spine as the dogs sniffed at my suitcase, which was between my feet. Big black German Alsations. Their tails wagged and one began to bark but bounded off to another suit-case. In my mind I apologised to Pablo for thinking of him as a bad guy.

When I got to Montreal, I was mysteriously directed by a taxi driver to a hotel room. The taxi driver pointed up from the Gauloise sign on the street. I took the lift to the seventh floor. Outside one of the apartments, Pablo was standing smiling.

'I've got a real partner,' he said patting me gently on the back. I noticed a very big diamond ring on his finger. 'Come on in to my home. I hope you will like it for your short stay with me in Montreal.'

He took the suitcase and laid it down on the sofa. His thumbs flicked open the clips and he lifted the top. He examined the dresses and smiled. Out of a coat in the wardrobe, he pulled a white envelope.

'For you, Cascarino, destiny has brought you to my hands. How will you spend the money?'

They were hundred dollar bills, not Canadian but American. I began counting.

'You're too slow Cascarino my boy,' he seized the money. 'I really have to teach you everything.' The dollars bent and made a sound of wind. 'Five thousand, it's all here. Always be fast if you want to be a businessman.'

I felt my feet deep in the carpet. I moved to the kitchen. The cooker looked like it had never been used.

'What business do you want to teach me?' I asked him over a delivered dinner.

He got up and walked over to the suitcase. 'Watch carefully,' he told me.

I noticed all the dresses had large thick buttons. He unscrewed the top of the first one, and blew off some red pow-der which smelled of pepper. Under this was a layer of paper, under which was a small plastic bag filled with white powder.

'Pepper's scent is stronger than cocaine. This is why the dogs passed you,' he said laughing.

He came over to me. 'Now you are my brother. I'll always make sure you are safe when you make a deal for me. I'll also keep this safe.'

He took the five thousand from me. With a small remote he opened up the wall. Into a cavity he put my money. 'It can sleep in good company. You are looking at two million and five thousand US dollars, Cascarino.'

The bundles were neatly stacked, bound with elastics. He pushed the remote again and the wall closed. A genius would never know the safe was there.

'Why do I show you this?' he asked. 'Because there is no turning back. I am part of you and you are part of me. But get this right from the start,' and he read me the rules from a notebook:

'Rule Number One: Never ask me any questions. Rule Number Two: I am always right, so do as I say. Rule Number Three: Never make any call from home or give our home phone number out. Rule Number Four: Never cook at home or watch TV. Rule Number Five: Never touch onions with your hands. Rule Number Six: Never look behind you in the street. Rule Number Seven: Always call me Pablo Acuna. Never ever call me Lorenza Morales.'

I said nothing and he kept talking.

'We are going to live in Montreal till we have the amount of money we are looking for,' he said. 'It shouldn't be later than December. Onions have bad smells, which can be used in tracking you. TV and home cooking will make you lazy, and if you have to look behind you, it means you did not keep your eyes open to the front and sides.'

That week I handed over a suitcase worth one hundred

thousand dollars to a man in ankle-high trousers, leaning on a black staff under an elevator. I learned to open the safe and code language. I learned to identify a cop even if she looked like an Irish peasant. I travelled to Halifax six times and I spoke to Anna on the phone most days. Pablo was as patient as a hyena and each day his fondness for me grew.

'When are you going back to school?' he asked me one day over bubbling aqua.

'School is a long-term investment, I have money now. What am I going to do in a classroom?' I said.

As each day flipped away, I felt myself getting taller. I prayed for December when we had agreed to partition the money. I'd open the safe and praise the money, two inches from madness.

'So you are also a gangster,' says Steven.

'No, I'm not, that was years ago and I lost a panoramic view of my predicament,' says Valentine.

'You watch too many movies,' says Pinky, accusing him of having an active imagination.

'True or not, your sense of suspense and intrigue is master-ful,' says Jonathan.

'Every single word is the truth,' protests Valentine.

'What happened? Did you split the money with Pablo in December?' asks Patrick.

'If you give me a chance to read my next window, and some benefit of doubt, you will find out soon enough,' says Valentine.

 SUSHI
by Valentine

It was early in November 1997. We were still living in the hotel. Pablo looked stressed and told me that we wouldn't be working for a month. I asked him one question, 'Can I go to Ontario to visit Anna?'

He gave me four thousand dollars and told me to come back in five days. I arrived in Ontario and looked at the students in McMaster University campus. I saw the blindest creatures on earth. Anna also hardly recognised me. Pablo had taught me to speak little and not to answer questions. After three days I gave her a wad of money and left.

'I'll be back in December to settle the score,' I told her.

She wept and wailed and grabbed my suitcase. Pablo was overjoyed to see me back early. 'Now you are a man. Women can only retard your progress. If you care for her, surprise her with your bucks and marry her but that's all.'

I could see he was edgy. He sent me out to patrol the street and to report changes in atmosphere. He himself rushed out to check people at the station. Something he never did. We were to meet in twenty minutes time.

The street had maintained the status quo of the day the taxi driver had dropped me off in front of the Gauloise sign. I entered the flat two minutes late. A kid flying down a rail on his skateboard had delayed me. It took me another four minutes to get to the seventh floor. The door was open. I pushed it open and found Pablo lying in a pool of blood. He had been stabbed through the neck with a Japanese sushi knife. I touched him with the back of my hand. He was still hot. There was sweat on his face like he'd been running. My world turned down side up.

Afraid the murderer was still around, I could not spend time looking for the safe remote. One thousand Korean won and another five thousand dollars were all I had time to retrieve from a coat and I dashed out the apartment.

In Ontario I fell at Anna's feet. She gave me a hot drink and I told her all. We walked hand in hand to a travelling agency.

My Cameroon passport was a free visa to Zimbabwe. Two days later I boarded a plane for Harare, promising Anna I would always write. Adjectives cannot describe the expression on her face.

This time I had no mother, grandmom, African food or well-wishers to see me off. I just watched two movies on the plane, and the earphones made me think of my walkman. I was flying back to Africa but both my parents were dead and I had become a criminal just like Lord Albert.

Prince demands to be taken to the toilet so I ask Valentine to stop and we take a short break. Once we come back, he picks up where he left us off.

'I've come for a holiday,' I told the guy at Zim immigration. He gave me a 14-day visa after I produced evidence of sufficient disposable income.

A month later, I crossed into South Africa illegally, using a forged Malawian passport but this is its own story. Nearly all of my money had been stolen by then. The driver of the van wanted money but all I had was Korean won. The denominations are very big but it is not powerful. He accepted a thousand to drop me in Hillbrow.

Believing he had been very well paid, this man who brought me to this country, gave me twenty rand to start my life. In my pocket I had $150 and 9000 wßon. The exchange rate was R5 for US $1, which meant I could pay one month's rent in advance at the Park Lane Hotel in Hillbrow. I ransacked the surroundings for my compatriots but could not find anyone I knew. The couple of Cameroonians I met, who'd been there about three years, were below the poverty margin. From the tall buildings in South Africa, many people have been deceived. A job, even peasant paid ones like waitering, is the most precious thing and of up-market quality here.

Let me bring this fish in to land. I began showing people where to change foreign currencies at a hotel in Berea. For this I always got a commission. A few days before my rent became due, I was as poor as church mouse. I was standing outside my hotel in frustration. Suddenly a Namibian came up to me. He showed me four thousand Namibian dollars and begged me to change it quickly for him.

He was breathing heavily. As we walked quickly along Olivia Road, a car screeched to a stop behind us. The Namibian started running. I took to my heels like a dog as the people in the red Monza gave chase. The Namibian dashed towards Abel Road and I headed towards Tudhope. They chased him not realising the money was with me. That was the last I heard of him.

I lay on my hotel bed staring at the ceiling after having paid my rent. Tears dropped from my eyes. I know I will never find rest until I rest in the Lord.

'I agree with Pinky to some extent,' says Jonathan, 'your story is so fantastic sometimes it sounds like you've been reading too many cheap novels, but I really love it. I especially liked the bit about the Korean won. That and the end bit gave it a wonderful dose of authenticity.'

'The whole thing is true, you can ask Anna, here is her phone number in Ontario,' says Valentine taking out a little diary from his bag. 'Those Korean won, I gave one of them to a Senagalese friend who lives here in Abel Road. I can get it.'

Pinky is smiling, 'OK we belieeeeeve you, it's just that it's so incredible.'

209

'The way Valentine talks and the bits about drug dealers, reminds me of some of my Nigerian friends,' I say. 'Sometimes they talk in pidgen English expecting me not to understand, but I pick up a lot. I've always wondered how they can afford so much from just a pap and stew restaurant on the pavement outside the Mimosa International.'

'The Mimosa,' says Jonathan, 'that's where I started doing research for the novel that I gave up and that eventually became this book.'

'What do you mean by *pigeon* English, Virginia?' asks Patrick.

'"No go gree" means "refuse",' I say.

'And "watta gwan" means "what is going on",' says Virginia.

'And "wisa ya mami deh" means "where is your mother",' I say.

'You could probably have a really good gossip about the rest of us,' says Jonathan. 'But let me get this straight, Valentine, you could not find the remote, nobody who walked in that room would know there was a wall safe, and those millions of dollars may still be there?'

'Let's go look,' says David, 'if Jonathan pays for our air tickets, he can get a big share if we find it.'

'I'm still planning to go back to that flat and get experts to drill the wall,' says Valentine.

'How much do you think is there?' asks Jonathan.

'Pablo was saving even before he met me. There was over one million dollars.'

'What if someone is living there?' asks Steven.

'If someone is occupying the apartment, I will use all my investigative powers to buy my way in, but this is not about the book,' says Valentine looking at me to bring order.

I bring the workshop to a close. Steven walks me home since we live in the same building. As usual, I feel like going

210

elsewhere because I hate my place, especially my little room. On arrival, I try hard to keep Steve as long as he can stay, because I feel a little better when there is company in the room. I'm already thinking of next Saturday because at this stage, the writing team is all that is keeping me interested in life.

"

Sixteen
Steven

I can hear Steve and David's voices. Steve is behind the steel grid in his tuckshop, while David is sitting on the snooker table. It came as part of the business plan for Steven's business. I peep at them and creep down the stairs. I know Prince always wants to call out 'Steefie' so he is silenced by my hand over his mouth and we get to the street unnoticed.

As we walk along Eloff Street, I hear a group of people laughing and someone screaming as if in pain. Stopping to look, the Chinese man sits on Eloff and President, with his big maroon briefcase full of watches. Each watch sits behind a strap of black elastic, on a cushion of red velvet. Even from where we are, we can see this kind hard working Chinese man jumping up and down.

'Why don't you take everything?' he cries.

Keys, coins, notes, and cigarettes land on the pavement. My eyes follow the congratulating laughter and shouts of the bystanders. A man with the maroon briefcase is running towards me. I pull Prince towards me to get him out the path. As the thief passes me, he looks satisfied with himself for a job well done. Like the cat that has eaten the cream. He is not running very fast but very alert, and could speed up any time he wants to. I feel we are all complaining when it is done to us, but if people cheer when a thug steals from other innocent people, who do they think will say no to crime?

I pull Prince and we take a different route as I struggle to hold my tears. The Chinese man knows me and I don't want to be linked with the applauders.

"

When I get to the room everyone is there before me. Prince starts fussing. I give him my bag and he finds a banana. I always keep a good supply of them because he likes them more than other fruits. He starts peeling it quietly, which gives me a chance to do my job undisturbed. Not in the mood for small talk, I get Steven to begin reading.

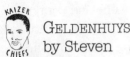

Geldenhuys
by Steven

You can't keep a good man down and, as it happened, boxing officials remembered me when they had a shortage of boxers in my division. The week of the big Interstate South African Games, they found me trying to take the weekend blues (or babbelas) away with a six pack, and a half bottle brandy.

'We need you fit or unfit,' the one official in the Dolphin BMW shouted at me from his steering wheel.

I was like a clown when I donned my training kit and begun road training. People had seen me drinking the last three months and they laughed. Although very unfit, I managed to run twenty kilos that first day. What worried me the most was the weight I had gained during my drinking spree. From 63 to 69 kay-gees. This is a move in the wrong direction from Welter Weight to Middle Weight and just thinking of one dangerous Namibian guy from Middle Weight, made me determined not to be a Middle.

No one realised the pain I was in, craving for even a spoon of drink. But the dieting boxer's motto is no food or drink, no matter what. Even on the train journey to Johannesburg, I put my mouth to the tap many many times, and just washed my mouth without swallowing.

The next morning, very weak and tired, my trainer took me to the hall for official weigh-in. I was 38 grams over. My long permed hair was cut and my trainer told me to take off my underwear.

Before the fight, I washed myself with the coldest Gauteng water to freshen up. I remembered my first boxing name, the Horrible Terrible, which I used when I was still a novice fighting like a mad dog. I decided to use it in my mind as a desperate measure.

To cut a long one short, I heard my name and a guy's from Venda. My God, I whispered through my heart as I saw that very fit dark guy. I had no proper fighting plan till the first bell rang. I ran to the guy like a locomotive and punched him like a punching bag. Tyson once said if you are afraid of someone, give him no idea of this, just punch him till he falls down. It was not a surprise when his corner threw a towel, signalling

214

that their boxer had had enough.

I used the same tactics till I met Geldenhuys four matches later. My good luck was quickly ended with this South African Champion and Springbok. My last fight had taken it from me and he had been watching me. There was no fear in him as he stood in his corner half smiling at me. Geldenhuys did to me what I had to others. I could not match his speed and he won the final. But what a remarkable performance for a man who many thought would be K-O'd in the first round of a tough Interstate Games.

'I'm confused. You should be going on to window 6 now,' says Valentine.

'OK, I'll make this window 6,' says Steven rearranging his unnumbered pages without any paragraph breaks.

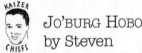 Jo'burg Hobo
by Steven

After nearly winning the Interstate I got my old mine job back. Beside being too hot for me, one thing that always gave problems was the chemicals they were using. They were so bad smelling that every time you blow your nose you bleed. But what worried us the most was the apartheid treatment us blacks were subjected to. Every day we were accused of being thieves and a metal looking thing was put in our anuses to check for gold. No living human could stand that every day for a twelve month contract. They expected me to stand this, plus heavy work, plus boxing. Maybe that was the beginning of the downhill to where I am today.

From Randfontein Mine, one desperate day, I phoned the boxing trainer of Rustenburg Mine.

'You can have a job if you pack your bags now. We need a boxer like you,' he shouted into the phone.

I packed then and there and boarded a taxi to Johannesburg to collect my Provident Fund money. Jozi was the place I was scared of but conditions forced me here. As soon as I had that Provident, I was going straight to my new job in Rustenburg.

After getting my hands on that money, I went to the post office to buy stamps to send some savings home. After that I was still left with seven hundred rand in my pocket. My throat was burning like fire, which demanded a bottle store. After a couple of pints I asked for the taxi rank.

'It is there, left, no right, first left, second right … No, second right, third left.' Many people were asked. Jo'burg can amaze you. It is so big, especially with a few beers inside. Sitting in a taxi for Rustenberg waiting for it to fill up, I went through my wallet and there was not even a single paper money inside. The punch I got when I saw no notes was harder than any boxing knock-out punch in the ring. I didn't talk to anyone and quickly got out. That was the beginning of being a Jozi hobo.

Wandering around with not a cent, without knowing what to do, my mind went back to days when I was working and seeing dirty-looking people sleeping on the floors of Park Station. With one blanket, and two two rand coins, that night I joined them on Platform 5, but sleep did not come with all the noise all the trains and passengers. The biggest problem was the unwritten law that you must sleep on your clothes or they'll be stolen. That first night of aching ribs and cold floors was like twenty hard lives.

Hungrier than a wolf when I woke up, I thought of selling my gold watch. It had been paid for in six months and it was worth four hundred and ninety-nine rand. Hungriness was tempting me to sell it for fifty or seventy rand. I got eighty from a certain guy passing to the taxi.

I took the eighty bucks and spent fifty-five on toiletries – a big vaseline and a big soap called Geisha. It was big as a cake and one guy teased me that if I slept with it on my head and it fell off it would break my toes. I also bought Colgate and toothbrush which was used up by everybody on the platform in one day. I gave the rest to these two guys who offered to show me Jozi's ways.

The two guys were called Chacklas and Mike. They met each others in prison. I was afraid of Jozi and just followed them when we woke up to see what they do the first morning. They took me to a place to park cars. On a good day we exceeded eleven or twelve rand and could buy some meat gravy and half loaf from a Greek café. Most days we just ate inkomazi (sour milk) and half or quarter loaf.

The only time I starved was the time I got sick because of sleeping on cement. When I came from hospital I couldn't even walk more than eight paces and when I lay down on platform 5, I didn't get up or eat for three days.

Next to me during that time was a real Jozi hobo called Oom Joe. He lived on home-made brew prepared with fast yeast and King Corn porridge in a bucket of hot water. Lying next to his bucket and his whale-sized bag of old clothes even though her never changed, he just sang over and over, 'Totsiens my pa, ek sal jou baba sien.' Oom Joe didn't ever remembered where his background is and now he is sleeping corner of De Villiers and Nugget after they threw us all out the station.

I still don't know what prompted me to write a story about what had happened to me my early days in Jozi. One day one guy Vusi Nkosi came and saw me busy. He was this tall guy who looked a bit like Cascarino with Rasta dreadlocks which are more popular today. He also liked to have some glasses high on his head as a fashion. Although he knew where to get soup for free, he liked to think of a better life and got some piece jobs as a gardener. He invited me to attend *Homeless Talk* meetings.

I called my story 'Jozi's Hardship' and every night I would sit alone in my sleeping place, looking at all those people going home or from work, writing what I saw. At that time the paper was two month old, and I submitted the story with a new title, 'Face to Face with Egoli's Life'. The Editor published it and asked me to write more.

Wahtever I saw and lived I began to write. I was in the paper every month and I moved off the platform and the street to the abandoned Drill Hall.

The Drill Hall is an old ex-South African Defence Force Headquarter along Twist Street.. It is where Baba Mandela was held in the early sixties. There is buildings on all four sides with a courtyard in the middle but one wing was caved in with no roof where a bomb went off by mistake. I always saw guard in uniform standing out there and I was tired of sleeping on the street and always being sick. He told me it had been closed for ten to twelve years and even let me in to have a look. On 17 August 1994, due to my experience of being an organiser on the mines, I collected 210 people from the streets and we toyi-toyied in front of his gate. We told him we would not fight and he said he would not shoot.

Within minutes the TV and the radio arrived and we were told them our demands to take over the old place for shelter in the new South Africa but we were told to wait for the Commissioner. We waited nearly the whole day and even the TV and radio went home. At 4 o clock we moved in and took others to the Red Cross down the road.

Soon after that I was elected Chairman of the Drill Hall but tragic struck me on 1 October 1997.

At about 6 p.m., already half full of Saturday night fever and spirits of Jozi, I stopped at Bree Bar Lounge, just near Joubert Park. Old habits die hard, and I sat so no one could pass behind my back. At 9, I went to the toilet leaving this friend of mine with four sealed beers. I took longer in the toilet as there were many people in the queue. When I came back, this Portuguese was trying to take the beers.

'We bought them, me and Steven,' said my friend.

I joined in pleading with him and at such a time the owner came jumping over the counter and hit me on my forehead with handcuffs. I turned to face him but got a terrible blow and quickly went down dizzy. He repeated hitting me on my head and someone else kicked my in the ribs till I passed out.

I was taken by my friends to my room at Drill Hall.

'Hospital is for weak people and not for a boxer,' I groaned to myself, over and under.

Around four hours later I had a dream, which forced me to get them to call an ambulance. I dreamed I was at home in 1978, sitting on the bank of a river. Everything was blue. The grass, trees and the water in the river. I was sitting with my girlfriend. She playfully hit me on the hand and ran over the water which had frozen to ice. I follow her but the ice melts and I cry out for an ambulance.

I stayed in hospital for four days without eating anything, and the doctor said, 'you'll never be the same again.' But I told myself being paralysed is not the end of my road.

I made a vow not to touch alcohol but I ended up being on the streets again sleeping near Joshua Doore furniture shop. The place was a sleeping place for many homeless people. To be in that life again was hard. But unlike Park Station, I had a good time of being close to the homeless community. I was an experienced hobo having learned and digested all hobo's way of life.

'I can't help notice violence is always present in Steven's life,' I offer, 'is it the influence of his upbringing or just misfortune?'

Steven gets up and goes over to Jonathan.

'Feel here,' he says bending his head down and taking one of Jonathan's hands, 'this is where he hit me with the handcuffs.'

He guides Jonathan's fingers deep among his longish hair, and only once Jonathan has caressed his scarry bumps, which I too have touched, does he sit down again.

'Why didn't you get the guy arrested?' asks Patrick.

'Because Portuguese is white,' I say.

'I'm still pursuing the case,' says Steven. 'The lawyers of this Portuguese have turned the story inside around.'

'Why didn't you somehow get back to your newly offered job in Rustenburg?' asks Jonathan. 'If you could have done that, do you not think you could have avoided becoming a hobo, as you call it?'

Steven takes too long to answer.

'Maybe you fell in love with Jo'burg, or with its beautiful women and its posh shebeens?' I suggest.

'How could he get money for booze and women?' asks Valentine the investigative journalist.

'It was destiny,' I say, 'Steve needed to take a halt from boxing and manual labour and fighting, so he could discover the writer in himself.'

'You are all talking as if I'm not here,' says Steve who has been politely waving and bending two fingers from each hand in the air. To me this means inverted commas, but to him it must mean he wants to insert his own comment.

'I agree with Sis Virginia,' he says. 'Terrible as this thing was, I still cannot answer it certainly, that is why I didn't just take my-five rand from my watch and get back to my new job. The only thing I can offer is to say it was God's way of getting me to stop drinking.

You were at you lowest almost like Oom Joe; ready to eat out of bins and to live off home brew porridge and then things changed and you almost died,' says David.

Before Steven can respond to all this gossip about him, I call it a day. Trying to be a facilitator with Prince demanding my attention, plus the sad stories that keep reminding me of my own life and experiences, these things make me feel like sleeping and forgetting about everything.

Seventeen
Jonathan

TIPS TO GET OFF THE STREET

Tip 1: Believe that you are naturally endowed with above average intelligence. You are clever, you've got the brains, so what the hell!

Tip 2: There is a belief that what goes around comes around. There is the superstition that the gods (or God) conspires up above there once in a while to change the rules ... and you find yourself at the short end of the stick. You and I know better, we do not believe in these kinds of watchamacallit ... superstitions. Throw salt over your shoulder, man, and cross your heart.

(Sipho Madini, Unpublished)

I hate my place even more. On Wednesday, when I had no money to buy Prince new shoes, I was thinking that I never write articles for *Homeless Talk* anymore. Every time I sit down to write, I just cannot. These stories are always about poverty, homelessness and crime. I do want to be a writer but I want to write children's stories.

Photos, that's it. I can take some photos for *Homeless Talk*. They pay almost as much for a photo as for a story, even though it is nothing, I tell myself.

I get up from my bed and open the bag where I keep my cameras and photographic equipment. The automatic camera that I saved for and bought and the manual one, my favourite, was given to me by an old couple in Washington when our theatre group went there. I have already learned the basics and my intention is to specialise in landscape and industrial photography. Until then, *Homeless Talk* will have to do.

I pull the bag from under the bed and open it without look-ing. When I put my hand in, it feels nothing. I get a fright and look more carefully. My equipment is gone.

"

Saturday. I am depressed and late.

'When are you going to read again, Jonathan?' asks Valentine as I come in, 'or have you not written your windows?'

Jonathan smiles, 'I wrote them even before I met you all, and I have them right here.' He pats the Billabong bag at his feet as I sit down.

'Well, get them out and read them,' I say. Actually my mind is still on my stolen cameras. I consider everyone I live with in Cornelius House a friend, and one of them has stolen from me. Still I agree with Valentine. I used to love it when Jonathan used to write stuff about us. What we do, wear and say in the group. He has stopped and has become a sort of Baas.

The group has also grown small. In the beginning with Sipho and Fresew there were about ten. People were all around the table. Now Robbie and Patrick have stopped coming. We are scared to ask where they may be. Jonathan looks around to see if it's OK for him to read and he then gets out some notes from his rubber file made out of shoes soles.

Before he begins reading, he pauses for a minute which makes me wonder why.

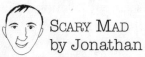 SCARY MAD
by Jonathan

Plop, through my cornea, and my iris, into my lens, and Hlupp, back out again. No pain and no blood but in that instant it all came rushing in, the glare, the sky, everything.

223

'Give yourself time,' I tell Jeremy Kagan who is seriously depressed, 'I've given myself twelve months to get over this eye thing, what happens in-between and till then is of no consequence. I'll reassess in a year's time.'

We were standing in front of the Wailing Wall in the old city of Jerusalem. A month later he was dead. Eight years later the sky and the world and the past are still rushing in.

'Do you sell syringes? I'm going to Angola on business and I was told to bring my own clean syringes in case of a medical emergency,' I tell the pharmacist on Rocky Street, Johannesburg. Eight years is enough. Can't say I never tried. More than wanting to stop life, I just want to kill the pain.

He brings me a tiny little one. 'Don't you have bigger syringes?' I ask. He raises his eyebrows and shakes his bald head.

In my flat, I write letters to the other five people in my immediate family, and one to Emma. I leave all my money to her. I don't spend much so I've got quite a bit. The worst thing for Emma when my parents sold their house, was that she lost all her friends and shebeen customers. She went back to White River to her mud hut and started a shebeen there but I heard it's not going too well. With the syringe, I get into the bath and try shoot air into the veins of my forearm. In Platoon, a Vietnam movie, a traumatised GI tripping on acid, sent a huge bubble of air to his heart and popped. Easy peezy. With me it doesn't work. There is blood all over and my heart is still pumping. The syringe is too small.

Uncle Joel, ex-Mandela defence lawyer, unintentional billionaire, banned at the time of the Rivonia trial, comes to the rescue. I board a plane for London. I refuse to go to Tara 'cause I know all the psychologists. They used to be in my class at Wits.

Those first few moments coming in through the glass doors

into the overheated foyer, nurses in uniforms, the reception desk, suitcase in my hand, Dutch honing in on me asking me something incomprehensible and unanswerable, were as difficult as leaving was. You could see Dutch was mad straight away. In a place like that you've got to stick close to your self even if it feels like you haven't got one.

A nurse takes my name and details and shows me to my room with a number on the door. It is to be my room for four months. It's been six years and still I can't stop the world rushing in through my bad eye. I put up some pictures from an Oxfam calendar my aunt has given me.

'Colin the psychiatrist will be in to give you a physical,' says the male nurse.

Colin brings another one with him. She is tiny. I'm asked to undress and she just stands there and watches. Did he bring her in case I attack him? He is fat.

'You're very fit,' he says. 'Your heart beat is very slow. Are you an athlete?'

St Michael's, a private hospital for the mentally ill north of London. Lots and lots of madness here. Unquantifiable uncontrollable energy spiralling unimaginably behind dilated pupils and anguished faces. Thanks to medical insurance both the haves and the have nots can be mad here.

I meet them in ones and twos. Elwin. He gives me a lift to London on my first weekend out.

'How come you're in here?' I ask.

'Got into a barney wiv a bloke oo it me owver the bleedin ed wiv a steel pipe. Don't remember much no more, get depressed but this new stuff ey've got me on elps.'

'What's it called?'

'Mmm, kills me sex life wiv ve old lady if ye know wha I mean.'

William. He'd been kicked in the head by his father's horse

when he was 5. Didn't stay very long.

Heads seem designed to be bumped and bounced and flattened and fucked with.

If I had a photo of all of us, we'd be standing out on the lawn, in rows holding a banner 'Class of 97'. But we were not allowed cameras. Imagine if one of us makes it out here, I mean really makes it, like becomes President, or really normal or something? Why even Dutch maybe, and there he is in front of the ECT sign, taking his imaginary dog for a walk. Somethings are impossible to capture. Had to be there.

Ron. It was easier to focus on, and to laugh at others, and we took our cues from the professional helpers.

'I know exactly how you feel Ron,' says Colin the fat psychiatrist in a group, 'you're always looking backward and upward and sideways and forward, but all you ever see is a dark red tunnel you can never see the end of.'

Ron's face lights up. The corners of his mouth held so tightly relax into a smile. Oh, to be understood!

Colin isn't finished, 'it's because you've always got your head up your own arsehole Ron.'

In St Michael's, I get to be recognised as a master of mad and cruel humour in my own right. I'd begun honing these skills around our yellow-wood table twenty years before I was admitted.

My weekly routine is punctuated by two 45-minute psychotherapy sessions, and many more pill-popping pit-stops. Nights are heavily sedated blackouts, which blur into occupational therapy, day planning, week planning, life planning, death planning.

The more I slow down, the more the world speeds up and continues to rush in and break up. After supper, a long queue in tracksuits and pjs, hold out our hands for coloured pills. Once we are out we are woken up twice every night to check we are alive and haven't done anything stupid. There we all were, in ways that are not the way, and that cannot be named, but are, but wrongly. I never bothered to steal a look in the file and look up my diagnosis.

In OT I make a key-ring with my room number on it, made out of ceramic and copper. I bake it in a kiln. I paint stripes on my white shirt. I am free to leave but I cannot. The hospital grounds are beautiful to visitors. I like to sit in the unactivated sauna for hours staring at the tiny glass window.

Lois moves her body to a timer buried deep near her heart. No one here moves very fast but she is the slowest. She is 17. Amphetamines can't speed her up. She tries to, but she never can catch me. Her wavelengths are far too long. Only at night does she slip into my disturbed and drugged stories.

'I dreamed about you last night,' I tell her at breakfast.

Blushing, she asks, 'what was I doing? I mean, what happened?'

'You past me eighty-five times in the corridor without greeting me.'

Before the thorn went in, it would have been, 'you were sitting naked on a garden swing and I was pushing you first from behind and then I moved to see how it was from the other side.'

In the group I listen and watch. It always goes like this. Everyone except the one talking, can see and hear what is going on. Round and round, week after week. We all know Dutch has no dog except him. We all know Alice should leave her husband except her. You become more and more subjective. The more you protest the deeper in you get driven. I begin listening for what I can't see. I begin to play with the idea, just the idea, that I may be wrong, even if it feels horribly right. This little huge shuffle is the one that stems the tide and I take the corner.

I'm in the sports complex. I'm overtaken and locked in by a mob of young loud people. I am put into a team.

'These kids can be violent,' says the nurse, 'are you sure you want to play?'

'Play what?' I ask.

'Volleyball.'

'Sure,' I say.

'What are the rules?' I ask a skinhead beside me.

'None mate, none whatsoever,' he says grinning, 'but get up there will you.'

He points at a folded trampoline stacked against the wall. I ignore him and move towards the net. The server, a giant teenage Rasta, stands on the other side waiting for the whistle to blow. The ball falls out of his hands, a feeble little attempt, then his green Doc Marten comes up full tilt, and the ball ricochets off the ceiling and wedges itself behind the trampoline.

His team cheers. Mine BOO at me like it's my fault.

The skinhead climbs up and seals our side's structural weakness.

Their side is made up of at least seven giants, and one severely handicapped woman in a wheelchair. If it wasn't for her, we would have lost for sure. She continually breaks the only apparent rule. No catching the ball when it is in play. Whenever the ball bounces, she goes ballistic, screaming and knocking people over, and getting penalised for catching it. Our team loves her.

'Ooh, Sarah, Sarah, Babyyyyyyyyy!' we scream.

Everyone is playing a different game, but it becomes my best therapy, and I get to become a regular. The skinhead starts calling me 'Doc'.

I'm lying on the lawn trying to let some summer in and some dread out. I squint at the oak branches through my good eye. My damaged iris still can't filter bad stuff out.

'It's all in your head,' say the group.

'I see too much even through my eyelids,' I tell them.

'He's hypervigilant and stimulus bound,' I overhear Rona the therapist say to Colin.

At 9 a.m. every day, ten of us shuffle into the group psychotherapy room – eight patients, one therapist, and one psychiatrist. The chairs are arranged in a circle. Only the select few are admitted. Firstly you need to have pretty serious problems. Secondly it is expected you will be responsive to therapy within one year.

Ninety per cent of the patients were excluded. When the door was shut, we told each other stuff we would never tell mothers and brothers and lovers. If a non-group member wandered in, we stopped talking. If we didn't improve, we were relegated out of the inner circle to the no-hopers and to shock treatment. Whoever's pain was the loudest got to hold the floor. In each other's madness, we groped in and around.

I make a hundred breasts out of plasticine, and hurl every one of them at Colin. He doesn't stop me but he ducks. They flatten on the wall.

On my day to choose, I make the croup watch 'One Flew Over the Cuckoos Nest'. I become our bull goose loony. We share a golf course with the public. I enjoy scaring them.

'Roll up, roll up. Do it yourself ECT,' I shout with Steve holding sparkplugs under the raised bonnet of his Bentley in the parking lot.

Eventually I've had enough and I chain my ten quid bike to my chair in the group room. I'm no better really, but I got fight in me. Lots of it. I've still got the key.

'Is your eye alright now?' asks David.

'Sort of,' says Jonathan. 'I can see out of it, but only far, not near. They had to put in an artificial lens, which cannot change its shape like a natural lens.'

'You mean like a contact lens?' asks Valentine.

'Not really,' says Jonathan, 'this one is deep in my eye, not on the outside like a contact lens.'

'If the syringe wasn't too small, this book would never have happened,' says Patrick, 'don't you regret it?'

'I'm really happy I failed,' says Jonathan smiling, 'but at the time it felt like the only way. The hardest thing is that you have to split yourself in two. There's the part of you that makes your heart keep beating and your lungs keep drawing breath. The other part of you that wants to die feels like a murderer.'

'I once watched a film from a hidden CIA camera,' says Valentine, 'it captured students and youths who had lost hope and who were taking grade A cocaine. They pump it inside them and struggle for about twenty second before dying. It was horribly frightening. Their bodies shake and dance involuntarily and they take in turns but will not rest their eyes on their friends.'

'I watched Platoon,' says David, 'it was a black sergeant who killed himself like that right?'

'Mmm, I think so,' says Jonathan.

'Were you formally discharged from the mental hospital, or did you just walk out?' I ask.

'Are you suggesting I should still be there?' Jonathan asks me and we all laugh.

'In our African culture, we believe that madness is either caused by a spell cast on you, or by studying too much,' says Pinky.

'I am more interested in the spell side,' says Jonathan. 'I now feel I've broken that spell. By the way, you people have helped me with this a lot. Thanks. I mean it.'

I get him to read his other window.

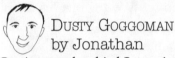
DUSTY GOGGOMAN
by Jonathan

On August the third I married Kyoko. Since then I have been married three more times.

Two months before I met her, she gave birth to Masego who is half Tswana. Masego's Japanese name is Shiho. It means to give direction to your mind. Shiho has countless other names, my favourite of which is Dusty Goggoman. When she was 11, in Japan, Kyoko won a Little Black Sambo reading contest. At school she was teased for being a shade darker than her classmates. When I was 10 I had longish straight black hair, and was called a Chinaman by the other Jewish boys. The little South African Jewish boy who to some looked Oriental, and the little Japanese Buddhist girl who dreamed of Africa grew up, met and got married. Our first wedding was a Buddhist one. The next day we queued in a huge pale green room with rows of hard wooden benches at the Magistrate's Court. The three hours were punctuated only by periodic purchases of single chocolate éclairs from a hawker called Johannes. Eventually we were summoned into the solemnising room whose walls were hung and covered with bridal lace, plastic flowers, and pin-ups of dark women wearing nothing but bikinis and bridal veils.

Orthodox Jewish law demands that both bridegroom and bride produce their pedigrees of pure-blooded Aryan Jewish ancestry, and that all four poleholders be Jewish and circumcised males. My great grandfather Avram Zvi Idellson, composed Havanagilla and first introduced Reform Judaism into South Africa. For wedding number three, in Sandton, I took his pioneering efforts to their logical conclusion. I married a non-Jewish American princess wearing a kimono under a talis held by two females and two Afrikaners.

For wedding number four we fly to Tokyo. Kyoko instructs

231

me to call her father Otosan (Father). We arrive at his house. Still bearing luggage, I watch people in socks moving around, bowing and speaking very fast. I am introduced to Otosan and to Kyoko's brother, Taijiro, who works for Arms Control and Disarmament Division, Foreign Policy Bureau, Ministry of Foreign Affairs, Tokyo. His present assignment concerns the cult leader who released nerve gas in a train station. Taijiro prances around with Minnie Mouse and gets Shiho to join in.

In the morning we chant in front of the Gohonzon, which is a scroll on to which Nicheren Daishonin, the 'True Buddha' who lived seven hundred years ago (as opposed to Shakyamuni, the more famous Buddha who lived three thousand years ago) inscribed the embodiment of the essential law of the universe, 'Nam-Myo-Ho-Renge-Kyo'. (Life and Death. Out of difficulty, beauty can come. We are responsible for and have the power to change any difficulty we may find ourselves in.) Shiho's imitative skills are blooming. She has learned to sit on a cushion, clasp wooden beads in her hands, rub them together and to intonate Nam-Myo-Ho-Renge-Kyo. She has also learned to sound the gong, a deep metal bowl, which stands beside the Gohonzon. The night before, I placed the gong stick out of Shiho's reach. When it comes to the point when Otosan needs to gong, he reaches for the stick but it is not in its place. His hand finds the TV remote control instead. Unfazed, he strikes it against the metal bowl. The others giggle.

Otosan is 67 years old. He used to be captain of the karate team at Tokyo University. He was sent to America in 1961 by the Japanese government to investigate the advent of computers. Otosan wears old suits whose trousers are too short, allowing his long johns to show above clapped-out, unbuckled fake leather sandals – day in and day out, to go to work in and to garden in. He hates wasting and wears underwear purchased decades ago, indelicately held together by heavy black string.

Otosan, an eccentric Ghandi–Bruce Lee–Einstein genius of sorts, is deeply interested in world peace and anti-nuclear efforts. He donated one million yen to a remote Chinese province to stock school libraries with books. Otosan is best understood against an appreciation of modern Japanese work and spending habits. As far as I can make out, Japan is in the grip of a frenzy of workaholicism and consumerism. Productivity is over the top. Poverty has been licked. Zen simplicity and asceticism have all but disappeared. What to do with all those yen? A workforce of sixty million highly energetic and disciplined individuals buzz around producing, adding value, spending, consuming, discarding, producing, spending, consuming, discarding. The young girls in the malls of Tokyo make Sandton kugels look shabby.

Masego receives a gift pack of Mickey Mouse disposable nappies manufactured by Disney Baby Enterprises, and some Minnie Mouse chopsticks. Each nappy is elasticised, lacy, fits on like adult underwear without any folding or fastening, and has a faint reddish print of Mickey on the butt. Towards the lacy bit is a darker red dot. When the absorbent padding reaches a critical wetness, and the colour of Mickey matches the colour of the dot, it is time to change the nappie. There is also a cord you can pull, which releases a few centimetres of cellotape to seal and wrap the soiled nappie. In the street, I see a twenty ton truck, which is chrome plated and covered with Mickey, Minnie and Pluto. It is as if this vehicle is an exact replica of a child's toy.

At the doorstep to Otosan's toilet are a pair of slippers. These belong to the home and are worn by anyone using the toilet. As I squat over the low elongated un-Western bowl, staring at the red slippers which my feet barely fit into, I feel connected to Otosan and to the three young single women who live in this house, rent free in exchange for cooking Otosan's meals.

Kyoko explains to me that when I exit the toilet, I should leave the slippers facing inwards making it easy for the next person to step into them. What she doesn't make clear is that when I squat, I should be facing towards the wall and not away from it (European style). Had I known this, the whole balancing, wiping, flushing time-and-motion sequence, would have been much easier. Kyoko tells me that many women in Japan are embarrassed about the sound of urine splashing into a toilet bowl. To prevent others hearing this sound, they flush the toilet before urinating. In an attempt to save water, sonar triggered devices, which reproduce the sound of flushing, have been installed into factory and public amenities. Fresh out of a station toilet, Kyoko excitedly reports that she peed to the sound of virtual flushing. In Japan I receive an e-mail sent via South Africa from a hospital in New Zealand offering me a job. Geraldine from Christchurch, with whom I have struck up a correspondence writes, 'What a contrast it must be to go to Japan from South Africa. It sounds to me like going from chaos to order.'

I take photos of Shiho, walking over a stop sign painted in white katakana characters. Just as my eyes have come to know, take for granted, and to filter out much of the environment I have lived in forever, Kyoko's do not rest on the interestingly shaped letters. Kyoko's background becomes my foreground. Perhaps it is because I no longer have to listen for meaning that I see so much. Baskets with jerseys and other semi-valuables in them are left on the back of parked bicycles and motor cycles outside stations. There is no need to steal such things. Everyone has them. When Kyoko was a child, she found the equivalent of a hundred rand in the street. She handed it in to the police station where her name and address were recorded. After two months no one had claimed the money. The police contacted her and the hundred rand became hers.

Kyoko also used to shoplift as a child. Her father's stance against consumerism impaired her ability to compete at gift-giving at her friend's birthday parties.

The next day we go visit Obaachan, Kyoko's granny who is 90 years old. When she heard Kyoko had fallen pregnant in Africa, and that Kyoko's child was of mixed race, she cried and cried. She considers me the great white saviour of her sinful grand-daughter and her halfu (Japanese word for mixed race child) great-grand-daughter. She is almost a century old, but she still puts on a kimono every day, ties an elaborate bow behind her back, and takes walks along the beach in wooden sandals. We walk to a nearby restaurant. Masego squelches her toes in the oily sea sand and Obaachan treads carefully in her sandals under an umbrella held by Kyoko. We celebrate our fourth wedding in the seaside restaurant with very low tables and no chairs. Obaachan asks me what I would like to order. I am able to communicate to her without Kyoko's help since the menu comprises of photographs of each dish. I wonder if this is in any way linked to the alphabetic phenomenon whereby each character is a type of picture of the thing it represents. This helps explain why there are so many Kanji letters, more than five thousand, almost a one to one, letter-subject representational ratio. For example, 'big' is represented by the Kanji character 'dai' which is a person with outstretched limbs. 'Small' is represented by the character 'sho' which is a person with legs together and arms held close to the sides of the body. I am familiar with both these characters as they appear as choices beneath the flushing handles of many toilets.

On another afternoon, gifts of Rooibos tea are delivered to various neighbours. I notice bottles of colourless liquid standing on doorsteps. These are cleaning detergents left by the municipality for housewives to scrub and clean the streets with. In the supermarket, I come across very white artificial-looking

235

eggs, each with a little red sticker, informing the consumer of the date on which it was laid. Good old katauba grapes, which grow on vines in Johannesburg's back gardens, have been hybridised to the size of kiwi fruits and are sold in fancy boxes for one hundred rand a kilo. In a health food shop we find brown eggs and health bread, which is about as unrefined as white bread in South Africa. I develop a craving for the German sourdough bread I buy from a bakery in central Johannesburg. For oranges purchased by the bag for R5.99 sold by Portuguese men who ask you 'eating or squeezing?' And for giant mangoes.

Kyoko leaves us and spends the afternoon in a Buddhist meeting. Masego insists on travelling on my back wrapped in a blanket. We visit a museum. People are more intrigued by the spectacle we provide than by the exhibits. A tour guide opera-tor who is offering information regarding a Ming vase to a large of group of Taiwanese women asks me where I am from. 'Johannesburg, South Africa.' He says something to his group who begin to applaud. I imagine they imagine I am a typical African man. I do not have a big enough bum or any breasts to speak of and Masego begins howling and slipping down towards the back of my knees.

On the trains Shiho loves rushing up and down the aisle trying to keep her balance. She also grooves on pressing her-self through trousered legs, flinging herself onto laps and sali-vating on stranger's clothing. Grim-faced businessmen look up from their pornographic magazines, and they don't seem to mind having their suede shoes bottle-splattered with soya milk formulae. I read in the *Japan Times* about a high-ranking bank manager who molested a schoolgirl on a train on Monday. She reported him to the guards and he confessed. To reach out and touch the schoolgirl sitting next to you as you perve over pho-tographs of similar aged teenagers, is but a small jump.

In most train stations, in a big glass cabinet, sits a flower arrangement (ikebana) with a small almost unnoticeable sign signaturing the master or school responsible for the arrangement. The one I liked the most was two vases out of which quite tattered, insect eaten, and weathered branches of pears and autumn leaves, entwined with sword-like river reeds. At first I thought it was rather shabby and that perhaps it had been left there unattended in need of replacement for many months. Just then two old women left the stream of commuters and took time out to contemplate the arrangement. I understood not exactly what they said, but I understood that they were happy and that what stood before me was fine art.

Early one morning in Kyoto, while Kyoko and our hosts chant, I push Masego in a borrowed pram along a pedestrian avenue lined by indigenous forest. After some time a side path leads off the avenue onto an open area covered with loose pebbles. At the end of this space is a tomb which I later learn is an emperor's. As Masego fills her pockets with pebbles, an elderly woman carrying leafy vegetables in a shopping bag enters the area. Near to where I rest she puts down her shopping. She takes a few steps and to the Emperor she bows. I watch as she straightens her back, widens her stance and allows her hands to float up from her sides. Silently I move across the pebbles and my hands too float upwards. With her head she gestures that I should stand a little forward and together we complete the 'Nine Pieces of Silk'. After stretching our neck muscles (Rhinoceros Stares at the Moon), and standing on one leg (Attitude of Waiting Fish), out of the corner of my eye, I watch her collect her packet. Pebbles crunch.

On our way out of Japan, in the shopping mall engulfing Tokyo station, I wander into a kimono shop. A man sits at a low Singer sewing machine tailoring kimonos. Most of the fabrics are traditional, and include images of petals and butterflies.

237

One stands out. It shows the trails made by traffic photographed from a skyscraper using a very slow shutter speed at night. We have been here for fifteen days and not a single postcard has been sent home. Kyoko buys several. Leaning and pressing against a pillar on a train platform, we scribble off our haiku impressions and post them. Boarding the Cathay Pacific flight back to Jo'burg, I grab a newspaper with a red star on it. The alphabet characters go from left to right and are identifiable. A hidden video camera in a South African post office captures a postal worker sorting mail. He lifts an envelope to the light, he squints, he lowers it to table height. He tears it open. Torn envelopes with no money inside them go into the trashcan. Here is one he cares for. He places it under his cap.

'Are you not glad to be back?' asks David.

'To tell you the truth, I love and I hate this place,' says Jonathan, 'so the answer is yes and no.'

'Computers that are two years old get left on the street when people buy the latest ones,' says Jonathan. 'I feel stupid that I still cannot type and use a computer.'

'Is it the same with cameras?' asks Steven who knows about my loss. 'Maybe your wife could get Virginia a new one?'

'In Cameroon those people in the post office are everywhere,' says Valentine, 'we call them rats, and every time I write a letter to the receiver that he will be lucky to get it and to beware the rates.'

'I was surprised to hear that there are mkhukhus there also,' says Steven.

'What do you mean?' asks Jonathan.

'Mkhukus, you know, shacks,' explains Steven.

'Did I way that?' asks Jonathan frowning, 'are you perhaps confusing this with my wife's name Kyoko?'

Steven puts his hands over his face and everyone laughs.

"

I walk home with me head full of crazy thoughts. I think about Japan and how much seems to go around there. And about suicide and the Christian belief that you will never go to heaven if you do it. The other day Valentine told me he was worried that Jonathan will not be going there because he is not Christian and is not willing to become one.

Eighteen
Virginia & Gert

When my friends in Cornelius House, who are all accusing each other of stealing my things, talk and be friendly to me, I get annoyed. The only ones I feel comfortable with are Steven, David, Rodwell, Sarah and Di. It's unbearable for me to carry on living there. When I see people laughing, I take it that they are laughing at me for being so passive, just letting them take my stuff. They all think I am better off than them, and I expect to be mugged by my own neighbours. Perhaps this feeling of not feeling safe, and of not being able to call my home a home, can drive me mad.

"

Today I think I will read first. I just feel like it.

BIG BOETIE
by Virginia

The last time I saw Boetie was 1985. He was about to finish his army service and to study medicine. We were both about 20 years old. Missie has summoned me to Kensington to come see him. I just hated the look of him being all military. Just like that I stopped liking him. I knew he was going to become a Baas or, even worse, drive around Soweto shooting and killing innocent black children.

I had my matric but there was no money for me to study so it was back to Venda. I didn't know what to do with myself? I

240

had never prepared myself for life after matric because I took it for granted I'd go to college. I couldn't think of myself as anything but a school teacher.

'Please give me money to go to Johannesburg by train to look for a job?' I asked my father.

The Nzhelele River is a river that takes its name because it flows opposite to other rivers. Nzhelele means up-side-down. It flows parallel to the Tswime Mountain, which is part of the Soutpansberg. The sight is beautiful. Green grass, trees, flowers, the sound of the river water, birds and baboons and many that I couldn't identify. I walked further to be closer to the hot spring where they were adding the finishing touches to the newly built Mpehepu resort. I looked at the contour lines I had been taught about at school, and for the first time in my life I felt good about belonging to this beautiful land. I wished I'd paid more attention to my geography teacher, I wished I could stay there and be with my brother Eric.

Early the next morning the train comes to a standstill in front of me. People board slowly chatting to each other. As soon as we settle in, someone plays some music loudly. It is hot and dry in the train and we are packed in. I am shy about using my inhalant in company and pray I don't get an asthma attack.

Others are playing music too. It is mostly Zimbabwean music. Most Venda people are fond of it. Quite early, people start taking out their food – cloth-wrapped pap, dried meat greens or mopani worms. Some of them offer me food but I decline saying, 'Ndolivhuwa.' (I'm not hungry.)

By the way I pronounce the word they guess I don't know the language well. To adjust they start chatting to me in Zulu and Sotho. I don't feel like talking but end up enjoying them. When I bring out my sandwiches, they feel pity for me, 'Why didn't you say you don't have food?'

I eventually doze off having adjusted to the noise. Then a

241

blast of fast-beat music jolts me awake. A man who looks middle-aged has decided to entertain us. The passage has been cleared of all luggage, and the speakers of his big hi-fi are on the luggage rack one on each corner. He takes of his clothes and gets into a blue overall and takkies. To the full-blast music, he starts dancing with all his energy, different styles, jumping from side to side, falling on his back and spinning around. All the way, twelve hours to Joeys.

'You come from the farms and still you think you are smart,' says my Aunt when I arrive and enquire about courses, 'papers won't get you a job. Go out and market like other girls.'

I choose nursing because they pay you while you are being trained. When I get to the Training Centre, the only class that is not full is for security guards. Even before the course is over, Callguard Security Company come looking for female security guards. I am the only girl so I get the job. The next day I am checking for bombs in people's handbags as they enter Checkers in Steeldale.

And so it went, working and saving and finally getting into nursing. Not as a trained nurse but as a Nightingale Care worker for Hospice. I do a lot of moonlighting in private houses. This gives me enough money to buy a small house in Katlehong, a segregated suburb outside of Jo'burg.

When I sign all the forms and the bond is granted, I cannot believe it. I have my own home! I put up curtains. I grow lawn. I bake cakes and I invite friends and cousins. And when I wake up in the morning and go to work, the door I lock is my own wood.

When the fighting between the Zulus and the ANC loyalists gets worse, I send my cousins who I asked to come live with me home to the countryside.

The necklacing of suspected informers, by trapping them in car tyres doused with petrol and set alight, and the burning of houses, and the chopping of people gets closer.

One day I come from work. My job is to look after Trevor Huddleston, the well known ANC freedom fighter. Where my house stood, is a pile of black beams and bricks with dirty smoke rising. My unpaid-for-furniture seems to have been taken before the place burned completely.

Innocent people are accused of informing and are destroyed just like that, I remind myself as I sob. Looking to the left, I see a gang of youths at the end of my street. I just run and run through a border area between our house and an Asian neighbourhood called Palm Ridge. Exhausted, I realised I have nothing, no money, no ID, nothing.

'God if you don't want to help me, that's OK, I don't care anymore, it's up to you.'

I look down and there in front of me is twenty rand, enough for bus fare and some food, and a phone call to the bank where I have some money saved.

'Is that how you became homeless?' asks Jonathan.

'Yes,' I say, 'I still had some private nursing jobs so I moved to a cheap housing project at St George's Church in Joubert Park. But the trauma of losing my house made me not care and I began missing rent payments.'

'Did you end up sleeping on the street?' asks Patrick.

'Nearly, nearly. One day at the Hillbrow Recreation Centre, I met the Muka boys, who were at that time sharing a blanket and whatever food they could find. Peter, the leader, was born in South Africa. His father had been active in the freedom movement so others had hunted them forcing the family to flee to Zimbabwe. Peter had a vision calling him back here. When he arrived, his father's family were afraid to have him around, so he slept on the streets. It was hard for him because he was

243

not used to what you have to do to survive. But he had some experience with drama and music and believed people would pay to see a play about homeless life. After one meeting, he invited me to join his drama group called Muka.'

'Was that a turning point?' asks Jonathan.

'Definitely,' I say. 'I had only been with them for a short time and we were invited to go to Washington DC in USA. To participate in a play. We performed at the Source Theatre, and several churches, and a Correctional Services Centre. In Virginia, a place with my name and not the Orange Free State one where my father disappeared to, a minister, called Sonja Dyer encouraged me to go and fetch Prince before the bond is completely broken.'

'Yes,' says Valentine, 'he is so much here but so little in your life stories.'

'As I began to recover, my brain started to recall things that I had deliberately blocked out. I began to acknowledge his existence. You see I'd conceived Prince just before my boyfriend Freddie Lavele was shot dead in the taxi faction fight. I sent Prince to to Venda to live with my stepmother and my father because I needed to stay where there was a chance of a job.'

'Did you unite with him?' asks Patrick.

'In 1998, just before I joined this group, I went to find him. He had such a bad case of allergies which especially has affected his eyes. Remember how in Herschel my eyes were pricked by prickly pears and became and infected and how thin I was when Gogo rescued me?'

'It seems you finally came to be proud to be Venda, the way you describe your homeland,' says Patrick.

'Mmm, maybe,' I say, 'firstly Vendas are highly educated, which I like, and we are less in numbers than other tribes, and unique in many ways. But the main thing I really regret is not having learned to speak Venda properly so as to be able to communicate properly with Prince.'

Valentine points to his watch and asks me to proceed to my next window.

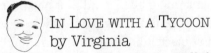

IN LOVE WITH A TYCOON
by Virginia

There he was as if by magic. 'Tall dark and handsome' as they say in fairy tales. I looked up and he was still there. Without him moving his lips, by his eyes I knew he was smiling at me.

I've always considered myself level-headed but all that vanished with Siphiwe. He spoke to me but I heard nothing but the sound of his voice. He took my hand and led me walking on air into the Wimpy in Kotze Street in Hillbrow. It was just after 10, so it must have been breakfast, but I don't remember what we ate or spoke about. Besides staring at the good-looking man, I must have given him my address because he became a regular visitor. I couldn't figure out what he saw in me.

Apart form his perfect looks, Siphiwe seemed to be in the money. For the first time in my life I went into real restaurants and ordered food without having to worry about prices and costs. As I regained my senses, I realised that I did not have any contact addresses. I would miss him after he had spent some days away from me, and he never gave me his cellular phone number. I tried bringing this up but he shrugged me off and changed the topic. Apart from this he seemed to feel about me as I did about him.

One day, whilst walking near the bus terminus in Bree Street, I met one of the so-called older street kids that I know. He tried to be fresh with me so I told him where to get off. Laughing he said, 'look here, I respected you very much but you disappoint me.'

'What are you talking about?' I asked

'If you can play hanky panky with one street kid, you can do it with another,' he said.

As I stood there wondering what he was talking about, he let off a shrill whistle and someone whistled back in answer. Another boy came staggering along glue in hand. If it had been at night I would have been frightened. This other boy looked vaguely familiar but I couldn't place him; after all I, know quite a few homeless people of different kinds. As he got nearer I couldn't believe my eyes. I blinked at the tall staggering dirty figure. It was Siphiwe. It took him a moment then he ran off.

Tears came to my eyes as I stood there. I heard a buzzing sound in my ears. The surroundings turned red then pitch black. Everything disappeared, except for me and the blackness and the noise.

I don't know how long I stood there but fortunately everything came back to normal. I was on my way back to Hillbrow where I lived.

It took some days before I got my final visit from Siphiwe. He was wearing reasonable but not very smart or very dirty clothes, but he could not look me in the eyes.

'Virginia, I don't know how to start but firstly you must know I love you,' he began.

I said nothing.

'I'm not who you thought I was. I am Siphiwe Buthelezi, born in KwaZulu-Natal. I never went to school. I preferred looking after my grandfather's cattle. When I got older I longed to come to Johannesburg to find my father and perhaps a job. Getting here I realised I needed more than a train ticket to find him. People whom I asked kept asking me, "what is his address?" I hadn't thought of that.

I met some guys who taught me how to survive without a home and I learned how to write. Then one day a Nigerian man came up to me and gave me a job. I was to take an envelope to the licensing department to a certain man. He gave me another brown envelope in exchange, which I took back to my boss. I expected at least ten rand in payment and was surprised when I was given a lot of money and a cell phone and told to buy good clothes. I was only allowed to wear these on a job. These were the times I came to you and acted like a tycoon.

I'm not allowed to stay smart away from the street too long. I have to be myself until he phones me and tells me what to do. Lately my boss has been promising that if I introduce a clever boy to him I'll be promoted. That means getting a house and living freely. I don't want to tell you too much detail because you might get into trouble. The good part is that the boss approves of you.'

'What?' I shouted, 'what does your dirty boss know of me?'

'He has seen you and says I can live with you when I get promoted.'

It feels eerie to be known by shady people who don't come out in the open to meet you. I ask myself even now if the so-called boss is any of the Nigerian men I know. As for Siphiwe, I politely asked him to leave and to forget that he ever knew me.

I miss him but I've put him down to history. To try and forget him I wrote an article about him for *Homeless Talk* entitled, 'Street Tycoon'.

As I was reading, I felt my fellow writers become tense. Am I boring them? It is rare since we started these workshops for Jonathan to comment first.

'You've made me cry yet again Virginia,' he says.

'Do you consider yourself unlucky in love?' asks Patrick.

'I never gave it a thought,' I reply, 'men don't like me in a romantic way.'

'Who are you kidding?' asks Jonathan, 'I know at least half a dozen contradictions to that statement.'

Everyone laughs. He can be quite funny sometimes.

'Have you ever seen Siphiwe again or around?' asks Valentine.

'Once when I was walking Nokuthula back from a Muka rehearsal to her shelter. She is our youngest member. We were walking down Edith Cavell and we just walked into him. It was like there had been nothing wrong between us.'

'Did he look like a street kid?' asks Jonathan.

'No he looked nice, like he was on a mission,' I say, 'who knows? But it was very nice to see him. We were all over each other. Nokuthula still asks me now about the nice man, but it's easier if I don't answer her.'

'Nigerians keep popping up in everyone's stories,' says Jonathan. 'I wish we had one in our group to get beyond this view of them as all being criminals.'

We talk about this for a bit. Then we run out of things to say. We don't even talk about Sipho anymore. No one has got anything to read so Jonathan takes out one of Gert's windows from the time he interviewed him. I wish Gert would come. I feel like I know him but not that he knows us. He has never heard our stories.

POTE
by Gert

I called him Pote even though birds don't really have paws. I was working as a steel stitcher and I was living in a flat in Mayfair with him. One Sunday morning my father and brother came short on a scooter. The exhaust burned my father's leg and it never came right. Six months later it got gangrene. The hospital gave him a bypass but it didn't help so they took his leg off and he moved in with me and Pote in Mayfair.

One day, me and my sister's lightie, Tiny, saw these crows at Tony's Scrapyard by that old mineshaft. Just under the wheel there was a nest and we checked them going in and out with food. With a rope and a bag, I climbed under that wheel. I took out five chicks and kept the biggest one.

I raised Pote and took him to work with me. I'd buy pet's mince and carry him to work in my bag. There I'd leave him in the showers in a bowl and I'd feed him both tea times and at lunch-time to build him up. When I didn't take him to work, he slept on top of my wardrobe and the windows were always open. You must check what the flat looks like when you come back from work if you leave Pote there. He eats and shreds all your cigarettes and even bites the heads off matches. Mustn't leave anything or it gets fucked up.

When I was smoking buttons, Pote would sit on my knee. These two lekker buttons were in my palm but I was scheming how to get some zol (marijuana). Next thing the fucken crow goes *pick pick* and grabs mos both buttons. Fifty bucks each. I tried to get him to vomit them out and he did one and kept it between his beak playing with it. After about a half hour, I got tired of begging this crow's arse and tried to grab the button but then he swallowed both properly. For two weeks his eyes tilted back but he didn't die.

There was a woman in the flat downstairs who only smaaked Pote and always called him Pote Pote. She always said his name double. He'd fly out my window and spend time with her which was OK by me as long as he came back and she didn't start to think she's the owner. She was a big fat woman with a big fat son was a speed cop with a big fat seven-fifty Honda.

After work, my dad and I used to sit there and I'd make a buttons pipe and Dad would dop brandy and Coke and give me a light and we'd watch TV and my fish tank.

'Check that,' I'd tell him if something happened on the TV

or in the fish tank. Sometimes a big fish would chase a smaller one or one would dive and dance. There was also a green shipwreck they smaaked to go into.

Then one time he was dronk dronk and my friend Elvin came to visit. My Dad needed to go the toilet so I helped him 'cause of his amputated foot. When we were busy in the bathroom, Elvin tried to take one hundred and seventy rand from my jacket but I heard him and I tried to stop him. We began squaring it, you know battling, and this oak fell on my Dad's legs and two weeks later he died from clots.

I'd come home from work after and just stand at my gate and not want to go in. After some minutes I'd turn round and go stay at my sister's place. The emptiness just worked on me. At her place I'd have a few dops and pipes and pass out, and go to work from there the next day. Eventually I invited two cherries and two okes, also on the outers, to live with me in my flat but the cherries were steamers, you know prostitutes. One time they put the jewellery they stole in the sand in my fish tank and my fish died.

I missed having my Dad just to say, 'Check,' or 'Hey Pa,' if something happens on TV or in the fish tank.

I stopped eating properly and one day I woke up just scheming about koeksisters my Ma used to bake. I decided not to go to work and to go visit her. She was in an old-age home in Triomf and had a stroke and kept escaping and knocking on doors asking, 'Do I live here?'

It was close to her birthday so I took her a dress and some fruit. When I knocked on the door this nurse told me she'd been deceased for six months.

I also missed work the next day and got fired but they gave me my pay and I spent it all on dop. It knocked me missing her funeral and after that I went blank, lost interest in everything, losing friends, baled out.

I struggle to hold back the tears as I picture Gert's father lying there frightened by the robber friend while his bowels let go. I've been trained to clean up messes like that in hospital, but I really admire Gert for his big heart.

How many young men would do what he did for his Dad? Not having buried his mother drove him to pieces. I relate well to this story. I am praying to God for people to read this book we are writing. I would like people to understand how we got homeless and jobless. It is not always laziness or inability. You experience things that overwhelm you. You stop functioning. It is undescribable.

'Virginia,' says Jonathan, inviting me back. He must have been watching my face.

I scoop up Prince from his corner and rush to the toilet pretending to be taking him there. In the Men's, I let out a torrent of tears.

When I come back Jonathan is talking.

'See you all next week,' he says smiling his lopsided smile.

I stay to talk to him and he invites me home for lunch with Kyoko and Masego. On the way home we stop at his post office box, which is opposite the place Sipho slept. The last lead to Sipho is to write a letter to his mother who may know something we don't.

'Can you get me Reverend Dianne Wicks's number?' asks Jonathan. 'She is the one who he left his money with to be sent to his mom if something happened to him. She also has his mom's address.'

EPILOGUE

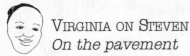# VIRGINIA ON STEVEN
On the pavement

Steve looks a bit tired as he settles before me. He has his mind on other things far away from here. I look at his face minus its usual toothless smile, the result of his boxing days I suppose. His complexion is lighter than the usual black skin. He could pass for a coloured. I can't help noticing the darker pigmentation blotching his cheeks and nose. I wonder if this could be an indication of liver problems?

He has bushy hair that seems determined to resist the effect of a comb. A camera is draped over his neck by a piece of string. He's wearing a white printed sweatshirt under a black leather jacket with a pair of jeans that also used to be black. My heart warms up to him. He is such a kind person and people don't really understand him. To me he is like a brother and I love him like one but today he is like a child crying out to be picked up. He would like us to be intimate and I always treat it like a joke. I just can't imagine us being lovers.

We are standing on a warm spot at Steve's former home, corner of Commissioner and Von Brandis Streets. His bed is a cozy corner, where he used to sleep with his feet facing Joshua Doore Furniture Store, 'Your Uncle in the Furniture Business', like they say on TV.

Virginia: What made you choose this place for the interview?

Steve: Because it is a place that always reminds me of the time when the stars and the street lights were my roof and blankets.

Virginia: And why this particular spot?

Steven: It's the warmest spot on Von Brandis.

[Steven says this kneeling down with difficulty and placing his palm on the pavement.]

Steven: Feel for yourself Virginia.

255

[I do and it is like there is underfloor heating. He cannot tell me why this place feels warmer. I picture him at night, curled up on a piece of cardboard, with other shapes snoring or talking in their sleep.]

Virginia: Do you think this project has made a difference in your life?

Steven: Yes, it gives me hope and strength as a writer. When people read the book, I will be recognised amongst other African writers.

Virginia: What are your chances and hopes in life since this project started?

Steven: My future seems brighter since we have been awarded some money to do some courses.

Virginia: Which course did you choose?

Steven: One called Rainbow in which I will learn computer skills, motivation, administration and English. It is a five-week course in Sandton.

Virginia: I know because I also chose that course. When should we do it?

Steven: I am not sure. I am worried because of my blood clot in my brain. I need an operation and I think I should get that out the way first.

Virginia: You got that injury from when the Portuguese barman attacked you, didn't you? When I was in your room the other day, I saw many hospital files and you showed me your X-rays and your EEG. How come your files were there?

Steven: I went to the General Hospital to book the operation last week. They messed me around so much I just took my files.

Virginia: Are you still planning to have the operation there?

Steven: I don't know.

[Steven has a piece cut off his little finger on his left hand. It's been cut off from the upper knuckle.]

Virginia: How did you injure your hand?

Steven: This is no injury. I'm the first son in my family so this had to be done when I was about a year old. If I had been a girl, it would have been on the second finger. On the mines, when a Xhosa injured their hand in this way, the mine would try get out of compensation by saying all Xhosas have it from birth, but this is a lie. Look at David, he has no joint missing.

Virginia: What difficulties have had you had in the months since you started this project?

Steven: Only my illness and the tornado, which destroyed my home in Ciskei. But I had the burning desire to attend the workshops even when the going was tough.

Virginia: What will you do if your hopes for the book are not fulfilled and it is never published?

Steven: When I was boxing I changed my date of birth in my ID book to make me younger. This was done easily by going to the Ciskei offices. If this book is a failure, I must change my ID back to my real date of birth, so I can get my pension earlier.

Virginia: So how old are you actually?

Steven: According to my birth certificate I'm 38.

Virginia: Jonathan is also that age. Still you have twenty-two years to wait for your pension. Do you believe this book has a future?

Steven: Well yes, because many people don't realise our trials, so through the book they will see that through determination, even the lowest of the low can succeed.

Virginia: Of all the stories you told, which one stands out for you?

Steven: There are two. Firstly, my arrest in 1987 for organising a strike on the mines. It was my first experience to taste the hardship of jail. Actually Jonathan never put that one in. That story gave me the power that I will never go back to jail even though I was only arrested for striking.

Virginia: And the second one?

Steven: When I lost to Geldenhuys in the South African Interstate Games. It was a dream come true.

Virginia: How can losing be a dream come true?

Steven: To lose on the finals of such an important tournament is an achievement by any standards.

Virginia: Any last comments about your hopes and dreams?

Steven: I hope to be the world's best writer and journalist.

Virginia: That reminds me of your ambition when you were a boxer and it took you to the finals.

Steven: Yes, when I'm dead, even if I'm in heaven or hell, I would like to see printed on my grave, 'HERE LIES MAN OF MEN'.

Virginia: What else would you like to tell me?

Steven: (yawn) I'm too tired. I've finished talking.

 STEVEN ON VIRGINIA
In the theatre

Monday 21 March was supposed to be a holiday – Human Rights Day. But it turned out to be a day of work for me. Ag, my mind nearly cursed my profession as a writer and my never-ending painful leg. Although I thought of sleeping on the historic day, I remembered the unfinished business of an interview with Virginia that Jonathan wanted so badly.

After washing myself, I dressed up and performed my little ritual. From the mining days I had this old habit of keeping my pocket-money in my jacket's inner pockets. In a hurry to get to Virginia's place, I checked my pockets and they were all as empty as a church on Monday mornings. My only option was to take all my clothes out my two metal lockers to check for the money. I hate doing it and I'm having to do it more and more often. Instead I took out my beloved Bible and read a verse,

258

which on the previous day people had me preach about. Then I checked again and found eighty rand blocked in one inner pocket.

My journey to the Hillbrow Theatre was not all that glossy because it started to rain hard but a job needed to be done. The theatre is attached to a block of flats and the name is written in big gold letters above the door. I buzzed and buzzed outside the flat entrance. Virginia didn't answer so I went to look in the theatre. It was open but no one was inside, which is not normal for Hillbrow. Brown seats filled up the whole floor. The stage is high and has black steps and black curtains are draped from the ceiling down. I walked up the aisle and noticed the new carpet but I began to feel like a thief so I turned round and started to leave without my story like a whipped dog. But then Virginia came from Checkers and shouted for me to join her.

As I enter her room I see a sewing machine near the door and it turned out that the evening before she was sewing Muka costumes for a play. Her room is much bigger than the one she used to stay in at Cornelius House. There is room to move and she has wardrobes made into the wall. My eyes go up and down to see if she still put a towel on the lamp, like we all do in Cornelius. In the bedroom I find the bed neatly made and a *True Love* magazine and small toy game machine lying there. An aroma smell wafts from the kitchen.

Before we interview, Virginia brings a cup of tea and a plate of pap and meat. We eat while we talk.

Steven: Virginia, could you please tell me what you liked most as a child?

Virginia: Singing was my first love as I did it every time I finished crying.

Steven: Tell me about the most horrible thing happened to you as a child?

Virginia: I was new in a location because we moved a lot.

259

Some new friends told me about new red sweets I'd never heard of. After buying and eating these red sweets they turned your urine red. The first time I tried them, I told my aunt very proudly. She forced me to use a bucket for urinating. Then my granny came home carrying bundles of newspaper on her head. I don't know why she used to bring those home. I looked in her bag for goodies and when I'd found them and eaten them, my aunt said, 'Hey this child of yours is having red urine, look!' and they started shouting and calling me names I'd never heard before. And they hit me. I'd never been so confused.

Steven: As an adult what are your most memorable moments?

Virginia: When I was nursing terminally ill patients to make them die comfortably, I was considered the best of the team.

Steven: In our windows, which one did you like telling the best?

Virginia: Every window brought back memories and made me happy to be with everybody there.

Steven: What are your hopes for the future?

Virginia: To write children's story books.

Steven: Predictions about this book?

Virginia: Hoping that readers get to know that homelessness is not brainlessness and is not a chosen career.

Steven: Thanks.

DAVID ON VALENTINE
In the movies

Today Valentine is wearing a leather waistcoast over a brick-red shirt. It is a shirt that he wore when the M-Net production team came to shoot. His veldskoens are usually worn by Afrikaner farmers but they fit him. His hair is cut like these African football stars with small dreadlocks. There is one gold-ish ear-ring in his left ear. The green trousers he has on are no different from the prisoner's uniform but he is not a bad person at all because under his shirt he has a white rosary. It perfectly matches his shirt. He is growing hair on his face on both cheeks, not bad for a youngster.

We are outside our favourite cinema called Good Hope. It is situated along Market Street and it is owned by Indians. We are five minutes early. The queue is more than one kilometre long. Valentine is feeling frustrated. He is insisting on going to Kippies to meet his new Canadian girlfriend, Colleen. I try to persuade him not to go.

'Where else can you pay only five rand for two movies?' I ask.

Most of the people in this queue are from Soweto. We are stuck behind a man on crutches climbing the old velvet carpet stairs. His armpits supporting the crutches drip each time he takes a hop. When he gets to the office to pay, in an Indian accent, the owner orders him not to pay by saying, 'You are just from sport, just go in.'

The film is *Ronin*, and it is set in France. Valentine's eyes are glittering in the dark. I look down at the translation but he looks at the top and the middle of the screen. The theatre is packed. Most late-comers sit on the floor. It is a pornographic movie almost. After some minutes I find myself ignoring the translation as do most others. Everyone is talking and jiving so I decide to ask Valentine a few questions.

David: How have you coped since the *Saturday Star* doesn't publish your stories regularly?

Valentine: Well I'm trying to freelance for many other papers. What *Homeless Talk* pays me doesn't even cover the rent.

David: Don't worry, my deal with MTN to support *Homeless Talk*, of close to one million, is materialising. We gonna make money.

Valentine: So will you leave *Homeless Talk* as you said?

David: Yes, they have promised to pay me twenty per cent of the deal for having negotiated. I want to start my own advertising company. Is Anna still sending you money from Canada?

Valentine: Yes, she sent me things on St *Valentine's* Day.

[He says this pointing to himself. We laugh and people look at us because it is not a funny part of the film.]

Valentine: She sent me this leather waistcoat and five hundred dollars.

David: What are your hopes for the book?

Valentine: I was spending some time with some musicians called Boo!, in Melville. An Australian journalist called Andrew, who sometimes writes for *Big Issue* in Melbourne, suggested the title be *Window Pain*. We discussed the title for five hours in a coffee shop and in the end everyone agreed on *Window Pain*.

David: Why?

Valentine: Because in all our windows we are talking about trouble and pain through life, and for the cover he suggested a naked woman, but not erotic, from knees to neck, with her back to the cover. She will be in front of that building with the broken windows in front of the Market Theatre, where we went looking for Sipho. Blood will come out all of the names of the writers.

David: Why do you want it to be like that?

Valentine: Because a well-designed cover contributes about sixty to seventy per cent to the sale of a book. The one musician's girlfriend, Kalli, goes to the mortuary to get pictures of people with bullet holes on their heads and body, and prints it on other pictures and it looks horribly frightened.

[The movie comes to an end and we go for a Castle in the bar.]

David: What has been difficult for you?

Valentine: The project was boring earlier. Before we got the focus of the spider. Waking early on Saturdays was also quite terrible. I also found the criticism quite hard. Some people couldn't take it, that is, the criticism we used to give each other to improve our writing. I remember we all used to call Sipho the toughest critic, but he found this the most difficult, even though his writing was so outstanding.

David: What about the future?

Valentine: The future is not in my hands but I plan to establish myself as a journalist. My gran wanted me to become a reporter. That opportunity has not come yet. When the money from the book starts coming in, I will go home and look at my mom's grave, make some improvements and write an epitaph on it.

David: What is that?

Valentine: A poetic verse. It is French and more popular there.

David: I remember you told us that your granny told you she only wanted to see you once you had built your own house and got married. She must be old now, and you have been published many times in South Africa, are you going back soon?

Valentine: At the airport she also said, 'No matter how slow the moon walks by daybreak, by morning it must have crossed the sky.' But right now I cannot afford it.

David: Just don't leave it too late.

  VALENTINE ON PATRICK
In a maid's room

We catch a taxi from town to Rosebank. Patrick pays as I paid when he visited my home in Yeoville. When we get there, two guys sitting on a two-metre black fence along Oxford Road greet him as he collects a key from one of them. He is Pat's brother from Venda. They start laughing at the pronunciation of my surname, Cascarino.

'Where is that name from?' Pat's brother asks.

In simple logistical quotes, Pat comes to my rescue, 'If you say Cameroon, you might be right. France, you might not be far from the truth, and Canada, you will be hovering around,' he tells them. There is a burst of laughter.

We take a lift to the third floor of a three-story building. Most of the occupants, I notice, are below middle class whites and coloureds. Except for the hooting of cars, the entire building is taciturn. We walk one more floor up to the little rooms on the roof. My heart stops beating fast.

A row of 23 rooms with red painted doors. One intercom serves all the domestic workers who live here. It produces a sound not easily distinguishable from the hooting of an owl. We push one creaking zinc door on the right which reveals a little room a quarter the size of mine.

An electricity meter using coupons waits for its thirty rand monthly bill. An old piece of carpet lying on the floor is washing away. Three little tables and one dwarfy bed are lying on it. The window is bathroom type allowing about one per cent of free air. On one of the tables lies a brown bread, which Patrick is pinching slowly but steadily. All the pots are empty. He drinks water as he eats. He sits on the bed and I sit on a single chair.

Valentine: What moments in the history of the group stand out for you?

Patrick: Especially on the very first day I came, I really didn't know that me and the other people there would be one of the great writers, but I always wanted to be one, and I sensed it was my very best chance.

[As he says this, pushing bread and water into his mouth, in this boxy room, I hide the tears in my eyes. A black and white fourteen centimetre TV set is on one of the tables with a Bible near it.]

264

Valentine: What were the high points?

Patrick: The upwards? To see the others simply write about personal experience and hardships, and that others found this interesting.

Valentine: And what was difficult for you?

Patrick: When I was stuck in Venda and I couldn't come to Saturday meetings because I had no money. I thought there was no other way to make it and I hadn't handed in all my windows. That was when I phoned Jonathan and told him to cancel my stories, but he said that even if I never came again, my stories were excellent and would stay.

Valentine: Have you handed all in now?

Patrick: No, but Jonathan said that just shows how difficult life can be.

Valentine: Why did you choose this place to be interviewed?

Patrick: This place was never visited by anyone in the group. It is the place I lived for three years whilst studying art at technikon, and it reminds me of all those hardships. Also, even though it is just one room that functions as a bedroom and a kitchen and a sitting room, I chose it because I want the whole world to know how I am living.

Valentine: Which story was the most important for you to tell?

Patrick: The circumcision one because it was like, as a Venda, we were being stereotyped as only brave if we went to initiation school. Through my passport story and my others I have proved you can be brave without having gone there. And the one about the stolen land.

Valentine: Why that one?

Patrick: Because it shows the roots of how my father and grandfather were living. Also, it connects to how I am living now. My father said some of his cows were taken by the Boers and maybe if they hadn't I could be having some wealth now.

[Patrick laughs as he says this but he is serious in his eyes.]

Valentine: What course have you chosen and why?

Patrick: I have chosen a driving license course because although I have a three year diploma in graphics and communication and computers, this may be the ticket to a job. They always ask for that when advertising in the paper for any job.

Valentine: What are your hopes for the future?

Patrick: I have unlimited hopes. I'd like to see myself as a great poet, writer and artist and art critic.

Valentine: And the book?

Patrick: I hope it goes very far and I think it can. The reader through our stories can be on the other kind of world and explore some things that didn't happen to him like in a movie.

[As Patrick talks I notice that above the Bible are two African Church uniforms, probably ZCC. One is blue and the other is light khaki green. In an old doorless wardrobe hang clothes belonging to Pat and his aunt and his brother.]

Patrick: Don't forget to note that all this furniture was given to my aunt by white people she had worked for. The three of us, squash ourselves here while trying to sleep on the ground.

Valentine: Do you see yourself as homeless?

Patrick: Yes and no. To have to sleep in a domestic room on the floor with my aunt and brother, on top of a building, yes. And the things and struggles of the people at *Homeless Talk* are my difficulties as well. I'm trying to raise R1500 to build a shack in Soweto. Then I can study or just live without having to pay rent.

Valentine: Thanks. It was interesting talking to you. Sometimes we are so busy with the past and the writing, we don't get to know each other in the workshops. [As I say this, I'm already crying inside.]

Inside a taxi, on my way to town, I burst into tears. 'Why are you crying?' asks a coloured teenager beside me, 'I've never seen a man cry.'

This made me sadder than Sipho's drain.

 ᴘɪɴᴋɪᴇ ᴏɴ ʀᴏʙᴇʀᴛ
In a ruin and on a bank

Robbie is wearing a black and red checked waistcoat with two different buttons over a Mickey Mouse sweater. His mafia shoes are reddish brown and they have little holes for air. He is missing socks but so neatly dressed. He is a gentleman. How would I describe his face today? GASP! It is handsome and I'm sure ladies think so, too. His smile is easy to understand because it is always there. It seems to be saying, 'do not feel sorry for me, I am just trying my best.' This is the first time we have spoken and I find him interesting.

Pinky: Robbie can you tell me how you got to be in this group. You did not come by the traditional route. I have not seen you around *Homeless Talk*?

Robbie: I was living in this abandoned house with Trevor and Gert for a short time. I had no direction and I wasn't having any luck getting piece jobs. Sometimes I knocked on doors asking for food saying 'I don't support crime,' and people would say, 'but you look clean, I don't believe you'. So sometimes for two-three days I wouldn't eat, but staying with others most days one of would manage to get something. For survival's sake, we learned to share, even though we were not always friendly with each other. Especially me and Trevor, who Gert and I called Clever Trevor.

[While Robbie is talking, I look around the place. The doors, the floor-boards, the toilet, the bath, everything, has been stripped. A smell of human, what can I call it, shit, comes from one room I will not go in. There is a big hole I am scared to fall into next to Robbie's place where he sleeps.]

Robbie: Don't look down, look up.

Pinky: So?

Robbie: Mine is the only room in the house with a roof.

Pinky: What happened to the other roof?

Robbie: A gruesome murder was committed so the owner tried to sell but no one as interested. People started looting but I hold on to this roof. See these built in wardrobes? They indicate this place used to be up-class.

Pinky: Why did you choose this place to be interviewed?

Robbie: Actually, I didn't. I wanted to be interviewed by the dam, which is just down the road, but I also wanted you to see this place. On Thursday nights, I hear very scary noises here and doors slam. I am thinking of going to stay with my girlfriend in Brixton. Can we take a walk down to the dam now?

Pinky: Which dam?

Robbie: The one where the double-decker bus full of schoolchildren drowned. Just down there.

Pinky: Sure, let's go.

[The dam is less than one minute's walk from the house. As we leave, I notice there is no front gate to the house. Robbie tells me that it was there two days ago. The dam is another world. Except for the litter, I feel like I am in the mountains in another country. As we walk down the bank to the water, a flock of about thirty big geese jump into the water. Some are white and some are grey and brown.]

Pinky: Why is the dam important to you?

Robbie: Well, I used to come here not to wash, because at that time the next-door neighbours still allowed us to wash at their place, but to get some peace of mind, and to get some contact with nature. One day I was here with Trevor and Gert just sitting on that bench just there, and I saw this guy walking around the edge. I was a little surprised, how can I put it, because he looked white and he had a little more like a coloured child with him. A girl. As I've learned from this guy, he always goes jogging around the dam, but that day he was just walking, talking to this little girl, only two or three years old. I remember Gert gave her a sweet and he was drinking water from a Coke bottle and she asked for a sip and took one. I wondered if her father would allow her to drink from the same bottle as him because you know, when you live like this, it is not so easy to stay and look clean to other people.

Pinky: You are talking about Jonathan and Masego aren't you?

Robbie: Ja. He told me he was a writer and a clinical psychiatrist, Dr Jonathan Morgan, and also about *Homeless Talk* newspaper, and he invited me to join a writing group.

Pinky: What did you think?

Robbie: Well, my mind was on lots of other things, so I just listened, but I kept on seeing him there at the dam, and he brought me pen and paper, and the windows. I ended up joining. Something made me become part of this very same project. Afterwards Trevor started telling me how he was going to write nice and beautiful stories. He never did and now he is in prison. I hear he broke into other people's houses and cars, and that some other people gave him a place to sleep. He found a gold and diamond ring in their bathroom and sold it for twenty bucks as I've heard.

Pinky: You were never very fond of him?

Robbie: Unless one forgives one cannot be forgiven.

[Just then, a man with four big dogs on very long leashes that seem to be able to stretch comes jogging past. When the dogs come too close, he jerks their necks back.]

Pinky: What difference did it make it to be part of the group in your life story?

Robbie: It was thrilling and I learned to strive.

Pinky: Did you know you were a good storyteller before you met up with this group?

Robbie: I can say no because self-praise is no recommenda-tion. It doesn't make me feel proud but people give an ear when they hear something new.

Pinky: But you are! When you tell or read a story, everyone listens. It's not just what you tell but how you tell it.

Robbie: At school I liked writing essays.

Pinky: Lots of your stories were about crime and you missed lots of meetings, like me. I remember Virginia once said to me we must try keep you distracted! We were worried you had gone back to old ways or to depression.

Robbie: Before I was less observant about this and that, now I'm more inquisitive. I wasn't a guy who worried about others. I was more interested in friends and nice times. Now I'm still a lone ranger, but I know the difference between good and evil more.

Pinky: How did the group help with that?

Robbie: Well before if you said to me, let's stab that guy with a knife, I wouldn't even ask why. I didn't know how to stop from doing something. Even though I don't know God per-sonally, maybe he knows me and it's him who knows the answer to your question. Before I never had a soft spot that could help you to negotiate with a person. Now I'm able to discuss part of my feelings with a person. Also I never liked to tell the truth about myself, and I always wanted to be the star, or the centre of attraction. Now I just want to be normal and ordinary. I never sat with people like this before.

[Robbie and I have now walked right around the dam. Some boys and men, most of whom talk Afrikaans, are fishing at dif-ferent places. The men often look at us with suspicion and unfriendliness even though their rods sometimes block our way and we have to go up the bank to get past.]

Pinky: What was the most important story you told through your windows?

270

Robbie: The one where I was arrested.

Pinky: Why?

Robbie: I saw my life was being wasted there. Even though the TRC was a waste of money, it was good how people were forced to confess.

Pinky: Was the storytelling in the group like the TRC for you?

Robbie: Ja, it did make a difference to be welcomed and accepted even when I told horrible stories, and to be able to discuss them. Actually I experienced great joy in my soul.

Pinky: What course are you doing with your share of the money?

Robbie: An air-conditioning course through Intec, and journalism. I want to be able to add to what I already know about air-conditioning but I also want to be able to write about daily events to inform people about what is going on. And I hope to get a camera. I see lots of things and I want to put pictures of them with my stories. Actually, I don't want to be rich. I just want to be somewhere between rich and poor and to help the under-privileged.

Just before we go through the gate of the dam area, under a willow tree at the water's side, we see a young boy with his one hand under his shirt. At a glance we both know he is sniffing glue, even though he is more than thirty metres away. Robbie and I just look at each other and pause in our step wondering to go talk to him or not. Without me saying anything, Robbie just shakes his head. We walk up the last bit of slope past an overturned dustbin through the gate. My stomach is hurting so he offers to get me Enos. Talking to Robbie Buys is interesting. It seems we will be talking more and more as I also gain a lot from him. Beside GASP gatherings, there is a man called Robbie.

VALENTINE ON JONATHAN
ON VALENTINE
On the top of Ponte

We are on the top of a cylinder, on the very rooftop, under the back of the biggest Coke sign in Africa. If we look down the middle of the building, we see circles of corridors and flats, and at the bottom we see litter on boulders at the bottom on the hillside on which Ponte stands.

Jonathan: Thanks for interviewing me and standing in for Sipho. You've already interviewed quite a few people for the signing-off-catching-up chapter. I have really appreciated your commitment to the project.

Valentine: Why did you choose to be interviewed here?

Jonathan: We decided on it together, don't you remember?

Valentine: I do, but you told me you wanted me to ask you that question.

Jonathan: OK, mostly because of the view. Look in that direction you can see mine dumps, which remind me of Kimberley and Sipho. And there is Sandton City, and there is town, and there is Soweto, and all down here is Hillbrow and Yeoville.

Valentine: So you wanted a bird-eye view?

Jonathan: Yes, but one I know well. When I was writing my novel, the opening scene was a Nigerian drug dealer called Ike, standing in one of these flats in this building with the Coke sign above him. He was looking down. I used to live in a block of flats on the ridge behind the water tower, and one in St George Street, and one in Isipingo. In Trinity Hall at night, when the Coke sign here on Ponte used to flash, my whole lounge would be bathed in red light.

Valentine: Did you know it weighs six and a half tons, and is made up of over two thousand individual glass units? Each one was manually manœuvered into shape and pumped with either neon or argon. Argon for red and neon for white, I think.

Jonathan: How the fuck do you know that?

Valentine: I researched it for a story for *Saturday Star*. At one time they were thinking of making this building into a prison. Look you can see my flat from here too. It's the one with the clothes lines on top, next to the Sputnik steel watertower.

Jonathan: I love that tower. It is pure Art Deco. Both sets of my grandparents lived in Hillbrow. In flats called Everest and Blue Haze. I used to stay weekends at my Granny Dena. She'd buy me huge boxes of wine gums in a café just round the corner from the Mimosa. I reckon it would be easier to find crack there now than wine gums.

Valentine: So the project has almost come to an end. How are you feeling?

Jonathan: Exhausted and proud and sad and relieved.

Valentine: Relieved?

Jonathan: Near the beginning of the book, about seven months ago, I wrote that in Kyoko's stomach there is a little creature, only four centimetres long whose nail pads would be complete by that night. Now we know he is a boy and he is almost full grown. In ten weeks, once he's with us, I don't know how much time I'll have for writing.

Valentine: You said proud, too?

Jonathan: Yes, of all the things I've ever been part of, this project must rank as one I'm the most happy about. Through it, I've strongly felt a part of Africa. Don't know if I'll always be here, but I'm here now and I've felt important documenting the era and the place from so many different angles.

Valentine: And what else made you feel good?

Jonathan: Coming across the incredible stories, first time round, in the person's own voice, and the ever richer versions that were handed to me on scraps of paper. Especially towards the end, it was like getting to the end of a sand-papering job, when the grain really begins to come out.

Valentine: You mentioned sad as well?

Jonathan: Yes, about the regular contact coming to an end and particularly that we have not found Sipho. I really expected to him to have turned up by now. My fantasy has been that he'll just pull in one Saturday, take the relay baton from one of us tired folk, and finish off with the most spellbinding dash.

Valentine: What is the latest place or dead end the trail has led you?

Jonathan: Well, I was going to empty my P.O. Box in Braamfontein yesterday, and I went past Sipho's drain slash home. A young man called Foster and a guy called Jewel were there. I've got to know Foster quite well and every time I park there, we talk about Sipho. The last time he told me Sipho is not in Diepkloof but in Leeukop Prison, and that his sister in Soweto has visited him in Medium A. I never even knew he had a sister, did you?

Valentine: No.

Jonathan: I've been disappointed so many times by false leads from unreliable sources, I'm not putting too much hope into what he told me, but I must say, there is something credible and likeable about Foster.

Valentine: Foster, that was who Sipho dedicated his last poem to?

Jonathan: What do you mean his last poem?

Valentine: The last poem he had published in January *Homeless Talk*. Haven't you read it?

Jonathan: January, no, he was already gone by then. I wasn't looking out for any of his poems. How come his poem was in?

Valentine: He handed it in November, just before he went missing. It was not published but Pinky and Ted found it and included it. I also nearly missed it because I was looking for unpublished stuff. We'd better be going now, the guard is going off duty at 4 p.m. Don't forget to look for Sipho's poem.

[Another Day in the boardroom ...]
Valentine: I brought the poem.
Jonathan: Yes, I found a copy of the paper in my bedroom, and I read it, but let's read it together. Do you mind reading it out loud to me. I'd like a tape recording of that.

A POEM FOR A FRIEND

Goodbye Foster
For the time being
Until we meet again
The youngest of us you were
Though your intelligence ran you by a mile
A smile, a grin and merry laughter
You could not fail to conjure

A standard 4 or 6 you had
Though you dreamed to follow up
English Afrikaans you spoke fluently
And rattled off Portuguese without a flaw
Zulu you did not dread
For a naturalised citizen you were

Your real name we never knew
For in the street is tight guard
With tales both true and tall
You could hang us a thousand feet
Puns you bore in your stride
And views easily swayed

You said the people ain't dangerous
But the place in itself is
Change goals and man himself
How true, we'll never know

A car they say you've broken into
Though no one saw you within
Or caught you with something unbecome

If you did it we don't know
That's between you and your god

A homeless is kept forever
Reminded for an eternity
To visit you we cannot do
For you lived under an assumed name

Where's the guitar that you brought here
Sold it by the roadside before the final applause
Has your truth come to roost
And the city got you at last

We know that you ain't dead
But to us you might as well be
And so we'll say my friend
Farewell until we meet again
(Sipho Madini)

Jonathan: I was amazed. Sipho wrote that poem for Foster who was missing, and who may have been in jail for allegedly breaking into a car, but now it's about himself. All we can do is say farewell until we meet again, that is if he's alive.

Valentine: Well, to find him might not be as difficult as you think. If, and only if, prison authorities can allow me in jail for a week. I've done similar stuffs when investigating a story. If it was in Hillbrow, I could commit a minor offence and be imprisoned.

Jonathan: Don't you think that is a bit risky, with you being an illegal immigrant?

Valentine: Mmm.

Jonathan: But it's like Foster and Sipho and so many others are all in the same force field. All of his poems so strongly traced and predicted his trajectory. But this one especially. Do you know, since we met on top of Ponte, and I read this poem,

I went looking for Foster? I wanted to show it to him. In our discussions he had never mentioned the poem to me so I wasn't sure if he had seen it. You won't believe what I was told?

Valentine: What?

Jonathan: Jewel told me Foster has been arrested again for the same thing and he's in prison.

Valentine: It's making me crazy.

Jonathan: I know, I feel psychotic myself. You know it's more than a little scary. I started writing a novel, which set out to describe a whole lot of marginalised Gauteng geography, characters and conversations. When I met you all, I gave up the fictional novel and allowed you to speak and write for yourselves, as well as telling my own story through this window of my life, which is the project. I also imagined, and to some extent prophesised, that some of you would go missing and I'd go look for you in the mortuary and the prison. In a way I feel responsible for Sipho. Actually one prophesy that didn't materialise was the one where I go looking for you in Lindela, the infamous immigrant deportation centre. It was the one of the places I wanted to describe.

Valentine: Actually, I have been there but only to bribe people out.

Jonathan: But getting back to what I was saying before, the more I write and live part of my life as a writer, the more I see how powerfully we shape our worlds through the language and stories we choose for ourselves. I'm also aware that privilege brings with it more power and choice when it comes to re-storying.

Valentine: What do you mean by re-storying?

Jonathan: Well, if you go to the average dinner-table in the northern suburbs right now, I mean tonight, or any night, you'll hear people having a conversation about crime in Gauteng. This exact same conversation follows South African emigrants to Sydney and London and New York. I've heard it everywhere. It's like people are no longer having that conversation. It's having them.

Valentine: Mmm …

Jonathan: In the same way that shit conversations can have us, so can shit stories. I like to believe we can choose to resist these, and write and be in new ones that we prefer.

Valentine: Did you do this with this project?

Jonathan: In a way that even surprised me. Through it I have felt part of a story or drama that is so good, and so full of plot and coursing narrative, I have felt completely over taken and energised. I've hardly ever felt more connected to Jo'burg, which can be a pretty overwhelming and disconcerting place.

Valentine: That sounds like Narrative Psychology.

Jonathan: Like me you are blessed with amazing powers of clairvoyance (laughs). Do you remember telling me that outside Diepkloof Prison?

Valentine: I do. Are you going to follow up on the Foster lead?

Jonathan: What are you doing tomorrow?

A New Wave of 'Truth' and Reconciliation

Narrative Therapy (as expounded by David Epston and Michael White) has richly informed this project and this book. As a school of practice it strives to honour clients as the principal authors of their own lives and acts to deconstruct any claims of 'expert knowledge' or 'truth'. It also encourages a perception that change is always possible by opening up spaces for story-telling and for a revisioning of history towards a carnival of possible futures. Unhappiness and struggle are viewed in a political and a social way, rather than in a pathologising and individualised way. Although Narrative Therapy has been widely embraced by psychology, many would agree that story-telling is best done outside of a clinical box where there is more space for wider audience participation and multiple perspectives. They would also agree that many of the issues discussed in therapy are public rather than private concerns, for example, the effects of poverty and patriarchy upon individuals.

Following on the type of work carried out by the Truth and Reconciliation Commission, in a national but decentralised way, a group of us are interested in pursuing narrative means to therapeutic ends, and in popularising story-telling (and documentation) outside of judicial and clinical settings. With the launch of this book, **Arc-Hive**, gleefully steps in as the first official African Story-Telling, Capturing and Lending Body. Its mission is to circulate stories of protest, survival and triumph, and to bring together a web of members for the purposes of consultation, information and support. By inviting stories of a particular kind, **Arc-Hive** will represent a rich supply of hard won knowledges and useful resources. In doing so it will honour the authors of such stories as consultants unto themselves, unto others trapped in similar difficulties, to researchers and to helping professionals.

The following organisations are some of those who have expressed interest and support towards this initiative: the Centre for the Study of Violence and Reconciliation, *Homeless Talk*, Zanendaba (Come with a Story), the Institute for the Advancement of Journalism, the Oral History Project (Western Cape).

If you or your organisation would like to find out more about **Arc-Hive**, please contact Jonathan Morgan at joko@netline.co.za or at P.O. Box 978, Melville, 2198.